The Watson Girl

LESLIE WOLFE

TDCJ APPROVED

ITALICS PUBLISHING

Italics Publishing Inc.
Cover and interior design by Sam Roman
Editor: Joni Wilson
ISBN: 1-945302-10-0
ISBN-13: 978-1-945302-10-7

LESLIE WOLFE

1

Cold-Blooded Beginning

Fifteen Years Ago

He knocked on the door with the barrel of his gun, then screwed on a silencer while waiting for someone to welcome him in. He checked the surroundings one more time. In the heavy dusk, shadows were long, and sounds were too few to disturb the suburban peacefulness. A dog barked in the neighborhood somewhere, and sounds of remote highway traffic were so distant he could barely register them.

The two-story house had warmly illuminated windows on both floors, with white sheers that made the soft lights shimmer, and gave the massive, Colonial Revival home a fairy-tale look. The distant sound of a cartoon made it all the way to the dimly lit porch. He recognized the guttural voice of Daffy Duck.

Only one car was parked on the wide, three-car garage driveway, the silver minivan Rachel Watson liked to use while performing the functions of modern-day motherhood, with one or more of her three children loaded in the back seats. Allen Watson's car was nowhere in sight. But Watson always garaged his Benz, careful not to get a speck of dust on the custom paint that must have set him back a small fortune.

Even if he couldn't see his car, he knew Watson was home.

He knew it because he didn't leave anything to chance. He'd waited patiently in his own car, parked discreetly around the corner and almost entirely hidden by the generous foliage of a thriving palmetto. He kept his eyes glued to the street, watching, stalking his target. Now he was ready.

He heard footsteps approaching the door, and he tightened the grip on his gun, hidden behind his back. The door swung open, and Allen Watson stepped quietly to the side, a tentative smile on his lips, and a hint of an intrigued frown creasing his brow. He waved him in and he obliged, his gun firmly in hand. Watson closed the door, then looked at him inquisitively.

"What are y—" Watson's question faltered mid-word, as he registered the weapon in the now-visible hand and froze, taking wavering steps back until he hit the wall behind him. Watson's eyes, rounded in surprise, drilled into his, while words failed to come out of his gaping mouth.

"No... No..." he finally managed in a hoarse voice, weak and choked.

He hesitated a little and took his time to raise the gun higher, aiming for Allen's chest from only a few feet away. Then the sound of tiny feet pattering on the hardwood upstairs preceded a high-pitched voice, resounding loudly above their heads.

"Who is it, Daddy?"

He looked up briefly and saw two of Watson's kids staring down at them, dressed in colorful pajamas, their hands gripping the newels supporting the balcony handrail above the main living room.

"No..." Watson whispered. "Please..."

He couldn't delay anymore.

He pulled the trigger twice, in rapid sequence, and Watson fell to the ground in a motionless heap, as the terrified shrieks of the two children pierced his ears. He lunged up the stairs, climbing three steps at a time, then ran toward the bedrooms. Within a few leaps, he caught up with the two screaming children. Then silence engulfed the home once more, as he searched the house room by room, looking for the third kid.

Soon he was finished upstairs, and ready to go back downstairs, when a knock on the front door made him freeze mid-step. He pulled back, closer to the wall, and held his breath. Worried, he checked the windows next to the main door, only partly covered by curtains, then he shifted his gaze to Watson's body, collapsed just a few feet from that door.

The visitor might see his body through the open curtains. All he had to do is want to peek inside, and lean to the side a little. Damn!

The knocks repeated, a little louder and longer this time, followed by the doorbell chime. Then he heard a man's voice, suppressed by the massive door.

"Hey, it's Ben from next door. I have your cordless drill." The man stopped talking, knocked a couple of times more, then continued, "I'll leave it here, on the porch. Thanks!"

The unwanted visitor went away, his footsteps loud and heavy, but almost undistinguishable against the sounds of the cartoon on TV. He breathed slowly, calm, calculated.

A moment later, he made his way downstairs cautiously, looking for Rachel Watson. He listened intently, and somewhere beyond Daffy Duck's nasal voice, he heard clattering noises coming from the kitchen. A hint of a smile stretched the corner of his lip and curled it upward as he headed there with silent, feline steps.

He didn't know how long everything had taken, but it was time to go. The sound of sirens in the distance brought an urgency to his departure, and he left the home quietly and hurriedly, after checking the undisturbed, peaceful surroundings once more, paying thorough attention to every detail. The home across the street had its main floor flooded with light, with all the curtains pulled aside, allowing the light to overflow into the street. The family there was on display while they went about their business. He frowned. People should be more concerned with their privacy.

He decided to sneak behind Rachel's minivan and screen the surroundings once more, before heading back to his car. He crouched a little, and within a few steps, he was hidden behind the minivan, careful not to touch it. He looked at nearby homes and listened for any sounds that didn't belong. His frown deepened with the nearing sound of police sirens, but then he looked up and froze, feeling his blood turn to ice.

On the back window of the minivan was a decal, the stick-figure caricatures of a happy family, showing a man, a woman, a boy, two girls, and a cat, all exhibiting anatomically impossible smiles.

He had a big problem. He was fairly sure he'd killed two boys and one girl.

He crouched closer to the ground and groaned, rubbing the deepening frown on his forehead furiously, as if that friction would solve any problems or hold any answers.

"Think, think!" he whispered angrily.

There was no way Rachel Watson had made a mistake when she'd ordered the decal for her car. Everything else matched, including the cat, whose threatening, phosphorescent eyes had followed his moves from the top of the kitchen cupboard as he'd dealt with Rachel. He'd let the cat live; it wasn't worth a bullet, because cats can't talk.

But this? This made no sense, he kept thinking, his eyes glued to the decal. It clearly depicted two girls about the same age, because the respective stick figures were identical, down to the double pigtails with bows. The boy figure was a little larger than the girls' size. What was Rachel doing? Replacing the damn stickers every year? Probably. And sure as hell, she didn't make mistakes about the constituents of her family.

Then, what was going on there? He'd found a girl in one of the bedrooms, playing with some Legos by herself on the floor. She could have been five or six, or about there. Then the two other kids were a tad older, maybe seven or eight, but not more.

Both were boys.

Something was terribly wrong.

He listened some more, trying to pinpoint the location of the approaching police cars. Had someone called the police on him? He was sure the gunshots had been quiet enough, but maybe someone had seen the flickers of light through the windows. Maybe the neighbor returning the cordless drill had seen Watson's body through the open curtains. Maybe.

But maybe there was still time to set things right.

He stared for a second at the back of his hand, slightly trembling in the dim light of dusk, then he decided to do what he had to do. He sneaked back inside the house, closing the door gently, quietly. Then he started searching it, moving quickly, room by room, gun held tightly in his sweating hand.

2

Back to Work

Present Day

Special Agent Tess Winnett leaned forward, closer to the mirror, studying the circles under her eyes with a critical, disappointed glare. Unforgiving and dark-hued, the subject of her disdain circled her eyes generously, tinting her eyelids and making the blue of her irises appear hollow and lifeless. She looked pale and her face drawn, her skin taut and almost translucent against the high cheekbones.

Makeup wouldn't hurt. Too bad she wasn't into that stuff.

It was her first day back at the office, after taking three endless weeks to recuperate after injuries suffered in the line of duty. A dislocated shoulder. Torn ligaments. A couple of broken ribs that still stabbed her side with every breath. But she was back, unwilling to spend another single day bored out of her mind, counting the hours, and pacing the floor between the 300 channels of crap television and the stack of novels she just didn't have the patience for.

It wasn't the physical injuries she thought to be the source of her pallor; it was the monsters that lurked inside, in the deepest recesses of her weary brain. The memories she wanted gone forever, but which refused to fade, the raw memories of that one terrible night, more than ten years before, when her life took an abrupt turn for the nightmare. A night when she was the powerless victim fighting for her life, not the fearless FBI agent she had become.

Those wounds were still painful, still making her go through life in a constant state of hypervigilance, although her assailant couldn't hurt her anymore. Those wounds hurt much worse than a bunch of cracked ribs could ever hurt.

Focused on her physical fitness and most likely oblivious to the rest of her baggage, her doctor had prescribed six weeks off, with the last two spent in daily physiotherapy sessions, strength building, and mobility exercises. She had pleaded and threatened, but he'd already spoken with her supervisor, FBI Special Agent in Charge, or SAC Pearson, as she liked to shorten his title, advising him she couldn't return to duty for medical reasons. When she'd heard that, she'd flipped, turning on the doctor with the full force of her irrational anger, and accused him of everything she could think of, from violating patient confidentiality to simply being an inconsiderate, selfish, cover-your-ass kind of jerk, the type who shouldn't be allowed to wear a doctor's badge at any time in his life.

That didn't get her too far. The doctor scoffed hearing about patient confidentiality violations, and reassured her he'd only shared the six weeks' rest order with SAC Pearson, and none of the details. Yet, miraculously, later that same day, he agreed to let her off with three weeks, if she were to perform only light duties, as in sitting behind a desk and doing paperwork.

Hell, no.

But at least she could set foot inside the federal building again; the FBI had restored her credentials. The rest was up to her, right? A crooked smile appeared shyly in that bathroom mirror, then extended to a full-blown grin, engulfing her eyes and making her dark circles almost disappear.

She was back. That was all that mattered.

"Welcome back, Winnett," a woman greeted in passing, then slammed the door of the last stall behind her.

Tess jumped out of her skin. She hadn't heard the woman come into the bathroom; she just heard the voice behind her, too damn close when she thought she was alone and safe. Her heart raced and her hands shook a little. She focused for a few seconds on her breathing. In. Out. In. Out.

"Thanks," she finally replied, a little hesitant, then let out a long breath, steadying herself some more.

Was she really ready to be back? She'd better be. Wake the hell up, Winnett.

She stared at herself a little more, building confidence for the meeting with SAC Pearson. She'd come in that morning to find a sticky note on her desk, with a quick message, "See me first thing." The message was signed by Pearson, his scribbled name evolving from block letters to a pseudo-signature, overall illegible. But she knew who it was, anyway.

SAC Pearson. Ugh. Her boss, who'd put her on notice a few times already, and who wasn't going to take any more crap from her. A man who'd completed twelve years of service as a profiler with an enviable case record, a case record only she exceeded. He scored 98 percent; she scored 100 percent. Tiny difference, great meaning. She was sure the two percentage points were front and central on her boss's mind, at least some of the time. But, most of all, Pearson was an experienced profiler who would take one look at those black circles under her eyes and send her packing, out for three more weeks of going nuts in her apartment.

She pursed her lips, considering her options, then cleared her throat quietly.

"Hey, Colston, would you happen to have any makeup on you?"

"Uh-huh, here you go," the woman replied, offering her purse under the stall door. "Knock yourself out."

"Thanks," she replied.

She took the offered purse and put it on the counter, but hesitated a little before unzipping it. She struggled invading someone's privacy like that, despite being invited to. How different other people were. How... unsuspicious, and trusting, and open. Calm. Caring. Unassuming. As she unzipped the purse, she felt a pang of envy. She just wished she could be like that, like everyone else out there who shared, trusted, and let their guard down every now and then.

Colston's purse held a treasure trove of makeup items, and she stared, puzzled at the pile of little objects, unsure what to use.

"This is what you'll need," Colston said, picking up a concealer from the pile. Her hand dripped water into the open purse, but she didn't seem to care.

Tess's breath caught, but she swallowed and managed to thank her. How come she hadn't heard Colston flush, or seen her wash her hands? She'd definitely washed them, seeing as she was now drying them thoroughly with a paper towel. What kind of field agent lets people creep up on them like that? She needed to get a grip.

She hid her frown and applied the concealer quickly, with her finger, and smiled with gratitude.

"I'd also put on a little bit of blush. You're too pale. Here, let me," Colston offered, and quickly touched up Tess's cheeks with a thick brush, bringing color to her alabaster skin. "Perfect, there you go. Much better."

They walked out of the restroom together, but then parted ways, as Tess swung by her desk to grab her notepad before heading toward Pearson's office.

There he was, sitting at his desk, with his completely bald head lowered, as he read through the pages of a dossier, flipping through it impatiently and pressing his lips together, a definite sign of annoyance. He'd taken off his jacket and rolled up his shirtsleeves, which meant he was going to be in the office for at least a few hours.

She knocked on the doorjamb and waited silently. He waved her in, without lifting his eyes from the pile of paperwork. She stood and let her eyes wander on the few items adorning Pearson's office. Behind him, taking a shelf in a half-empty bookcase, a cluster of three framed pictures showcased Pearson's family. His wife, a little overweight, was a warm, affectionate woman who held his hand with confidence in a family picture that included their two children.

The other two images were college graduation portraits of his sons, the professional type that higher-end colleges offer on the day of the ceremony. Both boys had their mother's kindness in their eyes; they were younger, milder versions of their father. She wondered if the harshness in Pearson's features was genetic or acquired. She studied the two vertical ridges that flanked his puckered lips, the permanent frown lines on his tall forehead, and the tension in his jaw. Probably his nature.

Finally, Pearson looked up and frowned a little deeper.

"Sit down, Winnett."

She obliged.

"So, you're back. Early."

"Sir."

"Welcome back. Are you up for it?"

"Thank you, sir. Yes, I am."

He rubbed his forehead and pinched the bridge of his nose where glasses had left reddish marks on his skin. Then he leaned back in his chair, deep in his thoughts.

"I have a few things for you," he finally said. The tone of his voice didn't promise anything good.

She nodded, but didn't say a word. She shifted in her chair nervously, but then willed herself to sit still.

"First, there's the issue of your latest case. There will be a formal review of that entire development. It's scheduled to start in two weeks."

"A formal review? May I ask why?"

"My question is, do you really need to ask why?" He drilled his eyes into hers until she lowered her gaze and stared at the floor. "Yes, you've closed the case. Yes, you added one more notable notch to your belt. But the review committee has become aware that some of your stats are not that good."

"Which stats?" She knew she had an impeccable case record, so it couldn't be that. Then what?

"Your kill ratio's higher than everyone else's. You have been cleared in every shooting, but there was something about your last case that got their attention."

"Sir, I—"

"Let me finish, Winnett. I suggest you let the committee finalize the formal review and make their recommendations. Like I said, you've already been cleared in each shooting, so you're fine."

She waited for a full second before speaking.

"Sir, with all due respect, I'm not fine. A formal review can be a career killer."

He stood abruptly, started pacing the floor, and buried his hands deep inside his pockets.

"There's nothing you can do, Winnett. There's nothing anyone can do. Let things happen, and don't rock the boat. But it wouldn't hurt you to arrest a suspect for a change, instead of shooting them."

She stared quietly at the floor, feeling the sting of frustration.

"Understood," she eventually replied, managing to refrain from disputing everything that was wrong with the system.

Pearson sat back at his desk, and his frown deepened.

"Second item on the list is definitely not helping you with the upcoming review." He cleared his throat, then continued. "I would like you to work with a partner for a while."

"Oh?" she said, looking at Pearson with poorly hidden annoyance. She didn't want a partner, but she knew it was bound to happen, sooner or later. Pearson had been clear about it. But still. "We're not required to have permanent partners in the FBI, so I was—"

"Don't quote statute on me, Winnett. I still get to decide who does what here, and with whom. That clear?"

"Yes, sir. But that means you actually want me supervised, rather than—"

"Winnett!"

She froze. She didn't want to push him too far, but she didn't feel she deserved it either. Where could she draw that line, between taking direction from her boss and standing up for herself?

"For now, there isn't anyone available to work with you," he said, then glared at her as her relief must have been too obvious. "But I want you to consider having a partner as a next step in your career. It will help you a great deal, and it will help with people's perceptions about you."

"What perceptions?"

"That you're not a team player. That you don't care about how others feel, or about their results; just about getting case after case solved, as fast and as good as possible."

"Umm... and what's wrong with solving cases fast? That's my job!"

"The perception is that you don't care who you hurt in the process. You have to fix this perception, Winnett. You have to, and I'm not kidding. Regain the trust and respect of your colleagues, and make sure you can demonstrate you belong on this team. There's no room for solo artists here, Winnett, regardless of your case record. We're all part of a team, and we have to act like it."

How the hell was she supposed to do that? Interactions like she'd just had in the bathroom with Colston were so rare, they only proved the rule by being the exceptions. They were enjoyable though, she had to admit.

"I worked just fine with Mike. I think I demonstrated that. But Mike's gone. He's dead."

"Listen, Winnett," Pearson continued, loosening his tie with a frustrated sigh. "No matter what you, or I, or anyone else would be willing to do, Mike's not coming back. No matter how much you blame yourself, or how much you decide you can't work with anyone else. It's time to move on, Winnett. Don't let it destroy your career." He fell silent for a second, letting his loaded gaze say the words he didn't speak.

She lowered her eyes again, not sure what more she could say.

"Then, there's the problem with the governor," he continued.

Tess sighed quietly and refrained from visibly rolling her eyes.

"He called with your name, twice, while you were working your latest case. Twice!"

"He gets calls from all the ritzy people I happen to bother during my—"

"Winnett!" he snapped. "Don't you think I know how the wheels turn? But you have to be smart about it! At some point, he could call and ask me formally to make you another governor's problem! No other agent in this branch has your kind of track record. They all solve cases, maybe not with your record of achievement, but definitely with less noise and disruption. With fewer complaints." He paused for a little while, as if trying to figure out what to do with her. "Be smart about these things, Winnett," he eventually continued. "Don't allow your behavior to cast a shadow on the reputation of this team, internal and external. Do you understand?"

"Perfectly," Tess managed. She was going to have to figure out how to get people to like her, to accept her. She had to change, and that was never easy. She needed to soften around the edges a little, but somehow still be able to do her job, maintain her edge. She had no idea how to do that, or where to start.

"I'm giving you an assignment," Pearson moved on.

She lit up, feeling anticipation and excitement elevate her gloomy spirits.

"There's a serial killer on death row at Raiford; Kenneth Garza."

"Ah, The Family Man," she added.

"Yes, The Family Man," Pearson confirmed. "His execution date is set and it's approaching. It's in three weeks or so, on the twenty-second. I'd like you to study his file, and go there for an interview. Make sure everything rings right, that we've crossed every T and dotted every I, and we're not going to have any surprises in his final hour. Are you familiar with his case?"

"No, just with his reputation. It was before my time."

"Jeez, Winnett, you're something else. Before Winnett and After Winnett, is that it? How arrogant can you get?" The irritation in Pearson's voice was discernible, almost physical in the unusually elevated pitch.

"No, sir. I meant I am familiar with all the serial killer cases closed during my tenure."

"Of course, you are," he reacted, "because you closed them!"

"No, sir. I meant I'm familiar with all serial killer cases closed by the Bureau, regardless of who closed them, since the day I joined the FBI ten years ago."

Pearson's jaw dropped a little, but then he regained his composure, apparently unperturbed. She felt the urge to smile, but knew better and didn't.

He continued, "Okay, so get familiar with Garza's file, and go have a chat with him before he fries."

"Yes, sir," she said and stood, ready to leave.

He pointed at a stack of boxes, already loaded on a dolly and parked in the corner of his office, near the door. She raised her eyebrows.

"Garza's file," he said, then resumed reading the documents he was studying before her arrival.

She grabbed the dolly's handle and winced. Sharp pain stabbed her side. She shifted the handle to her other hand and managed to roll out of there without hitting the walls or denting any furniture.

Relieved, she focused on pulling the dolly awkwardly on the thick carpet, looking behind her at each step to make sure the stack of boxes still held on. Then she ran into someone, head-butting into a muscular chest, white shirt clad, and boasting a colorful necktie. She gasped, as the impact sent a wave of pain into her shoulder.

"What the hell, Winnett, watch it," Donovan said. He was the best and brightest on their analysis team. An analyst, not a field agent, despite his numerous applications, and his solid, unwavering enthusiasm.

She tightened her lips and swallowed a long, detailed curse.

"Sorry, Donovan. Are you okay?" A hint of sarcasm seeped in her voice. He shook his head.

"And to think you wield a weapon for a living. Huh... I wonder who approved that," he replied with biting humor.

That stung, and, within that angry split second, she felt the urge to tell Donovan it was the same people who'd denied him his application to become a field agent. But then she remembered her commitment to herself and Pearson and swallowed that angry comeback.

"Um, once again, sorry," she said softly, then turned to leave.

Donovan's face dropped, seemingly unsure how to react. The Tess Winnett he and everyone else knew would have ripped him to shreds for far less. He stood there, riveted in place, watching her wince while she struggled to pull the loaded dolly.

"By the way, in case you want to know: you push the dolly; you don't pull it with loads that high," he offered, then turned away and resumed his course toward the elevators.

Gah... She closed her eyes for a second, trying to envision a space where she could let the angry cuss words she felt like shouting at Donovan's broad shoulders actually be articulated, to let off some of the pressure she felt. No such place.

She turned the dolly around and started pushing it, seeing how easy it was to make it across the wide floor to her desk. She smiled, almost forgetting about the review committee and the weight of the thousands of pages detailing the many gruesome murders perpetrated by The Family Man.

She was back. That was all that mattered.

3

A Letter

The recipe for pasta primavera can be tricky for those who don't spend enough time in the kitchen. Laura Watson didn't aim for culinary perfection; she just wanted a quick meal for Adrian and herself, something to be a little different from the monotonous sandwiches grilled in the toaster oven, or the long list of microwave dinners gulped down in front of the TV.

Typical youngsters, the two of them shared an apartment that reflected Laura's financial well-being, but also her chosen profession. At least twice the usual number of lamps and light fixtures adorned the place, every single one of them bearing the WatWel Lighting logo.

A particular wall sconce in the shape of a stylized seashell held special meanings. Laura had designed that lamp when she was fifteen, and her adoptive father/business partner had built the prototype. A year later, that particular model sold like hot cakes to hotels and resorts on both coasts. On her apartment wall, seemingly out of place, the prototype wall sconce was rarely turned off. Looking at the lamp's gentle light reminded Laura of her family legacy, the company her biological father had started with her now adoptive parent, Bradley Welsh.

Brad held a special place in her heart; he'd been a terrific adoptive father, who'd broken all the rules and had not placed her legacy in a trust; rather, he'd involved her in decisions at a very young age; he'd been there to kindle her interest for the light fixture manufacturing processes, teaching her how to lead, letting her sit in high-level meetings and big-dollar client negotiations. Together, the two of them had become media darlings.

There were pictures of them on the apartment walls, the oldest going back to when she was seven or eight years old, and he took her to the inauguration of the new manufacturing facility. She'd cut the ribbon herself, struggling with the huge scissors, but knowing she had him by her side. On a special place above the fireplace was the only photo of her long-lost family, five happy faces that shared one of many moments of closeness together, hiking in Yosemite. On the opposing wall, there was another cherished photo, of her father and Brad Welsh, taken the day they'd incorporated WatWel Lighting.

That's why, following the family tradition, she'd chosen a degree in electrical engineering, a difficult specialty that suited her future role with WatWel Lighting. She'd raced through the curriculum in a hurry, and she was bound to finish her degree early by several months. Yet following a simple pasta recipe posed issues for her.

Laura read the instructions again, and groaned. The recipe was marked "easy" or "beginner" on two of the most popular online recipe sites, yet she didn't have the necessary patience to execute all the things that needed to be done to achieve the colorful bowl of pasta. She let out another frustrated groan and decided to cut corners, the corners she had the most issues with. Zucchinis? She didn't have those and wasn't about to leave the house and go shopping. Adrian wouldn't know the difference anyway. The surviving red pepper in her fridge had endured in there for a long time and was mushy in places; definitely a candidate for the trash can, not her glamorous Saturday lunch.

She checked the time, throwing a worried glance at the digital clock hanging on the dining room wall, and decided not to waste any more of it. A little nervous, she ran her fingers through her long, sleek hair, tugging a few rebel strands behind her ears. Adrian's workshop was about to be over, and she wanted to be done with the meal. Okay… she was going to cut a lot of corners.

She drained the pasta, mumbling something unintelligible as a few rogue farfalle made it past the drainer and plunged down into the garbage disposal. She put the drained pasta into a large pan just as the phone chimed. She shot a quick glance at the phone's screen and saw a message from Adrian, saying, "On my way, be there in ten." Then she opened a small pack of frozen, mixed vegetables, and poured it on top of the pasta. She added olive oil without measuring it and turned on the stove.

Laura loved gizmos of any kind; maybe a trait inherited from her father's technical brain, or an acquired preference, she wasn't sure. Her apartment held an entire collection of small appliances and electrical tools of various kinds. Her best friend and adoptive sister, Amanda, teased her by saying that everything in her apartment had to have a power cord, or it didn't belong. For the task that most people endure without thinking, the part of the recipe that reads, "Cook on the stove, stirring constantly," she had a new device, an automated stirring machine that clamped on top of the pan and did the stirring for her. At least that helped a little.

She cleaned the table quickly and set the placemats, then plugged in a small electric grater and threw in a chunk of fresh Parmesan cheese. She was about done, when she heard the key in the lock.

"Hey, baby," Adrian greeted her with a smile, then pecked her on the lips. "Mmm… smells good in here!"

Boo, their tabby cat, circled his legs with his tail straight up, like a banner.

She chuckled lightly. All the cut corners were going to remain her secret; Adrian wouldn't know. He was an orphan, a kid who'd lost his parents to drugs and various prison systems, then grew up in street gangs and juvenile crime until someone took him in. A stranger... a neighbor who was willing to put up with the troubled teenager and had brought him to his senses before he could completely ruin his life.

They had that in common, the two of them, losing their parents early in their lives. Laura had the better deal though. She hadn't seen one day of street living, of poverty, or of foster care at the hands of the state. Her father's business partner and his family had been there from the moment her parents were so tragically taken from her, when she was only five years old. She had been the fortunate one in that respect, having grown up with the love and care of a family that left nothing to be desired.

Adrian, on the other hand, still had that ruggedness, that fierceness of the street survivor, of the boy who was forced to grow up overnight and fend for himself, when others his age still wrote letters to Santa. His heart was in a good place, but he could become overbearing and too protective at times, his fears and inner monsters fed by who knows what nightmarish experiences he had lived through. It drove her crazy.

That's why Laura averted her eyes as much as she could that day; she couldn't bring herself to tell him she was pregnant. She'd confirmed it earlier that morning. She'd waited for him to leave for school, then rushed to the corner drugstore to get a test, and came running back home. She'd only been a few days late, and she still had hope. She was taking her birth control pills every morning without exception, so she expected to see one line on the test, the one line that would put her fears at ease.

She saw two. She didn't believe it; couldn't. She waited for another hour, then ran another test. The same two lines that confirmed the unwanted truth: she was pregnant. In shock, she rushed to her laptop and typed exactly what she was feeling. She searched, "On birth control and pregnant. How is it possible?" Then added several question marks after her search phrase, not for any rational reason; only so she could refrain from breaking things.

The search results returned various possible causes that didn't quite match her case, but the fourth one on the list sent shivers down her spine. Apparently, if you take antibiotics when you're on the pill, it could reduce the pill's effectiveness. Then she recalled the strep throat she'd had three or four weeks earlier, and the full regimen of antibiotics she had taken. Someone should have told her!

Swallowing her tears, she weighed her options. She wasn't ready to start a family, to get busy with diapers and everything. She wanted to get her bachelor's degree, followed by her master's, then join her adoptive father at the helm of WatWel Lighting and open the new line of digital, LED fixtures. There was no room for a baby in her life plans. And Adrian? Probably not the best father material. Not the worst either, but someone so overbearing can drive a kid, and its mother, completely nuts. Still, abortion was not an option; she couldn't even bear the thought.

By mid-morning, it had become simply too hard to swallow her tears, and she just let the floodgates open. She cried herself out, then decided to cook a special meal, just so she could have something different to prevent Adrian from seeing something was, in fact, different about her. A decoy, a culinary smokescreen. As for her pregnancy, she needed to think and decide what to do. She missed her mother, her real one, the one she could barely remember. She wished she could run to her and ask her what to do, and cry some more, curled up in her lap.

She touched, in passing, the antiquated voicemail system on the counter, a system that worked with cassettes. She held on to it, because it was one of the very few relics she had from her real parents. They had touched that very machine, some fifteen years ago. She swallowed with difficulty, then turned around and faced Adrian.

"How was school?"

He scoffed. "You know… some of these folks can be so damn arrogant, it takes away from the material. I keep daydreaming about kicking their asses back into reality."

She smiled, a crooked smile filled with tenderness. That was her Adrian. Two parts engineer, two parts teddy bear, one part mule, and one part street thug.

"Simpson, huh?" she asked, referring to the electromagnetic fields professor.

"Uh-huh," he said, then sneaked his hand into the pasta pot and stole a couple of farfalle covered in fresh-grated Parmesan. She slapped him across the buttock.

He still held on to a bunch of mail with his other hand. No way had he washed his hands before touching the food.

"Ouch!"

"Hands off," she said, "it's not ready yet. And wash your hands."

"Looks ready to me," he replied, then dropped the pile of mail on the table.

"Take that away, I just cleaned the table. Anything interesting?"

"Just this," he replied, sorting through the mail above the trash can that ended up receiving most of the mail items, unopened.

He handed her a white envelope that bore her name and address in handwritten, cursive letters. She wiped her hands against her jeans and took the envelope, studying it on both sides before opening it. The letter was postmarked locally, in Miami. She opened it and took out a one-page typed letter.

She read the first few lines, then had to sit down, overwhelmed by a wave of emotion. She leaned her forehead into her hand.

"What's wrong, baby?"

She struggled to speak. She took a deep breath and cleared her throat a little.

"Um, it's a letter from a Dr. Austin Jacobs, a neuroscientist. She's conducting some studies in memory, um… here goes, 'cognitive memory recovery and memory distortion in childhood trauma,' and she'd like to speak with me."

"Why the hell would she want to do that?"

"She says I make a great candidate for her study. She says she could help me remember. I will call her on Monday."

"The hell you will," Adrian snapped and stood up abruptly. "It's over, baby, that part of your life is over. Let it go."

She clenched her jaws, swallowing the biting response to his outburst. She didn't like it when he tried to run her life like that.

"I will call her on Monday, Adrian. It's my only chance to remember. I want to remember... I need to."

They both fell quiet, each deeply immersed in their own internal turmoil and too troubled to want to speak. The silence between them felt heavy, uneasy, like a foreboding.

Laura folded the letter and stuffed it in her jeans back pocket, then stood and put the bowl of pasta on the table. Then she continued setting the table, adding plates, cutlery, and glasses.

"I'm not hungry anymore," Adrian said, pouting and gloomy.

Sometimes he behaved like a spoiled child.

"Don't be silly," she replied calmly, yet firmly. "Whether you eat or not, I am calling Dr. Jacobs on Monday morning."

4

Reflections: First Kill

I remember the night of my first kill as if it were yesterday. I remember preparing for it in detail, getting ready for it, from both a tactical point of view, but also emotionally. They say killing is hard; it can break a man. It can destroy him forever.

It liberated me.

But let's not get ahead of my story. The first thing that happened was the need to kill. You see, with me it wasn't an urge; not at first, anyway. Or, maybe, to be completely honest, I'd felt the urge to kill before, but I didn't understand it. It felt like waves of restlessness, of suffocating anger without a precise, well-determined object, that I didn't act on because I simply didn't understand what I needed to do. Not until that first kill.

Yes, so I had the dire need to kill Allen Watson. The reasons were many, too many, yet irrelevant to what I want to share with you. But, please, believe me when I say I tried everything I could to avoid having to kill him. He didn't give me much choice. I was backed into a corner, with no other alternative but to end the bastard's sorry life.

Once I understood I had no other choice, I started to think about how I should do it. You see, going to prison wasn't—and still isn't—an option for me. I kept thinking, looking for a solution that wouldn't land me in a cell. As I was tossing and turning for nights in a row trying to create the perfect murder, something happened. Fate intervened and opened a door for me.

A serial killer, dubbed by the media with the ridiculous name of The Family Man, had murdered a family of four, just miles away from Watson's neighborhood. I learned about it on the news. I saw everyone on TV fretting about the killings, calling it a gruesome repeat of some other murders, done in about the same way, in about the same area, that I'd somehow missed hearing.

What an opportunity!

I remember sleeping like a baby for the rest of that night. The next morning, refreshed, I started researching everything there was to know about that serial killer. I was careful not to leave a trail. That's what libraries are for, to research things anonymously, protected by a hoodie and some thick-rimmed glasses, and looking so grimy my own mother wouldn't recognize me. If I knew who invented the hoodie, I'd send them a check. On second thought, no... I'd be leaving a paper trail; big mistake. I'd send them cash instead.

Soon I knew everything there was to learn about The Family Man from the media and the Internet. Of course, police probably had held on to some details, to prevent perfect copycats from happening, but I didn't care. Maybe police had even lied about some of the details they released; I still didn't care. Copycatting The Family Man was still my best shot. I studied his handiwork and noted all the factors, taking them at face value: how he killed his victims, how he gained access to their properties, what kind of gun he used, what caliber and what brand, how he went about doing it. Every little thing.

There was only one problem with copycatting The Family Man: I had to kill Allen Watson's entire family. Oh, well... That was going to be on him, not on me. He's the one who pushed me to do it anyway.

Getting the right gun was tricky. I needed to buy a Beretta 9 mil, unregistered, of course, and from a reliable street vendor. Getting to the right street corner near Liberty Square proved more challenging than acquiring the actual gun. I couldn't drive my own car. Cabs have cameras onboard these days, so there I was, using public transportation for the first time in years, with my phone turned off and my hoodie zipped up, despite an early heat wave. I kept my face hidden behind a newspaper the whole time, and once I was in the neighborhood, I chose to walk the last leg of my trip.

The first person I asked about a gun sent me to hell. He was a well-built black man, who took my question personally and assumed immediately it was because of his race that I was asking him about contraband weapons. Honestly, it was, but I didn't admit that to him; I just apologized profusely and didn't stop until he said, "Whatever, man," and moved on. I'd learned a lesson.

I walked around Liberty Square for a while longer, then approached another young man, a white guy this time; well, at least the skin under his tattoos had been white at some point. He made these quick, twitchy movements with his entire body; he was probably a meth head. But he knew someone, and for a twenty he said he'd point me in the right direction.

He did, and a minute later, a third man approached us and led me to a car, whose trunk held a variety of firearms. He had the exact pistol I was looking for, and swore it hadn't been used for anything nasty before. Sure, like I was going to believe that... or maybe he spoke the truth, who knows?

He asked for two hundred. Unfamiliar with the street rate of illegal weapons, I'd come prepared to pay two thousand, and there I was, struggling to extract the two Benjamins he wanted, without them noticing how thick my roll of cash really was. Delighted I didn't bargain, he offered two boxes of 9-mil ammo, and I made a mental note to wipe the prints clean off each and every bullet. One can never be too careful.

I was ready, and I couldn't delay anymore. Allen Watson wasn't going to go away or learn to shut up; he was becoming a big liability for me. I went there and parked on the street parallel to his cul-de-sac, hidden behind a bush. I waited patiently for him to come home from the office, and then waited some more for dusk to set in. Then I made my move.

He let me in, just as I'd expected, and I didn't even let him finish his question. There wasn't any point to it. The time for conversations had come and gone. I pulled the trigger twice and watched him collapse against the wall, leaving a thick smudge of blood against the caramel wood paneling.

The thrill of the kill hit me like a shot of heroin to my vein, going straight to my brain and reverberating into every cell in my body. Whew! What a rush! I remember inhaling the metallic scent of fresh blood with flaring, lusting nostrils, and feeling the exhilaration of the adrenaline surge turn me into something else, a superhuman, a predator set on the scent of blood. You see, I'd expected to feel sick after killing Watson, because that's what I heard others feel; I'd even brought along a plastic bag to barf in, just in case I needed to. But no, that wasn't my case.

I heard the kids shriek, and I didn't want Rachel Watson to barge in and turn things messy. I leapt up the stairs and caught up with them easily. I didn't mind doing the three kids, but didn't enjoy it either. I felt… nothing. But again, I had no choice, being that The Family Man killed entire families, not just the adults.

I'd saved the best for last, and it was time for me to find Rachel. A neighbor came by and gave me a scare; I hated that. I hated feeling the fear gripping my throat and twisting it, choking me. Real predators don't feel fear, so why did I? I shrugged it off and went looking for Rachel Watson, feeling a forgotten, yet familiar feeling arouse me, making me eager.

When she saw me, she dropped some dishes and screamed, walking backward until she hit the kitchen counter, then begged me. "No, no," she kept saying, much like her husband had said, moments before dying. But I couldn't pull the trigger; something wouldn't let me. I wanted to; I wanted her dead, and I needed her dead. But not like this… it felt like a waste, a terrible waste of what could be an intoxicating experience, an exhilarating memory to cherish for years to come.

I put the gun down on the counter and grabbed a large knife from the wooden knife block, then took one step closer to her. Her eyes, rounded with fear, stared at the large blade. She gasped and continued to cry, louder and louder, "No, no!" Right… Like that was going to change my mind. Seriously, what did she expect? That I'd suddenly drop the knife and say, "Well, if you don't want it, I'll just go home." How ridiculous.

Yeah, thinking back, I didn't expect to enjoy killing that much. I remember seeing Rachel in a pool of blood at my feet and feeling exalted, thinking that I had to do this again sometime. Soon.

Then I heard the sirens.

I didn't care that The Family Man spent days with his victims; I wasn't going to do that, copycat or no copycat, although I had to admit, I would've wanted to take more time with Rachel. I rushed outside and hid behind Rachel's minivan for a short while. Then my whole world came apart. The stupid decals... I should have checked the decals first. The stupid decals showed two girls and a boy, and that didn't match the reality inside the Watson's residence. Did I miss a kid? Did I leave a witness? You've got to be kidding me, right?

You see, I don't pay attention to kids; not ever. To me, they simply don't exist. They're a source of noise and nuisance, and I can't even bear to look at them. They just irritate me, regardless of age and gender. In that case, I should have paid more attention, at least to Watson's goddamned kids, considering what I had planned to do.

So I went back inside and looked everywhere, checked under every bed, and opened every closet. Nope, there was no one else. With the sirens blaring closer, I had to leave, but I felt confident that I didn't leave any loose ends.

It wasn't until the next morning that I learned just how mistaken I'd been.

Laura Watson had somehow survived. Damn her! The press called her The Watson Girl, and that somehow became the moniker for the sole survivor of yet another horrifying Family Man attack.

How the hell did I let that happen?

In hindsight, considering the inherent stress of killing someone for the first time, it makes sense that I had to see the decals on Rachel's car to notice something was off.

But still, what a screw-up.

5

Death Row

Tess had floored it all the way to Raiford, the small town that houses the state prison, the home of Florida's death row. She'd turned on the emergency lights embedded in the grille of her black Suburban and enjoyed the thrill of being back on the road, blasting through traffic at eighty miles per hour.

SAC Pearson would have frowned, seeing her weave her way through the dense traffic on Interstate 95. Visiting an inmate on death row can hardly qualify as an emergency, but this was a typical illustration of the proverbial blissful ignorance. What Pearson didn't know, couldn't hurt him. Or her.

She finally left I-95 and had to make her way through a long, winding, country highway, and, after a long stretch of that, she finally made it to the prison grounds. She parked in one of the reserved spots and got out of the car slowly, feeling stiff and sore. Her shoulder hurt, and her ribs sent sharp needles of pain as she extracted herself from the SUV, but she was happy to restore some blood flow to her legs and reenergize herself.

She grabbed her briefcase and started walking briskly toward the main entrance. A series of endless security checks and she was in, after turning in her weapon to a corrections officer at the gate. Then she was escorted to see the warden, who made quick work of giving her instructions about how to interact with death-row inmates. Nothing new in what he had to say; she'd been there before. He knew it too and saved them both as much time as he could without entirely breaking protocol.

They'd already parked Garza in an interview room, and she asked the officer who was escorting her to let her spend some time in the adjacent observation room, studying the killer, and preparing her notes. Tess entered the observation room slowly, taking in all details. The faint smell of disinfectant, omnipresent since she'd arrived at the facility. The chill in the air, a humid, musty chill that got into her bones. The fluorescent lighting everywhere, with bluish hues and almost imperceptible flickering.

The officer offered her a steaming paper cup filled with coffee to the brim, and she accepted it gratefully. It was decent, considering where she was—not exactly Starbucks. She wrapped her frozen hands around the cup and spent a few minutes studying Garza through the one-sided mirror.

He was an average man; she probably wouldn't have given him a second look if she'd seen him on the street somewhere. His brown hair was shoulder-length and a little oily, and almost without a hint of salt-and-pepper in it, although he was pushing fifty. The only trace of gray was in his five-day stubble, and here and there in his bushy eyebrows. A furrowed, tall forehead emerged above those, the forehead of an intellectual.

So, that was what a serial killer who murdered thirty-four families looked like in person. Credited with 108 victims, of which 30 were children, Garza looked like an average person, and probably that's what kept him going for so long, despite law enforcement's constant efforts to catch him. Take away the prison garb, put him in a grocery store pushing a shopping cart, and he'd fit right in, waiting in line at the cashier's and making casual conversation with everyday people. But then again, that's why these predators were so successful in luring their victims. They didn't stand out; they were charismatic and appeared trustworthy. They fit in, everywhere. Anywhere.

She checked her file. Garza had not even finished high school but was self-taught. He'd been evaluated several times during the investigation and later, a few months after his incarceration. He scored thirty-two points out of forty on the Hare Psychopathy Checklist, and he was noted as a highly intelligent, perceptive, and cultivated individual. A certain psychologist had noted, almost six years earlier, that, "Garza enjoys setting the record straight and having meaningful debates of almost a philosophical nature." She was planning to use that.

He sat calmly at the metallic table, almost relaxed in his orange jumpsuit showing a white T-shirt underneath. His hands and feet were shackled, and a chain tied to his cuffs passed through a ring welded into the table. He stared at the mirror, almost straight into Tess's eyes. There was a state of peace, of calmness in his stare. Garza was accepting his fate, waiting to die. There was no anger in his eyes, no reveal of inner angst or turmoil.

She dumped the empty paper cup into a trash can and grabbed her files, then turned to the officer.

"I'm ready."

"We'll be here, watching. Just wave or knock when you're done," he replied.

He opened the door for her, and she walked into the interrogation room. Garza looked at her with a hint of a smile. She heard the door closing behind her, and then the clank of the electric locks secured it shut. She repressed a shiver.

"Hello there," Garza said. His voice had low tones, sounding almost baritone. Tess wondered if he could sing.

"Hello," she replied neutrally. "I'm Special Agent Tess Winnett with the FBI. Mind if I sit?"

His eyebrows shot up. He probably wasn't used to politeness from his prior interactions with law enforcement.

"No, please do," he replied.

"This is a routine conversation," Tess said, maintaining a neutral tone. "Considering the date of your execution is approaching."

"I see," he replied. "What do you want to talk about?"

"Actually, that's more up to you," she offered, deciding to postpone her standard list of questions, known internally and unofficially as the exit interview. If she could get him to open up, to relate, then maybe she'd have a better chance of getting her questions answered.

"Me?" he sneered. "There's nothing I have to say you people haven't heard before. This isn't the place where new, interesting stuff happens, you know. This is a place where death-row inmates prepare to die. Well, I'm prepared already. I've been prepared for eight years now."

"You have no regrets?"

Tess's question threw him off a little. He looked away briefly, then returned his calm gaze back at her.

"Everyone has regrets."

"Name one."

"One that's not in there?" Garza pointed at the file she held closed in front of her.

"Sure, why not?" She continued to let him be in charge of the conversation, already intrigued.

"My biggest regret is that you people don't care for the truth as much as you should, considering your line of work."

"How so?" Tess frowned a little. Was he going to be a cliché and start saying, "I didn't do it?" That would be very disappointing.

"I've told many others before you, that I only killed thirty-one families, not thirty-four. I would have expected some interest, considering the three families you pinned on me for no good reason were killed by someone who gets away with it. But no. No one gives a crap. They just want their cases closed, with no interest for truth or justice."

Tess looked at him intrigued. Why would he say that?

"So, you have an interest in justice?"

"Do you find that so hard to believe?"

She pursed her lips. There was an air of acceptance about him, almost of kindness. Yet this man had taken so many lives in cold blood. The disconnect between the man's appearance and his history was chilling. A true, absolute psychopath. She felt her hairs stand on end.

"Yeah, I do, actually. Can I be blunt?"

"Go ahead," he encouraged her, making a hand gesture restricted by the rattling chain.

"I'm thinking okay, thirty-one families or thirty-four, you still fry. What do you want? Do you want to open up a can of worms now and get a stay of execution?"

He laughed and leaned back in his chair, as far back as the restraints allowed.

"No, God, please, no stay of execution. I want this to be over." His laughter quieted and turned into a pervasive, lingering smile. "No, I just want what's true to be true. To be known as such."

"Nothing else?" Tess probed.

"No. That's it."

She thought for a few seconds, trying to think what type of manipulation could the psychopath in front of her cook up. She couldn't think of any ulterior motive, and law enforcement did make mistakes at times, more often than anyone cared to admit. She decided to keep an open mind.

"All right, I'm listening," she said, preparing to take notes on a blank page in her file folder.

"Well, you'd be the first. You have the list of families in there, I'm sure," he said, just as calmly. "Please take it out and follow along."

She complied, unable to refrain from shooting him a quick, inquisitive glance.

"The Meyers, the Townsends, and the Watsons, found them?"

"Um, yes," she confirmed, after marking the three names with her pen.

"These are the ones I didn't kill. The rest, I did. The rest are all mine, but these ones are not."

"Okay, but prove it to me," Tess said, staring him straight in the eye. "You were already found guilty by a court of law for the murder of these families, so I see no reason to believe you."

"What reason would I have to lie to you?"

"What reason not to?" she returned, impassible. "You have to do better than that."

"I'll give you two reasons for today, then I'll let you go back and work that angle. Then we'll talk some more, if you're interested."

"Shoot," she replied, seemingly only half-interested. She knew better than to show any interest or excitement with a psychopath in the room.

"First fact: if you go ahead and timeline my killings, the ones I really did, you'll see they're never closer than three months apart, from one to the next. I needed that much time to choose my targets, to study them, and to prepare for the kill. These three, the Watsons, the Townsends, and the Meyers, are the only ones breaking the pattern. The Watsons were killed only a couple of weeks after the Hamiltons. I killed the Hamiltons, but I didn't kill the Watsons."

"Most serial killers escalate, I'm sure you know that."

"That's what the other cops said, but I'm telling you that's not what happened."

"Okay, let's say I'll look into that. What's the second reason why I should believe you?"

He remained silent for a while, showing some signs of internal conflict for the first time. He clenched his jaws and bit his lip before speaking, while his hands clasped and unclasped repeatedly.

"I haven't shared this with anyone yet. It's very personal, you see."

Tess nodded quietly, waiting for him to continue.

"I like to kill women just as much as I like killing men and their offspring. This killer enjoys women more.... I may be a killer, but I'm no rapist. Check your facts."

There was sadness on his face, a flicker of gloominess coloring his features. Tess wondered why. She checked her notes. The file had Garza listed as a hedonistic thrill killer motivated by anger, whose methods did not include rape. His MO was quick and to the point. He shot his victims once or twice in the head or chest, killing them quickly, painlessly. What made him famous though was what he did after killing them.

"None of these victims were raped, the ones you're disputing: the Meyers, Townsends, and Watsons. What are you talking about?"

He sustained her inquisitive look for a few long seconds before replying.

"Check your facts."

6

Methodology

Laura paced the small reception area slowly, a little uneasy, doing her best to avoid the receptionist's look, although the young woman seemed kind and understanding, not at all judgmental after inviting her several times to take a seat.

She struggled to stay put. All kinds of random thoughts whirlpooled through her mind, probably a measure of her anxiety at the thought of meeting Dr. Jacobs, of taking a glimpse at her forgotten past. She checked the time nervously, then tucked a strand of her blonde hair behind her ear. She glanced quickly at the receptionist, who smiled apologetically.

She'd been waiting for almost fifteen minutes, her courage wearing thinner with each minute. Maybe her mind had closed up and swallowed all that horror for a reason. Maybe there was nothing to remember; maybe she really hadn't seen anything. Maybe Adrian was right, and she shouldn't try to fix the unfixable. Nothing she did now could ever bring her family back.

She turned on her heels and started for the exit, averting her eyes.

"Sorry," she said timidly, "I have to go."

"Please, don't leave," the receptionist said. "She's stuck on the phone with the hospital; there's an emergency. It's really not something she can cut short. Please. It will only be a few more minutes. I'll ping her again."

"Um, I'm not very sure I should even be here," she mumbled, in lieu of an apology.

"Please. She'd be very disappointed, because she knows she can help you. And you can help her."

Laura's head hung; she felt defeated. A few more minutes won't matter, she promised herself, watching the receptionist type quickly, probably a new message to Dr. Jacobs.

To pass the time, she focused her attention on the diplomas that hung on the wall, at the left of Dr. Jacobs's office door. Normally, diplomas hung inside the doctor's office, not outside. She found herself wondering why this particular office was the exception to that unwritten rule, but then became absorbed in the impressive list of credentials. PhD from UCLA, with honors. Board certified, specialized in behavioral and cognitive psychology. Awards for publications in the field of cognitive neuroscience. Worldwide recognition for her research. Dr. Jacobs could have worked with anyone she wanted. And yet, she'd invited her.

"You can go in now," the receptionist said, breaking her chain of thought. She knocked twice, then entered.

Dr. Jacobs's office was huge and decorated with incredible taste. Mahogany wood paneling, leather sofas and generous armchairs, and a massive desk. Fine art hung on the walls, gallery-level oil paintings of still nature and breathtaking landscapes. Yes, her black-framed diplomas would have ruined the look and feel of her posh office.

"Hi, I'm—"

"Laura Watson, right?" Dr. Jacobs approached her with a spring in her step and a friendly extended hand. "Thank you for coming, and most of all for waiting! It was impossible to get away, I apologize."

Her handshake was firm, and Laura enjoyed the friendship and warmth it conveyed.

"Why am I here, Dr. Jacobs?" she asked directly, eager to hear the answer.

Dr. Jacobs tilted her head for a second, giving her a scrutinizing look.

"Let's sit down," she offered, then led the way to a pair of armchairs seated in front of a lit fireplace. "I'm starting work on a new study, a new method to restore blocked or distorted childhood trauma memories. I think you'd make a great candidate for the study, because, well, you fit the profile we're looking for, and—"

"What is that profile, exactly?" Laura looked at her with serious, unforgiving eyes. Jacobs didn't budge under her drilling gaze, and her friendly demeanor didn't fade.

"Adults who have sustained significant trauma as children, under the age of seven, and who have no recollection of said traumatic events."

"I see," she acknowledged, then lowered her head a little.

"That's just the profile. You, however, make a terrific candidate for my new method because in your particular case, there is ample documentation of what went on during the traumatic event, and because we already have information about the perpetrator."

Laura frowned.

"Meaning?"

"Meaning we know who killed your family, Laura. May I call you Laura?"

"Yeah, sure. And that's important, how?"

"My method's primary use will be in assisting with the investigation of crimes committed against or in the presence of minors under the age of seven, whose blocked memories we can't extract or understand with traditional methods. To get this methodology ready for use, we need to demonstrate its validity, its reliability. In your case, knowing who the killer is will give us just that: validation of results."

"Um, I'm an engineer, or almost, Dr. Jacobs, not a doctor. I get most of what you're saying, but not all of it. Do you mean you'll help me remember?"

"Yes."

"Even what happened the night they died?"

"Yes. All of it."

She wrung her hands, afraid of what the past would uncover. Deep frown lines scrunched her brow. She had to remember. She wanted to remember, no matter how painful or how scary that seemed.

"I can only imagine what you must be going through, or how hard this is for you, but don't worry," Jacobs added, reading correctly the reasons for her anxiety. "This will not push you past what you're able to handle. We'll work gradually, and the moment you're not comfortable we will stop."

She frowned deeper, and for a few seconds she contemplated running out of there and not looking back. But she owed it to them, she owed it to her parents to remember. She wanted to remember how they looked, how they sounded, how they felt when she touched them. Her eyes welled up.

"Please, walk me through what you're going to do," she asked quietly, barely louder than a whisper. She stared at the fireplace, where a happy fire danced on real logs, reminding her of a distant past, another fireplace, another life.

"We'll start slowly," Dr. Jacobs replied. "I'll take a fact sheet first, listing all key details you remember or you know from third-party accounts. I'll add information from police reports and the actual case file for the, um, murder of your family, then we'll have weekly age-regression sessions."

"Hypnosis?"

"Yes."

"It's been tried before," Laura said, sounding almost apologetic.

"Not like this," Jacobs replied. "We'll add sensory details, to help trigger the buried memories."

"What sensory details?"

"Smells, sounds, images, perceptions."

Laura didn't hide her confusion. She looked at Jacobs with a renewed, deep frown.

"I'll explain in a minute. But first, why don't you walk me through what happened?"

Her voice was soft, gentle, supportive. Laura took a deep breath, steeling herself to go there. Long seconds of deafening silence passed by before she could speak.

"I don't remember, you know that. I will tell you what I know from other people."

"That's all right," Jacobs said softly, ready to jot down notes.

Laura swallowed hard, feelings and painful memories choking her. She took a deep breath, then finally found the words.

"They were killed on a Friday night and were not discovered until the next morning, when the housekeeper came. She worked weekends. I remember someone saying she took classes during the week, so that's why."

"Where were you when they found you?"

"They said I was in the laundry hamper."

"The laundry hamper? Smart little girl!" Jacobs reacted.

"We used to play hide and seek with Grandma," Laura smiled sadly, as she recalled, "and I drove her crazy, because I hid in all kinds of unusual places. My sister and brother hid like normal kids, under beds and in the closets, but I hid in suitcases, in the dishwasher one time, and in the laundry hamper. She used to tell me I must like filth and smelly socks," she chuckled lightly, then wiped a rebel tear at the corner of her eye.

"So, you recall playing with your siblings and your grandmother?"

"Yes, like it happened to someone else, but yes, that memory is still there."

"Great. What else do you remember being told about that day?"

"People didn't talk about it with me. Carol and Bradley, my adoptive parents, avoided the subject fiercely. I can understand why. The only thing my adoptive parents told me was that I didn't speak a word for a couple of years after that night. But I know Hannah, our housekeeper, was the one who found me, eventually."

"Why eventually? Do you know?"

"Yes, I do. I looked her up when I got older, because I wanted to find out everything I could about that day, and my adoptive parents didn't know much. She's still around; we stayed in touch. She didn't want to say, at first, but she said she'd known I was somewhere in the house, because she didn't find... um, they didn't find my body anywhere. She looked everywhere, knowing how I liked to hide, and got herself into trouble with the police apparently, for disturbing the crime scene."

"I see. Would you mind if I speak with her?"

"N—no, I guess not. What would you ask her?"

"Just more details, to help us with our sensory setup."

"Not sure I follow," Laura shrugged.

"For instance, what was for dinner that night? The smell of that particular food might trigger some memories. What clothes, if any, were in the laundry hamper? Socks or your mother's silk blouses? A particular fabric touching your skin could trigger a memory. Was the TV on? Or music?"

"I understand," Laura replied, "or at least I think I do." She drew a sharp breath. "When do we start?"

"Sooner than you'd expect. Are you free tomorrow afternoon?" Jacobs asked, flashing a charming, wide smile.

"I can be, why?"

"I was invited to speak about my new method on television, and I'd like to ask you to come with me. It's an interview with the Brandt Rusch, no less," she added, naming one of the most famous news reporters of the moment. "He's network, you know, not local."

Laura stood abruptly, getting ready to leave.

"Absolutely not."

Surprised, Dr. Jacobs stood as well, and touched her elbow.

"I don't understand," she said. "Don't you see the opportunity here?"

"This might be an opportunity for you, Dr. Jacobs, but it's my life, and I won't have it turned into a circus for anyone's benefit, including yours. I'm sorry for wasting your time."

She turned to leave, pressing her lips together to refrain from saying something she'd need to apologize for later. She couldn't believe she'd wasted so much time and raised her hopes like that, for nothing. For a stupid TV show.

"What if they hadn't caught him?" Dr. Jacobs said, asserting her voice just a little above the friendly, supportive level.

Laura stopped, frozen in place.

"What if the man who killed your family were still at large, out there? Can't you see? Your case is the baseline we need to calibrate a study that could bring hundreds of criminals to justice, criminals who prey on children. The fact that we know your family's killer with such accuracy is a one-in-a-billion chance, Laura. Please don't throw it away."

She turned and faced Dr. Jacobs, her features carved in stone. She felt her blood boil, as a wave of overwhelming emotion swallowed her.

"I won't throw it away, if you give up the TV circus. Why are you doing that? And why drag me with you?"

"Because this is how research grants are obtained. These methodologies, like everything else, are like products. At first, you invent them, prototype them, but then you have to publicize them, so the market can respond, and investors can put their money into your idea. TV interviews, media releases, articles, fundraisers, you name it. Taking this methodology nationwide, after proving beyond any doubt that it works and can be safely and fairly used in criminal investigations, will take serious time and effort. Financial effort."

Laura stood quietly, feeling her resistance vanish under the force of Dr. Jacobs's argument.

"Because," Dr. Jacobs continued, speaking softly again and touching her arm once more, "that's how grants are obtained. Through a goddamned circus."

7

Discrepancies

Tess left the prison complex at Raiford a little after lunch, driving just as fast as she had on her way in. She cut across the endless fields heading east on State Highway 16, eager to hit the Interstate, with the emergency lights on. Despite going constantly more than eighty miles per hour, driving back to Miami seemed an endless, nerve-racking task, mostly because what she really wanted to do was stop and review the case files for the three families Garza claimed he didn't kill.

Was there any mention of rape in those medico-legal reports that she, and maybe everyone else, had missed? How could Garza have known that the other killer had enjoyed killing women more, when all he'd had access to were a few crime scene photos? Was there really another killer out there, who patiently waited for Garza to fry, so he could be forever free of any consequence of what he had done?

Or was Garza playing tricks on them, after having pulled some names out of his list, by all appearance the names that didn't match his usual killing rhythm of one family every three or four months? Was he going to pull a rabbit out of his hat, after getting her all worked up, so they wouldn't fry him on the twenty-second?

Technically, no one fried anymore. In Florida, capital punishment was delivered through lethal injection, but the term had stuck in law enforcement glossary and was hard to shake. Details... Annoying little details, like Garza knowing the unsub liked to kill women more than men. How the hell?

She honked furiously at a distracted driver who wasn't letting her pass on a stretch of curvy road, more irritated by catching herself use the term unsub, which meant in fact her mind was already considering the possibility of another killer out there, on the loose. An unknown subject. A man who apparently liked killing women more than men. Or did he? How the hell did Garza know that? And why did the thought of rape make Garza sad? Why did it upset him? Her mind kept spinning and spinning, trying to weave some sense out of pure speculation and some half-known facts.

There it was, Interstate 95, a long stretch of asphalt that would take her all the way home to Miami. She checked the time and cussed under her breath. No matter how fast she drove, she wouldn't get there for at least another four hours. She couldn't wait that long; patience wasn't exactly her strongest suit.

She took the onramp and drove past St. Augustine, but then took the exit leading to Crescent Beach. A few minutes later, after refueling her Suburban and getting fresh coffee for herself, she pulled over on an undeveloped side road near the water, with the back of her car facing the Matanzas River. She got out of the car and inhaled the humid, heavily scented air, and felt her tension dissipate. She was going to get her answers now, not later.

She climbed into the back of her SUV, leaving the hatch open, and crossed her legs under her, seated among the four boxes of documents. The tall, coffee cup fit loosely in the side pocket of the cargo area above the left rear wheel, and she almost chuckled thinking how the Suburban's designers had failed, by not placing a cup holder somewhere in the back. People worked in there, and they needed their swill.

Curious and eager to replace speculation with fact, Tess sifted quickly through the boxes and pulled out the three case files, then started reviewing them in detail. She had already pored over the voluminous file on Garza himself and his methods, the particulars of his crime scenes, modus operandi, and everything else that distinguished The Family Man from the rest of the murderous psychopaths out there. In the particular cases Garza had named, she looked for discrepancies, and also how those discrepancies had been overlooked or explained away by the detectives who had closed the respective cases as Garza's killings.

Chronologically, the Watsons were the first murdered family of the three Garza didn't admit to killing. Fifteen years before, someone had entered the Watson family home and had shot Allen Watson, two of his children, and a little boy who was sleeping over that night. First discrepancy: the killer had stabbed the woman, Rachel Watson, instead of shooting her. Second discrepancy: a little girl survived, hidden somewhere on the premises. Third discrepancy: the killer hadn't posed the bodies and hadn't spent any significant amount of time with them, based on evidence left behind. Overall, the Watson murder seemed far less organized than any of Garza's, and missed a critical element. Or two.

The Family Man had earned his moniker by killing entire families, then staging them around the dinner table. He liked spending a significant amount of time with them, pretending to be a part of the family. He ate at their dinner tables, surrounded by decomposing corpses. He slept in the victims' beds. He lived in their homes for a day, sometimes even two. He always made sure he wouldn't be surprised by house cleaners, nannies, or other hired help coming to work; he did his homework thoroughly.

Most of his attacks happened on Friday evenings, before the weekend, when he could live out his fantasy without someone interrupting him or noticing that his victims were missing from jobs or school. He was highly organized, Garza. Whatever deranged fantasy drove him to kill, he kept it in check, doing careful work of his research before striking.

In the Watson case though, a fourth discrepancy surfaced. The Watsons were killed on a Friday evening, although the housekeeper's work schedule included weekends and excluded Mondays and Tuesdays. A handwritten note clarified that, and the writing was vaguely familiar. She flipped through the pages until she found the name of the detective who'd worked the case. Detective Gary Michowsky, Palm Beach.

She sighed. Good old Gary.

She had to admit that probably Garza would have never killed the Watsons. With them, he couldn't live through his sickening fantasy. Not for long enough. They didn't fit the profile. But there wasn't any mention of sexual assault anywhere in the ME's findings.

Tess leaned back against the window of the vehicle and closed her eyes for a second. Stabbing was a more personal form of killing than shooting. Pulling a trigger is done remotely, while stabbing requires proximity, closeness, passion. Yet, no sexual assault. The stabbing of Mrs. Watson had been attributed to the evolution of the killer's MO, despite the fact that Garza had continued to shoot, not stab, all the other families he killed.

Another finding, just as quickly explained away, was the ballistics that didn't match Garza's earlier shootings. People see what they want to see and fail to notice what's right in front of them.

Oh, Gary… What the hell were you doing?

She moved on to the next case, the Meyers. They were killed the following year, in February. That murder seemed more organized. None of the loose ends the Watson case was riddled with. The Meyer case stood out for another set of reasons though. They had no children, for one. Then Mrs. Meyer was stabbed multiple times and had died of exsanguination after what the ME had ruled, "three, maybe four hours of torture." No sexual assault on Mrs. Meyer either. A scribbled note on the edge of the medico-legal report, in Doc Rizza's handwriting: "Unusual skin distension pattern in stab wound. No trace elements found." She made a note to ask Doc Rizza what he meant by that.

She sighed again as she closed the Meyer case file. These two cases didn't fit the Garza profile either, yet somehow, they'd just been lumped with the rest of them. She reopened the Meyer file, checking for the detective's name.

"Oh, shit, Gary, not again," she whispered, then wondered how it was possible. Gary Michowsky was a good cop. His heart was in the right place, and he was experienced and thorough. She'd worked with him before, and, yes, she'd noticed some slip ups, but who doesn't slip up on occasions? It happened a long time ago, but she planned on confronting Gary about his decisions in these cases. Then she cringed, remembering Pearson's words about solving cases without caring who got hurt in the process.

She scoffed, a little bitter. Probably Gary was popular with his colleagues and deemed to be a reliable member of his team, while she wasn't. But he had screwed up big time on the Meyer and Watson cases, and she wanted to hear his side of the story. How did a good cop make such a bad, obvious mistake?

She opened the third case file, fearing she'd find Gary's name again, right there, on the signature page. It wasn't, and she felt relieved. The case had been worked by a Detective McKinley, Miami-Dade. She'd never heard of him.

The Townsend family was killed almost three years after the Meyers. This time there was a child, a young girl, only eight years old. Tess shook her head, feeling a wave of anger suffocate her. She almost asked herself what kind of man kills children, but she already knew the answer to that question. A man like Kenneth Garza. A cold, blood-thirsty psychopath, someone who deserved to die.

She ran her thin fingers through her hair, pushing it away from her face, and returned to study the Townsend case file in the dimming light of the disappearing day. The same notable exceptions to the typical Garza MO, but this time stronger, more prevalent. A stabbed female victim. Long-lasting torture. Then the surprise, right there, on the last page of the medico-legal report. A detail she'd missed on her first, hurried review. A two-line paragraph that had her gut in a twist.

Emily Townsend had been raped.

8

Dinner Talk

It was close to midnight by the time Tess made it into the city. The traffic had finally cleared up a little, making it easier for her to weave through.

Her jaws hurt from staying stubbornly clenched the whole trip. Could it have been so simple? Just because the women were stabbed instead of shot in the three murders Garza rejected, he could have figured out the killer liked to kill women more? Who better to understand the workings of the psychopathic mind, than another psychopath? Or maybe Garza was making a fool out of her, giving her bite-sized bait for her to sniff and chase like a perfectly trained hound dog.

She wondered why she believed he didn't kill the three families in the first place. Was the word of a psychopath ever good enough? Yet her gut told her she should believe Garza, and find the real killer. Fifteen years after the fact, it was next to impossible, but still worth trying.

Completely absorbed by her thoughts, she almost didn't notice when she'd arrived at Media Luna, holding little hope the blue "Open" sign would still be on in the window of the old bar and grill. It was, and the parking lot still held a few cars. She parked far to the side, unwilling to scare off the patrons who might shy away from the place after seeing a black, unmarked law enforcement vehicle in front of the building.

The moment she grabbed the brass door handle and let herself in, the familiar smells and noises kindled the angry growl of her empty stomach. She hadn't eaten anything the whole day, and her entire body was sending out signals of protest. She propped herself up on a barstool at the tacky counter and looked for the bartender.

He hadn't seen her yet; he was immersed in a conversation with a man wearing dirty construction coveralls, and, by the intensity of their gestures and the loudness of their laughter, they were having a blast. She smiled involuntarily seeing him so relaxed, enjoying life, enjoying making his customers happy. She noticed a little more slump in his back, and maybe he'd lost some weight too. His long, wavy hair had more salt and less pepper each day, but he still looked good for his age. Was he approaching seventy? Probably not yet; but he definitely had passed the sixty mark.

Men like him never aged. Whenever she looked at him or heard him talk, she thought of Willie Nelson for some reason, although his hair was a little shorter, and he couldn't carry a tune to save his life. But there was something in his rebellious, free-spirited, refuse-to-grow-old nature, something that spelled freedom, kindness, and friendship.

He still wore his signature Hawaiian shirts, with a couple of top buttons undone to let his tattoo show just a little, a tribal design of a tiger that took most of his tan chest. Only part of the design was visible through the opening of his shirt, the eyes and the nose of the tiger, but it was enough to have earned him his nickname that only a few close friends were allowed to use: Catman, or Cat for short. For the rest of the world he was Ricky, or Mr. Bedell for complete strangers.

He turned and looked her way, and a large grin stretched his lips, showing off white teeth that sparkled against his dark skin. He kept looking at her and smiling while his hands kept busy fixing drinks, and she waved and smiled back. His friendship had been the cornerstone of her troubled existence for the past ten years, an unlikely friendship that had started on the worst night of her life.

From a distance, he lifted a burger patty in the air and tilted his head just a little, in an unspoken question. She raised two of her fingers in the air, and his smile widened. Then he showed her the bag of frozen fries, and she nodded vigorously, laughing quietly.

"You're too pretty to be sitting alone. What's your favorite?" a man suddenly asked. She nearly jumped out of her skin, her heart thumping against her chest. While she'd been focused on Cat, someone took the seat next to her, and she hadn't even noticed.

Again, Tess chastised herself mercilessly. *Again, you let someone creep up on you like that. Wake the hell up!*

She turned and looked at the man who was smiling expectantly at her left, and pulled her jacket to the side enough to show her badge, still hanging on her belt since the prison check-in. The man's smile froze, and he disappeared without saying another word. She refrained from chuckling. No one wanted to have anything to do with law enforcement. If she had been even remotely interested in dating, she'd be worried.

Tess looked at Cat again, who was shaking his head humorously. She mouthed, "Sorry," realizing she'd just scared away one of his paying customers. He shrugged, and seconds later, he set two juicy burgers and a pile of crispy fries in front of her. She started wolfing everything down, too hungry to savor the exquisite flavors. Then she immersed herself into her thoughts, staring at the tall glass in front of her, mixing occasionally the herbs and tiny ice cubes with the two thin straws.

"What's on your mind, kiddo?" Cat asked, pulling her back to reality. Strange how his voice never startled her. "Bad case?"

"Aren't they all?" she replied, chuckling sadly. "Nah, nothing that bad, not tonight. I'm okay."

He scoffed quietly, almost offended, while looking her straight in the eye and challenging her lie.

"It's just work, Cat, that's all," she confessed. "Not a case, but work overall. I seem to screw up all the time, regardless of how hard I try. My boss... I don't know what it would take to make that man say I do a good job."

Cat pulled a chair over and sat across the counter from her, then popped the cap off a Bud Light and downed a swig.

"People," she continued, back at staring at the bottom of her glass, "that's my problem. I suck at people, and that's a fact."

Cat touched her hand gently and smiled tentatively.

"Cat, why can't I trust anyone?"

He put the beer bottle on the counter.

"You trust me, don't you?"

"With my life," she answered without hesitation. "Since the first day I met you."

"Why?" he asked quietly, and waved at a customer who was leaving. "You didn't know me back then. You didn't know anything about me."

Memories flooded her mind, catching her breath, and welling up her eyes. That night she'd stumbled through his door, barely alive, blood gushing from her wounds, her clothes in shreds, and had collapsed right there, on the dirty barroom floor. He'd asked her if she wanted to call 911, and she'd refused vigorously, so he took care of her himself. When she woke up the next day, her wounds were dressed neatly, and her pain had somewhat subsided, her physical pain anyway. The first thing she saw when she woke up was Cat, dozing off in an armchair near her bed, watching over her. She slept for days in the small apartment above the bar, while his patrons sought liquor elsewhere, finding Media Luna closed, day after day. Until she was ready to face the world again.

"I was a rescue mutt," she eventually said quietly, "who landed on your doorstep about to draw my last breath. You saved me, Cat. I can never thank you enough."

"Yes, you can," he replied gently. "Trust other people, or at least try. Just a little bit, and see what happens. You might find some friends out there. You might find a new life."

"Huh," she whispered, "that's exactly what he said."

"Your boss?"

"God, no, although he might know by now something's off about me. Another guy from work, a profiler. He figured out I have PTSD. He called me on it."

"I was surprised that didn't happen sooner, kiddo. These guys, that's what they do every day. You told me that."

"Uh-huh, I know," she replied, sipping some more of her drink.

"Are you in trouble?"

"I could be, you know. I'm surprised he didn't report me already. Procedures are clear; unmanaged PTSD excludes agents from field duty. He broke the rules for me, and he barely knew me."

Cat smiled widely.

"What do you know... someone broke the rules for you without even knowing you. Gee, I wonder how that could ever happen."

She looked at him, confused for a split second, then lowered her head to hide her tearful smile. That awful night ten years ago, when he hadn't called the cops to report her assault, he had broken the law for her. He'd broken the law, and that had given her a life, a career without shame, without the public stigma of rape marking every day of her existence.

She kept her eyes riveted on the counter's shiny surface, speechless.

"Yes, I'm calling you on it too, Tess. Trust someone tomorrow. Try. Then come on over for a burger and a drink, and let me know how it went. We'll talk about it."

She sat quietly, staring into emptiness, absorbing Cat's words. He checked to see if anyone else was left in the bar, then switched off the "Open" sign.

"I promise," she eventually said, and lifted her eyes. Cat wasn't there anymore, busy with closing the bar. He wiped the counter, then washed all the dirty glasses, keeping his eyes on the TV screen. Late at night, it showed a rerun of a prime-time interview with two women Tess didn't recognize, but the captioning caught her attention.

"Cat, turn that up, will you?"

He clicked the remote while she approached the TV in a hurry.

"Miss Watson," the interviewer was asking, "what do you recall of the night when Kenneth Garza, the serial killer known as The Family Man, murdered your family?"

Oh, crap.

9

The Interview

Laura Watson hadn't been in front of a TV camera in years, and she didn't miss it. She still felt nauseous and a little dizzy in front of the blinding, irradiating lights, and was grateful that most of Brandt Rusch's pointed questions were addressed to Dr. Jacobs. If her role was going to be limited to just sitting there, on the black leather armchair backed against the green screen, she had no objection.

She hoped the interview would end soon, as she struggled to sit still, holding her hands folded neatly in her lap, and her back straight. She projected a professional, composed image, complete with a frozen smile that made her facial muscles sore after the first few minutes. She looked tiny and frail, vulnerable in her navy blue pantsuit, and she felt just as vulnerable.

Dr. Jacobs was a natural in front of the cameras. She was excited to be talking about her new methodology and explained in detail the numerous benefits of extracting deeply buried, traumatic memories in a controlled, therapeutic environment. Then she moved on to explaining, in non-technical language, how the process would work and why. Finally, guided by Rusch's questions, she turned her attention to Laura and spoke a little about her background.

Laura found it even more difficult to sit still in her seat.

"Some of you might remember Laura Watson," Dr. Jacobs said, gesturing toward her as the camera zoomed out to include her on the screen. "She was known as The Watson Girl, the famously smart and brave little girl who survived Kenneth Garza's deadly attack on her family fifteen years ago."

Rusch smiled and nodded in her direction, and Laura made an effort and widened her smile, and acknowledged the greeting with a quick head bow.

"Her iconic survival presents us with the unique opportunity to use the new method to extract Laura's traumatic memories and compare them against known case data. The project team was fortunate enough to elicit Miss Watson's commitment to participate. Thank you for doing this," Dr. Jacobs said, smiling widely at the cameras. "I can only imagine how difficult it will be for you."

Laura nodded, also smiling, while the unwanted line of a frown appeared on her forehead. She just wished the whole thing were over and done with.

Then Brandt Rusch turned toward her and asked her the first direct question, and she felt sweat breaking at the roots of her hair, and a sudden urge to throw up.

"Miss Watson," Rusch asked, "what do you recall of the night when Kenneth Garza, the serial killer known as The Family Man, murdered your family?"

Laura conjured all her willpower and managed to take in a breath of air, hot and dusty in the projector lights.

"Not much, I'm afraid. I'm guessing that's what makes me such a good candidate for the study. I've been told I was hiding in the upstairs bathroom laundry hamper. No one else knows anything else, and I can't remember." She choked a little at the end of her answer. She quickly recited Rusch's earlier instructions in her mind. "Short, simple phrases," he had said. "Keep it to the point, and remember to breathe."

Good advice. Hard to put in practice though.

"We've seen a lot of you on camera, especially after Garza was arrested," Rusch said. "Your survival story was inspiring. Then you suddenly disappeared. What happened?"

"I grew up," she said, almost chuckling. "I finally got to have a say in it, and my say was no."

"You don't like the publicity?" Rusch pressed on.

"Not at all," she replied with an apologetic smile. "The reason why everyone wanted me on camera, and today is no exception, was the fact that my family was killed. Not a reason to celebrate, at least not in my book."

Rusch made a gesture with his head, and his eyebrows shot up, while a smile of admiration lit up his face.

"And modest too," he said. "Our viewers would love to know you better, Miss Watson."

She shot a quick glance at Jacobs, and she nodded an almost imperceptible encouragement. She repressed a sigh.

"I remember being happy, growing up with my brother and my sister, playing, having fun. It's like a blur today, but the memories are still there. Then nothing… Like a cloud of darkness engulfed a few years of my life. Then more recent memories, of my new family, my new sister, Amanda, and my new parents, Bradley and Carol Welsh. Bradley was Dad's business partner and cofounder of WatWel Lighting. I was privileged to be raised by them, to be able to grow up so close to my family's legacy, to be a part of what my parents had built and left behind."

"What are you hoping to gain from participating in the study, Miss Watson?" Rusch asked, flicking a quick glance at Jacobs, who leaned forward a little, in anticipation.

Laura thought for a second before responding.

"I—I want to remember," she said, feeling the claw of tears choking her.

"I want to remember everything. I hope I will finally see the killer in my memories, and remember what he did, and what he said. Maybe that will—" she stopped abruptly and cleared her throat quietly, "that will bring an explanation as to why. Maybe I'll understand why they died. Why them, not others," she finally added, overwhelmed. "I know it's a terrible thing to say, but I want to know. And I want to remember them, my parents, to be able to see images of them in my mind."

"You've done well in life so far," Rusch abruptly changed the subject, making her frown a little. "Are you concerned what your participation in the study might do to your own well-being?"

She shot Dr. Jacobs another quick glance.

"Honestly, I am," she replied. "I'm already scared of looking in there, of opening this—this chest filled with monsters that hide locked inside my head. But I feel I owe it to my parents, to my brother and my sister, even to myself." She paused for a second, but Rusch didn't interrupt with a new question. "I'm sure I saw something that night. I'm sure that's why my memory is gone. I *know* I saw him. There's no way they all died, and I didn't see or hear anything. That can't be. I just have to remember."

The moment she finished talking, she felt a pang of fear wring her gut. She tried, but couldn't shake it.

Rusch nodded a couple of times before moving on to the next question.

"Kenneth Garza was arrested four years after the death of your family. How did his arrest change your life? Did it bring closure?"

She frowned pronouncedly, not caring that her frown was televised. That question wasn't on the preapproved list.

"It changed my life to the point where my adoptive parents stopped being afraid the killer might come after me and tie up the loose end. He never did; in retrospect, I think it had become public information that I didn't remember anything, so I wasn't at much risk after all. Closure? No. I don't think there could ever be closure; not for me." Her breath caught, and she covered her mouth with her hand. The camera operator promptly shifted the angle and focused on Rusch.

"There's a strange timing between your study and Garza's upcoming execution. Wouldn't you agree, Dr. Jacobs?"

"I agree, Brandt, and I have to admit I'd prefer his execution was postponed until we finish, but that's not going to happen. We do, however, have the case files and numerous interviews, evaluations, and notes of Garza himself to help me establish the reliability of the methodology. I think we're good."

"Miss Watson, what would you like to say to Kenneth Garza?"

The camera refocused on her, bringing her anguished features at the center of the screen, up close.

Laura felt a wave of unspeakable anger toward Rusch, who put her through such hell after making numerous reassurances that he would stick to what they'd agreed. Goddamned attention-seeking bastard, that's what he was. A shark, preying on people's misery. Yet ultimately, it was her fault for being there. She should have never agreed to do the interview.

"Nothing. I have nothing to say to Kenneth Garza," she spat, unwilling to share anything anymore. She shot Rusch a murderous look, then watched on the control screen how the camera zoomed out and moved away from her face.

She remained still for a few more minutes, waiting for Rusch to wrap things up with Dr. Jacobs. Hours later, the feeling of doom curled inside her gut still kept her awake, and she couldn't explain it.

10

Reflections: Memories

I turn off the TV with an angry press on the remote button, then send the remote flying across the room. It crashes against the wall, then pieces scatter everywhere on the thick carpet. My fists are clenched so badly my joints crack, but even that gesture fails to bring any relief.

I want to wring her neck, right then and there. I'm pining to go out there, to find her, and silence her careless, troublemaking mouth forever. If only I could.

"Goddamned, stupid, motherfucking bitch!" I let myself mutter under my breath, more subdued than I want. I wish I could let my anger roar, to relieve the burning pressure I feel in my chest, but I can't.

This shit ain't over yet. This shit could still hurt me. Talk about mistakes of the past coming back to haunt me.

I let myself fall on the sofa and close my eyes, trying desperately to remember. It's been fifteen years, yes, but I can still recall that night with plenty of details, mostly because I screwed up so badly, and I spent countless nights afterwards wondering how the hell that happened. Well, now I know.

I remember going upstairs twice, not once, and both times I passed by the upstairs bathroom. Not the master bathroom. The one in the hallway, the one the other three bedrooms shared. Was she hiding in the master bathroom and that's why I didn't see her?

There's a burning sensation in my eyes, and I rub them furiously, getting very little relief. I recall checking the master bathroom at least once. The light was on in there... I recall that much. I keep my eyes closed, trying to visualize the master bathroom. Yes, I can still see it. The lights were on, two powerful sets of six lights above each sink. The shower stall was empty and its glass walls completely clear of steam; I could see clearly that no one was in there. The tub was empty, and that's it. There was nothing else in that master bathroom. No hamper, no small closet, nothing that could hide that girl. Definitely she wasn't hiding in the master bathroom.

I let a frustrated sigh escape my parched lips, then pour myself a generous shot of bourbon and sink it down in one thirsty gulp. Suddenly, I'm pacing the room like a caged animal and I hate the feeling. Not even the bourbon can wash that feeling away.

Why didn't I check the hallway bathroom? Why?

I recall the door was open. The bathroom was dark; the lights were off. The only light that made it inside was coming from the hallway. I focus my weary mind on that faint flicker of a memory. The bathroom door is right there, open, and passing by I see nothing. No one.

First time I didn't hesitate or stop to look; I just walked by it in a hurry. I'd just found and shot the three kids I thought were all Watson's; so there's no reason for me to keep looking. The second time though, I looked. I was pressed for time, of course, with the cops' sirens blaring, but I still opened every closet and looked under each bed. I even opened the pantry, the massive fridge, the double oven, and the dishwasher.

Did I stop to check the bathroom?

My head suddenly hangs low, heavy with the burden of guilt and humiliation. I fucked up badly.

No, I'd barely slowed down my pace, passing by that bathroom. The door was open, and the lights were off. I assumed... Yes, I know just what you're going to say. I assumed. And it could cost me my life.

But now I remember. I can visualize. I can see that blue laundry hamper, large enough to hold laundry for a family with three kids. Large enough to hold her, Laura Watson, the biggest mistake of my life.

My sweaty hand clutches the bourbon glass and suddenly shoots it across the room, sending it crashing into the fireplace.

She needs to die. Now. Today.

My reasoning is fear-driven, and that's really bad. Real predators stay calm in the face of a threat. The bigger the threat, the calmer they get. Have you ever seen a tiger freak out? Or a lion?

If I kill her now, everyone will know that Garza didn't kill that family. They'll know that with more certainty than ever. I would provide them with the proof they need to exculpate Garza for the killing. You see, he must have told them he didn't kill the Watsons, but apparently, they didn't listen. Or maybe he *did* confess to the killing, to add one more notch to his belt. Hmm... You never know with people.

I continue to pace the room, feeling more and more caged, trapped, about to be caught and killed. I hate that... I hate that my life depends on some psychological mumbo-jumbo that might be entirely bogus science. Who the hell knows... Maybe the years Laura believed Garza killed her family will have overwritten her real memories, and she'll reveal she saw Garza doing it, and that will be the end of it.

But how would I know? How could I find out what she does in those, whatever the hell it was she called it... regression sessions? I can't just sit here and wait for the police to break down my door and drag me out in chains.

Stupid, stupid girl. She's got everything a girl could want, but no, she has to open the can of worms from hell. She must die… there's no other way. And I better not break my neck in the process.

I can't kill her; that's for sure. No matter how much I want to. No matter how many nights I've dreamed of plunging my blade into her, again, and again, and again. No, I must be strong and deny myself.

She must have an accident, one that will be above anyone's suspicion.

11

Direction

It was still dark when Tess pulled over into a parking spot reserved for visitors and went upstairs, to the floor that housed SAC Pearson's office. She was the first one there; normal business hours didn't start for at least another hour.

The entire floor was dark, except for the night lights. Sensors activated the ceiling fluorescent lamps throughout, the moment she opened the glass doors. Yet she didn't bother to pass by her desk; she just grabbed the nearest chair, rolled it in front of Pearson's door, and took a seat, waiting impatiently and tapping the sole of her shoe against a desk.

Two minutes later, she decided in favor of a hot cup of coffee and the Watson case file, to pass the time with some usefulness while she waited. She checked her watch two or three times a minute and promised herself that she'd call Pearson at precisely eight, not a second later.

"I've never been stalked before, Winnett," Pearson's loud voice almost startled her, resounding and echoing in the silence of the deserted office. "Have you heard of using a phone?"

She sprung to her feet and followed him inside his office. She noticed his shoulders hunched a little, making his jacket's fine fabric stretch over his back, although it was loose enough to be a comfortable fit. He carried an old leather briefcase, his all-time favorite most likely, because he could afford one in better shape, one with fewer scratches and a shinier look.

He put his tall Starbucks on the desk, and loosened his necktie just a little.

"I didn't want to call so early—"

"Well, next time call. What's up?"

"We need to reopen three cases. I have reasons to believe these three cases were attributed to Garza in error. I'm talking about the Watson, Townsend, and Meyer cases."

Pearson took off his thick-rimmed glasses and rubbed the bridge of his nose between his thumb and index finger, slowly, thoroughly, taking his time. His face scrunched up in a multitude of deep lines. He obviously wasn't thrilled with the news she'd brought, but Tess expected no different.

"How strong are your reasons?"

She hesitated a little, thrown off by his phrasing. She bit her lip before replying and wiped her hands against her pants.

"I'm not 100 percent sure, but there's a strong enough likelihood that Garza didn't kill those families. There's a copycat out there, someone we missed."

"Are you sure Garza's not playing you?"

She looked away for a split second. No one could be sure of anything when it came to a psychopath.

"Again, not 100 percent, no. But—"

"Yeah, I heard you the first time. Do you realize what this means? It will be a public relations nightmare. We can't just say, after fifteen years, that we're sorry, we made a mistake. Just when the man we maintained for so long is the killer is about to be executed."

He ran both his hands across his shiny scalp, one after the other. If Pearson still had hair, he might have been tempted to pull some of it out, in a gesture of deep frustration.

"The Watson case is now a priority, sir," Winnett pushed.

"Why is that?"

"There was a TV show last night, featuring Laura Watson, the Watson family massacre survivor, declaring she's going to undergo experimental memory recovery therapy, or something like that. If the real killer's out there, he'll be coming for her."

Pearson's frown deepened. He extended his hand silently, waiting for her to give him the case file. Minutes later, he lifted his eyes from the pages covered in Tess's scribbled notes, his frustration even more visible.

"All right," he eventually said, "I'll give you forty-eight hours. See what you can find out, draw your conclusions, and let's put this mess to rest. Wrap it up in forty-eight, not a second more. I have a health insurance fraud case lined up for you."

She nodded once, although she thought forty-eight hours would probably not be enough. It was a stone-cold case, archived for fifteen years. No new witnesses, no new forensics, no new evidence of any sorts. Just something a death-row psychopath had said.

"Um, I need to place Laura Watson in protective custody."

"Absolutely not," Pearson replied firmly.

"But, sir, this girl's got a target on her back, ever since they aired her interview. Do you think the real killer will risk leaving this loose end out in the open?"

SAC Pearson clenched his jaws but remained quiet for a few seconds, thinking. He probably mulled over the implications of exposing the uncertainty of their findings in the Watson case, so late in the game. She understood his concerns, because she'd spent most of the night awake, tossing and turning, trying to make the wisest decision under the circumstances.

"Sir, I understand the media risk, but we have to," she insisted. "If she dies—"

"I don't need you to spell it out for me, Winnett. I can think for myself."

She promptly clammed up. No matter how much she tried, she couldn't get on his good side. She couldn't establish a real dialogue between them. Maybe his past frustrations with her behavior ran so deep that their relationship couldn't be healed anymore. Maybe her job was, in true fact, hanging by a thin thread, waiting to snap at the first gust of adverse wind.

"Listen to me, Winnett, because I'm only going to say this once. You're not going to place Watson in protective custody. Not until you have confirmed your theories beyond any reasonable doubt, and you have a tight case with a new name on it. Even then, you will run this by me first, for approval."

"But, sir, she's going to die—" she pushed back vigorously, standing up.

"I wasn't finished, Winnett, for God's sake," he reacted, visibly antagonized by her reaction. "For now, you have nothing, just speculation. Please, feel free to interrupt me if I'm wrong."

His condescending tone ripped through her self-imposed calm, making her blood boil. Regardless, she decided to shut up and listen, no matter how disheartening that was. Pearson was her superior, whether she liked it or not.

"I'm glad we agree on something," he continued. "You want to compromise the reputation of several police departments and their detectives on nothing more than speculation. Do you realize that every case those detectives have closed will have grounds for appeal? Do you realize the ripple effects of such a discovery, so late after the fact? Those detectives won't even be trusted to sign for mail, going forward... All they have, in their line of work, is their reputation. You'd completely destroy that, on nothing more than speculation coming from a death-row mass murderer. Not to mention the rift you'd create between us and them, between the regional Federal Bureau and local police. We're supposed to work like a team, to be on the same side here, Winnett. But then again, what do you know about teams, huh?"

His words fell like stones, as if she was caught in an avalanche of hurt and humiliation that she didn't feel she deserved. Was it that bad to put a woman's life above political bullshit? She let her head hang for a second, but then raised it and looked Pearson straight in the eye.

"I'm sorry, sir, but I don't believe any of this political crap is worth the gamble with Laura's life. If Laura were your kid, you'd probably agree more."

Pearson sustained her gaze fiercely, and Tess noticed his skin was turning a darker shade, probably his telltale sign for contained anger raising his blood pressure level.

"All I'm saying, Winnett, is get me some goddamn facts before doing anything we'd probably regret for years to come. Can you do that much for me?"

"Yes, sir, I can. In the meantime, would you please approve a protective detail for Laura Watson?"

Pearson stood abruptly and slammed his hands against the desk. Taken aback, she took a step back, reacting instinctively to put more distance between herself and his unusual outburst.

"There are no grounds yet, not until you get me some facts. I thought we just agreed on that. Dismissed."

12

Reunion

Tess trotted out of the federal building, eager to put some distance between SAC Pearson and herself, between her scrunched face and the inquisitive glances of her colleagues, who were arriving in endless files, pouring in from their morning commutes and lining up for screening.

She'd tried to get Laura out of harm's way and failed. She tried, to the limit of pissing off beyond repair her direct supervisor. Yet, she had to admit Pearson had a point. So far, she didn't have any facts on her side; just the words of a death-row serial killer and some observations, some details that would have made her investigate the cases more carefully.

Would have? Or might have?

Those murders happened fifteen years ago. Well, the Watson murders did. The rest were more recent, but not by much, a year or two. Back then, DNA was an emerging forensic science, and the tests were ridiculously expensive, rarely approved, and took forever. The Internet wasn't nearly what it was today, and neither were mobile communications, car navigation systems, or nationwide, integrated databases, such as the one she preferred to use, DIVS.

DIVS, or Data Integration and Visualization System, brought a single-source search that pulled results from literally hundreds of databases, making correlative deduction easy and accessible, and, more important, fact-based. It was easier for her now, immensely easier than it had been for the investigators who looked at those cases fifteen years ago. Still, they shouldn't have just discarded the discrepancies in killer signature, ballistics, and MO that easily. That—putting aside DNA evidence, DIVS, or any other technological advancement—was just crappy police work.

Take ballistics, for example. The gun used in the Watson killings was the same model used in prior Garza murders, a Beretta 9 mil, but it was a different gun. Yet the experts explained it away quickly, by stating that Garza must have used another gun for that murder. Later, with the Meyer killings, when again the ballistics didn't match the most recent Garza killing, they explained it away by stating that the gun matched the Watsons, an already confirmed Garza murder at the time of the Meyer family massacre. The evidence was there, but was it, really, anything more than coincidental? Was it that incomprehensible to assume that Garza might have used two identical guns, not one, over years and years of killing? Still, discarding MO and ballistics evidence so quickly didn't speak well of the police work done fifteen years ago.

Oh, Gary... What the hell were you thinking back then?

She dreaded the call she was about to make. She and Detective Gary Michowsky had crossed paths before, and it hadn't always been pretty. Her impatient, demanding style collided with his almost forgiving nature. He was a good cop, many times overworked, rushing through things, trying to do what he thought was best, and sometimes failing. Like everyone else, including her.

There was another side to Gary though. On the last case they'd worked together, he'd risked his life to have her back, even after she'd treated him harshly, irritated by the errors he'd made during the investigation. She cringed, thinking about what she stood to discover in the Watson case, and what that could mean to Gary, his career, his reputation, and his self-esteem.

She hopped in her Suburban and turned on the engine, then immediately increased the flow of cold air and breathed deeply a few times, curbing her anger. Everyone had done the best they could, under unusual circumstances. But she didn't feel that was nearly enough; not when a young woman's life hung in the balance.

Ah, screw the politics, and screw them *if they can't take it,* she thought, then dialed Gary Michowsky's cell number. Everyone did the best they could; but this time, it wasn't good enough. She had to do what was needed.

He picked up immediately, and the background noise told her he was in a car.

"Go for Michowsky and Fradella," he said, opening the call in his typical manner.

"Good morning, Michowsky and Fradella," she greeted them as cheerfully as she could. "Tess Winnett here."

A quick, loaded second of silence ensued. She could tell the two men were exchanging glances, wondering why she'd called.

She continued. "Gary, I need to talk to you about the Watson case and two others."

A roar of laughter erupted in Gary's car. She winced and turned the speaker volume down.

"What's so damn funny, huh?" She sounded almost irritated.

"Pay up, pay up," Fradella's voice cut into Gary's laughter. "We had a bet going, and I won. A tenner. Good money for a young, poor kid like me, right, Agent Winnett?"

"Yeah... he won," Gary admitted reluctantly, his laughter gone.

She pursed her lips and refrained from lecturing them.

"What was the bet about?" she asked instead, keeping her voice calm and neutral to encourage them to open up.

"Right after that TV show aired last night with The Watson Girl, I just knew you'd call, first thing in the morning," Todd Fradella replied. "I just knew it. But Gary, no, he said you're probably assigned to another case, minding your own stuff."

She didn't know how to react. Maybe she was too tense, too afraid for Laura's life. Maybe she saw things others didn't see, the possible truths hiding behind the words of a monster named Garza. Maybe she knew how the real killer, if he was out there, would deal with the risk posed by Laura regaining access to her memories. She didn't care which for sure... all she knew was she didn't feel like laughing. Nope, not at all.

"Okay... whatever. I'm coming over to Palm Beach. I'll set up shop in the conference room, like in the good old days. We'll catch up."

The two clammed up promptly, probably swallowing what they really had to say about her upcoming visit.

"What's going on?" Gary finally asked.

"I have reasons to believe the Watsons and two other families weren't killed by Garza," she replied, giving them the same canned phrase she'd given to SAC Pearson earlier. She hoped for better results with Michowsky and Fradella, but she wasn't holding her breath. No one liked dredging up old history.

Silence again, and the rhythmic sound of car tires running over concrete bridge segments.

"I see," Michowsky replied, not a trace of humor left in his grim voice. "Can I ask, how come you're looking into these cases now?"

"Garza's about to be executed. I did some due diligence; normal procedure prior to his execution. Some things caught my attention, that's all."

It was pointless to go into the details over the phone. There was going to be plenty of time to do that later, in a conference room, where they could all get together and dish it out freely.

"When are you coming in?" Todd asked, his voice marked by poorly disguised worry.

"Right now," she replied coldly. "I'm on my way."

No one replied. She felt like the unwanted relative visiting the family for a few days, but she didn't care. All she cared about was catching the killer who was out there, free, after taking who knows how many lives and getting ready to take another.

"You know, it's one hell of a coincidence," Gary said, "you looking into this case just when the survivor is supposed to have those regression sessions." He paused for a while, probably waiting for her to say something. "All right, see you later."

He hung up, leaving her free to mull over his words. Coincidence? No, that concept didn't exist. Not in her reality. She felt a tug of uneasiness in her gut, as if a scary monster curled up in there was about to awaken.

13

Argument

The dealership's lounge area was small, but well-equipped for people looking to kill an hour or two, waiting for their car maintenance to be done. There was only one other customer, and Laura enjoyed the peace and quiet, letting her mind wander as she flipped absentmindedly through the pages of the latest *Popular Mechanics*.

Across the floor, in the dealership showroom, a tall, slim man stood near the exit, looking in her direction through two glass walls. His eyes didn't budge; he stared at her with intense, drilling eyes, and his facial expression, unchanged, seemed carved in stone, emotionless. He stood out from everyone else, dressed in a black turtleneck and a jacket, quite the unusual combo, especially for Miami.

A little uneasy, Laura shrugged off the sudden pang of fear that pierced her gut and returned to her *Popular Mechanics*. All kinds of creeps were bound to stare at her after that damn TV show. Normally she enjoyed the magazine and read quickly through the articles that caught her eye. But nothing had been normal since the day she received Dr. Jacobs's letter. Pulled back into her dark past and thrown into an abyss of turmoil and anxiety, she couldn't find her bearings anymore.

She needed time to recollect her thoughts, to strengthen herself for what she was about to do. Sadly, she only found that peaceful time there, at the dealership. School was tough these days; a frenzy of difficult, final-year assignments, and hordes of young, carefree students, mostly boys, who tried to pull her into dates, parties, and whatever forms of pleasurable past-times they could think of. March spring break was near; where was she going to go? Did she want to join them on a diving trip to Key West?

Home wasn't much better either. Adrian had been more overbearing than usual, ever since she'd gone to see Dr. Jacobs. She tried to make excuses for him, maybe more than she should have. He was a kid who never had anyone but her. He was probably afraid to lose her, afraid of anything that could alter the frail balance of their life together. Probably, deep down, Adrian wanted to keep her from going forward with the regression sessions, even against her will. He knew better than to try that, because he knew her quite well. Laura seemed frail and carried the aura of her past around her like an ethereal cloud of pain and sadness, but she had willpower, and she stood for what she wanted, for what she believed was right.

Yeah… that was valid for those times when she didn't hide for hours in a car dealership, to avoid confrontation and find some peace.

She tightened her lips, angry with herself, then abandoned the unread magazine on the small table near her chair. It was time to go home, although she still planned to make a stop at the grocery store. She was going to cook something, instead of microwaving sandwiches again, and she wanted to make chicken piccata. She felt she was discovering a new hobby, stress cooking. Not stress eating; that would be terrible. No… just stress cooking. She chuckled silently, imagining a conversation where she'd say, "My hobby? I'm a stress chef." Well, stress chef or not, she needed capers. One more stop before going home.

A worried, impatient text message from Adrian got her to jump to her feet and ask her service advisor to put a rush on things. A few minutes later, her car was ready, and she took the keys from an attendant who couldn't keep his eyes off her body.

Before long, she stood in the checkout line at the grocery store, carrying a jar of capers and a small tray of chicken breasts. She put them on the conveyor belt and greeted the jaded cashier with a faint smile.

"That's $11.49," the cashier said.

She pulled her card and swiped it, then extended her hand for the receipt. At the corner of her eye, something got her attention, and she turned to look. Then she froze. There he was again, the turtleneck man, his eyes riveted on her. He was closer this time, too close, a mere few yards away. There were lines of tension in his chin, his mouth, and in the way his muscles tensed under his cheeks, as he clenched his jaws. She felt a wave of unspeakable panic but managed not to run away screaming. Instead, she tried to keep her cool and think. Who could this man be? What did he want?

"There you go, ma'am," the cashier said, but she didn't react.

She couldn't call the police; the man hadn't done anything wrong. But she couldn't take her eyes off him, petrified, as if she was staring into the hypnotizing eyes of a snake about to pounce.

"Ma'am?" the cashier insisted, holding out the receipt.

Laura took it with a trembling hand, finally breaking eye contact with the stranger. She started toward the door, trying to walk calmly.

"Ma'am?" the cashier called. "You forgot your bags."

She sighed and turned quickly to grab the bags, then disappeared through the automatic doors with a spring in her step. She tugged at the strings of her hoodie, and pulled the hood over her head, almost to her eyes. She was grateful for the heavy rain, compounding the darkness of the early winter evening. Afraid to look over her shoulder, but feeling the choke of fear strangle her, she walked faster and faster until she got to her car. She started the engine, pulled out, and floored the gas pedal as soon as she exited the parking lot. Only then she took a deep breath, but kept her head on a swivel, looking at the passing cars, checking her rearview mirror.

On the short elevator ride to her apartment, she had a few seconds to calm herself. She didn't want to freak Adrian out. Knowing him, he'd storm out the door and beat the streets, looking everywhere for the stranger who'd stalked his girlfriend. No, she didn't need any of that.

She unlocked the door and immediately locked it back after she got in, not forgetting to put the chain on. Then she leaned against the door, feeling a little safer.

"I'm home," she hollered, not seeing Adrian anywhere.

"In the shower," he replied.

Boo appeared, his tail straight up and stiff, as he meowed excitedly, then rubbed against her legs, weaving a complicated pattern.

"Hey, Boo," she said softly, then picked him up in her arms and rubbed her face against his. Boo purred happily.

Her moment of bliss vanished, dispersed by anxious recollections of her recent experience. Who was that awful man? And what did he want? She suddenly regretted not looking over her shoulder as she'd left the store, to see if he followed her. What if he followed her home? What if he knew where she lived?

Her stomach started doing a number on her, unrested, and she felt queasy. She let Boo drop on the table and took her hoodie off in a hurry. Seconds later, she dropped in front of the toilet bowl, retching violently.

She felt Adrian's hands grab and hold her hair out of the way. She heaved a few times more, then stopped, breathing heavily.

"What the hell, Laura?" he demanded. "What's going on?" He sounded angry.

"Nothing," she replied, "I'm just sick, that's all."

"That's all? Let me tell you, that's not all. It's the damn Jacobs thing, that's what's going on."

"God..." she pleaded, her frustration exceeding her nausea. "Don't be ridiculous. I'm just sick. Must be something I ate."

"Baby, you don't have to do it," he insisted, in a soothing tone. "Not any of it. It's making you sick, stressing you out."

She didn't want to argue. Almost every word she'd said since she'd come home had been a lie. Adrian deserved better, and one day she'd make it up to him.

"Give up this fucking madness, baby, please," he continued his appeal. "Don't do this to us."

She groaned.

"Adrian, I'm not doing anything to *us*. It's about my parents, my family. It's not about you. I need to know. I need to find out what happened that night, and some of these things Dr. Jacobs does are incredible. I feel I'm closer to remembering, closer than I've ever been, and I haven't even started the sessions."

"What are you saying?"

She still kneeled on the floor, leaning against the toilet bowl, afraid the dry heaves might return.

"She taught me to remember smells, sounds, and the house—how everything felt, before I try to remember anything else. And it's working!"

Adrian's eyebrows shot up. "You're saying you remember?"

"No, not yet," she said, letting all her sadness come out in her voice and her misted eyes. "But I'm starting to remember things from *that* time. I'm starting to remember them, my parents, my brother and my sister, and how it felt to be with them."

"How about the rest? You know… that night?"

"I can't," she said, lowering her head, defeated. "Not yet. It's like a dark closet that's there; it's scary, and I'm afraid to open it and look inside. That's how it feels."

"Maybe it's scary for a reason," he said softly. "Maybe you shouldn't look. Why would you want to relive the death of your family?"

"I—I just have to, Adrian. I must. I don't know why, I can't explain it, but I've always felt I had to see for myself, see that killer with my own eyes."

"He's going to be executed in a few days; isn't that enough?" he asked, seemingly irritated.

"No… I need to remember. Don't do this, please."

"Do what?"

"Keep pushing me like this."

He stood and took a few steps back into the hallway. "This is ridiculous. You're being ridiculous," he said, shoving his left hand into his pocket.

She fell quiet for a while, saddened and feeling powerless.

"You know, you're probably one of the very few men out there who'd argue with someone who's sick, right by the toilet bowl," she blurted, a little more bitter than she'd wanted.

He turned and left without a word, then she heard him drop onto the sofa and mutter curses under his breath.

She had to keep on lying, at least for a while. She couldn't bring herself to tell him she was pregnant. Not like this, not with his attitude. He'd go completely bonkers.

She repressed a shudder. She couldn't bring herself to tell him about the man in the turtleneck either or how frightened she really was.

14

Sensitive Ego

Tess pulled her Suburban right next to the entrance, ignoring all the open visitor parking spots. The two-story building that housed the Palm Beach County Sheriff's Office had a new sign in stainless steel, replacing the old, rusted one she remembered. Other than that, nothing had really changed since she'd last been there.

She went straight for the reception desk and pulled out her badge.

"Special Agent Tess Winnett, FBI. Please have the four boxes of case files in my vehicle hauled upstairs to the conference room, will you?" She dropped her car keys on the reception counter, under the rounded eyes of a young man, not a day older than 23.

"Um, I can't... Sorry, I can't leave my post, ma'am," he said stuttering, then turned red in the face.

Her eyebrows furrowed and drew closer to each other, showing her frustration with how difficult everything seemed to be lately. She leaned over the counter, not even attempting to disguise her irritation.

"What do I have to do—"

"Just say yes, Jimmy," she heard Michowsky holler from the second floor, at the top of the stairs. "Trust me, it will help your career more than you know."

She nodded once in Gary's direction, her quick glance long enough to let her notice he wasn't happy to see her there. He'd propped his hands on his hips, and he wasn't smiling.

She climbed the stairs a little slower than she liked, under his scrutinizing eyes, then walked right past him on her way to the conference room. Her ribs were shooting painful darts every time she exerted herself.

"Good to see you too, Gary." She heard him scoff behind her. "Hey, Todd," she greeted Fradella, Gary's younger partner, as she passed his desk. Fradella pushed away his chair and turned toward her.

"Hey, Tess."

She waited in the conference room doorway for them to catch up, then closed the door.

"Imagine my surprise," Gary said, "when I got a call from my captain this morning, right after you and I talked on the phone. He took us off our caseload and assigned us to whatever goose chase you're up to now. To whom do we owe the pleasure?"

His sarcasm attempted to be biting, but she didn't flinch.

"That would be my boss, SAC Pearson. I think the two of you have recently met, in case you want to thank him in person."

Gary stood uneasily, shifting his weight from one foot to the other. Todd repressed a hint of a smile that curled the corners of his mouth.

"We done with the bullshit yet?" Tess asked coldly.

Michowsky lowered his angry gaze and pulled a chair. Fradella followed suit.

"Okay," Michowsky eventually said, letting out a long breath, "What's going on with the Watson case?"

Tess delayed taking a seat for a second more, then sat and pulled out her notes.

"Short version? I told you on the phone. The Watsons, Meyers, and Townsends weren't killed by Garza. We need to find out who killed them, like yesterday. Laura Watson's a walking target after that TV show."

"You're sure? Why? Those cases were closed years ago," Michowsky pushed back, sounding a bit worried.

"There are discrepancies you missed. Two of the cases were yours, in case you forgot."

"No, I didn't goddamn forget, Winnett!" Michowsky snapped.

She stared blankly at him, then continued unperturbed.

"The third one, Townsend, was worked by a Detective, um, McKinley, from Miami-Dade. I don't know him."

"That's because he died a long time ago. Massive coronary," Gary said.

"Crap... I was hoping he could clarify why he pinned the Townsend case on Garza."

"*Pinned* it?" Michowsky reacted, his high-pitched voice sounding almost strangled. "You think that's what we did, McKinley and I? Pinned cases on people, instead of working them?"

She repressed a frustrated groan, this time irritated with herself. She managed to say the things that made people blow up and turn defensive, even when she tried her best to be diplomatic. She'd forgotten just how sensitive Gary could be. One word was all it took.

"You know what I meant," she replied quickly, apologetically. "I meant attributed to Garza."

"Yeah, right..." Michowsky replied morosely. "Tell me, Winnett, is your career so badly adrift they don't assign you real cases anymore? Is that it?"

Her breath caught. Could that be true? She felt a sudden urge to call Pearson and ask him why he'd assigned Garza's interview to her, and what was up with that strange coincidence Gary had mentioned before. Logic took over, and she stopped her descending spiral into the abyss of anxiety, remembering she could have been on medical leave that week and two more. She was the one who insisted to return to work early. It was her decision, and hers only. No coincidence, nada. So much for Gary's conspiracy theories, all fizzled out flat. She almost smiled.

"Let's just work the cases, guys. That's all I'm asking. Let's just put the cases on a matrix, and map the discrepancies."

"You're digging up old cases based on the say-so of a convicted serial killer, Winnett. You know that, right?" Michowsky continued to push back. "You don't care one little bit about what it does to me, to us here, at the precinct."

"It doesn't have to do anything to you, Gary. But if there's a killer on the loose, out there, wouldn't you want to know? Wouldn't you want to be sure?"

"I *am* sure," he fired back, raising his voice. "I'm sure Garza nailed them, and now he's messing with you, seeing how you're in a hurry to cause trouble and throw us all under the bus. I'm sure he's enjoying himself right now, having a blast."

He suddenly seemed older, tired. Tess knew he'd just returned to work himself, a week before, after the concussion he'd suffered trying to help her. Some reunion. They should be downing mojitos and sharing war stories, the three of them. They'd been through a lot together, and had done some good work. Instead, they were ripping at each other. Fradella watched their exchange quietly, with an expression of gloomy disbelief pasted on his face.

"Gary, this killer will kill again, and it's not Kenneth Garza," she said softly, trying to appease him.

"Says who? A convicted killer?" he bellowed. "And no surprise, Special Agent Tess Winnett of the FBI takes his word over mine, after twenty-five bloody years spent on the fucking force!"

A few heads turned outside the conference room. People stared at them through the glass wall with disapproving looks. Jimmy approached hesitantly and struggled to knock on the door, carrying two of the four boxes in his arms. She opened the door to let him in, thankful for the interruption.

"Todd, can we have the room for a minute, please?"

Fradella nodded and left, a second after Jimmy.

"Sit down, Gary, please."

He stood stubbornly, pushing his chin forward in a gesture of defiance. His chin trembled slightly, a sign of deep emotional turmoil.

"Please," she insisted.

He finally obliged, and folded his arms on his chest.

She studied him for a second, taking in the circles under his eyes, the tiredness he seemed to emanate, the stiff gait, probably from the same pesky sciatica that kept him wondering about old age, and envying his younger partner. She cringed a little, knowing what she was about to say.

"Gary, there's no easy way to tell you this, so I'll just go ahead and say it. Catching a potential killer on the loose trumps your ego and your concern with covering any mistakes you might have made. It's that simple; I'm sorry."

He stared at her, astounded. Then he spoke in a low, loaded voice. "You self-righteous bitch! I heard that about you, and I didn't want to believe it. It's true, damn it, so true. I'm a goddamned idiot, that's what I am."

She expected his reaction, and took it impassibly. "Work with me on this case, Gary," she continued just as calmly as before, "and I promise you I'll do the best that I possibly can to make you look like a hero in the end."

"Huh?" he reacted, a little surprised. "Why the hell would you do that?"

"Because you're a good cop, Gary, and a good man. The rest is life, details, chaos happening to us. Psychopaths playing with us. Sometimes we get deceived, trapped into situations that aren't our fault."

He fell silent, biting his lip and clasping his hands together. He stood and paced the room, slowly, keeping his hands in his pockets. He didn't say a word, just stopped his pacing after a while and looked her in the eye before making his decision.

Then he turned to the phone and dialed an internal extension.

"Jimmy? What the hell's keeping you with the rest of those boxes?" Then he hung up and looked at her with a flicker of curiosity in his eyes. "Let's map the damn cases."

15

Reflections: What I Want

What I want is clear, since the day I killed Watson. Since that exhilarating moment fifteen years ago, I've known exactly who I am, or at least I started to discover. I'm a predator, a deadly one. A skilled hunter with sharp instincts and a fearless heart. One kill, and I was hooked for life. I live for the thrill of the kill, anticipating whom I will choose next, how I will do it, planning every little detail over and over in my head. Counting the minutes until the day of the feast.

Hooked, that's what I am. Entirely hooked. Addicted, down to the last bone in my body, but not out of control. I know I have to be patient and pace myself. Best meals are savored slowly and in small quantities. The biggest change Allen Watson brought to my life is the fact that I can finally see it clearly and accept who I am. I'll be grateful into eternity. His, not mine.

You see, I'm not like you; not in the slightest. You might have struggled with accepting yourself too at some point, maybe you and I have that in common, but that's where the commonalities end. I'm a taker, the ultimate seizing machine. I see something I like, I don't hesitate; I just go after it, right then and there, grasping the opportunity. I've always been like that, always understood and loved that about myself, way before Allen Watson and I even met.

Ever since I can remember, I always knew what I wanted. Some people are ashamed of their wants and needs. Some are indoctrinated into guilt by religious precepts; others by their society; and finally, some by the education they receive from their families and communities. That's not to say they haven't tried it on me... only it didn't take, not a single iota. I could close my eyes right now and recite from memory some of that senseless horseshit that turns men into sheep, generation after lame generation.

No, you can't want to be rich, not openly; people might think badly of you. No, you can't fuck a different woman every day; that's a sin. Always forgive, it's good for the soul.

Good for the soul, my ass. Have you tried killing the man who fucked you over, to see just how good for the soul *that* would be? Well, maybe not for you... I keep forgetting, you and I are not the same. It could destroy you, put you over the edge of an endless abyss from which there's no return. Not ever.

Yes, I always go after what I want. My problem back then, right after the Watsons, was getting better at securing what I wanted. Because, whether I liked to admit that or not, with the Watsons I'd screwed up badly, leaving a live witness behind. And I'd screwed up before.

But that night with the Watsons was filled with revelations; Rachel Watson was another surprise. She reminded me of my youth, with its almost disastrous mistake. She reminded me of that long-forgotten feeling of sublime exultation that comes with exerting absolute power over another human being. Over a woman's vulnerable body, lying helplessly at my feet, ready for my body to take.

What I want is messy, and that's the truth. So messy, it almost cost me my life, back in college. Her name was Donna, and she was a beauty, a magnificent creature who didn't know I existed. I wanted her; I craved her body like the junkie craves the fix that could end him, with trembling hands and sleepless nights. So I did it; I made my stupid, rushed move, riddled with juvenile, inexcusable mistakes. She had a tight little body that fought mine with every fiber, making my senses vibrate with pleasure every time I penetrated her. She gave me a night to remember, a night that fulfilled my wildest dreams.

Well, she didn't exactly give it to me, per se. Let's say I *took* from her a sexual experience like no other. That's what I do… I take what I want.

The following day, Donna deeply disappointed me; she reported me to the police. Unbelievable. Statistics say that a vast number of sexual assaults go unreported, the victims being too ashamed to step forward. My astonishing Donna refused to be such a statistic, unfortunately. In retrospect, maybe I'd pushed things too far, and she needed medical attention. She didn't know who I was, of course. I'd visited with her at night, in the dark, and had been careful not to leave bodily fluids behind. The cops didn't have much to go on.

Imagine my surprise when the cops banged on my door a day later. I had a flimsy alibi, only half-thought through, because… well, because I was young and careless. An hour later, they had me in a lineup at the station, and what I felt then is indescribable. My life, as I knew it, was about to be over. It took tremendous amounts of effort to maintain the appearance of innocence and calm, to hide my burning rage, to wait it out, to hide the sweat beads that constantly emerged at the roots of my hair and rolled down my forehead.

I don't feel fear like you do; not at all. It's hard to describe, but I do feel when things are about to leave my control and enter someone else's. It makes me angry, and most of all, it makes me tense. It's a nuisance. For instance, knowing that I could be locked up for years for my adventurous night with Donna gave me a feeling that could be described as fear, although it wasn't. It was more of a concentrated state of readiness, of alertness. All my muscles were tense, and all my neurons were firing at the top of their game, going through countless scenarios to identify opportunities and analyze my captors' behavior, searching for clues. During these times, unlike you, my heart rate stays level, instead of escalating, and my breathing slows down, deepening, oxygenating every fiber of my body that needs to be ready to pounce.

All stars lined up for me that day, and they let me go without even a single word of apology. Fucking bastards… Later, I'd learned that dear old Donna had picked the precinct's accountant out of the lineup. Although grateful for that twist of favorable fate, I was a little frustrated too. The man looked mediocre, almost humble. The only things we had in common besides gender were hair color and height. How could any woman I'd been so intimate with, for so many hours, confuse me with… *that?*

Good that she did, nevertheless.

Unfortunately, after that wonderful night with Donna and the ensuing near-disaster, I didn't dare try again, not for the longest time. I had no idea how the cops had found me, no idea what I'd done wrong. I learned to curb my urge, and hoped that one day I'd stop feeling its unsatisfied burn deep inside the very core of my being.

It never stopped burning. That fire would kindle repeatedly in my groin, demanding action. Demanding me to possess someone completely, urgently.

You see, what I want is primal. Total, absolute power over a woman. Remember, I always take what I want. You might struggle to understand why I do that so freely, without any concern for the human being I choose to enjoy. Let me explain that as simply as I possibly can.

Have you ever enjoyed an apple? Have you ever sunk your teeth into that crisp, fresh skin, freeing the juices that quench your thirst so deliciously? Ah, so you have… In that case, here are some questions for you to ponder: Have you ever apologized to that fruit for possessing it, for consuming it? For the infinite pleasure its demise had brought to your senses? Have you ever felt bad about your craving for its savor? Has that conscience of yours, that you take such pride in having, ever bothered you with long-lasting remorse for every apple you've ever relished?

I didn't think so.

16

Questions

Fradella helped Tess list the three cases up on the case board. They placed them around the center of the board, in chronological order. Tess hoped to uncover the unsub's before and after killings, and possibly some in-betweens, so she made sure she'd left space on the board for any such findings.

A little to the left was the Watson case, with several pictures showing the bodies, how they were found, and close-ups of their fatal wounds. Allen Watson was shot twice in the chest. The children were shot in the head, point blank, execution style. Finally, Rachel was stabbed three times in the abdomen.

With the Meyers, things differed somewhat. The man was shot twice in the chest, much like Watson, but the woman had been tortured before being stabbed to death. The trend continued with the Townsend family. The man was shot twice, the daughter killed quickly and painlessly with a bullet in the back of her head, and the woman visibly tortured, then stabbed.

Tess stepped back and looked at the board. She thought through all the images and analyzed all the details, as if it were the first time she saw them. She frowned and muttered something under her breath.

"What's wrong?" Michowsky asked.

"This doesn't happen," she said, gesturing vaguely at the board.

"Sure it does. Look at Garza. He's done a lot of these."

"No, I meant these empty spaces before the Watsons and after the Townsends. No way was this his first crime. No way Townsend was his last. We have to find his first victim. I'm willing to bet everything I've got in my wallet that Watson wasn't his first victim."

"Because of how organized he is?" Fradella asked.

"He's organized, careful, and precise. He's nowhere near Garza's level of organization, but he's up there. The Watson family is as low risk as they come. But look at his evolution, developing from murder to rape. That doesn't happen. History, statistics show us serial killers evolve from rape to murder, not the other way around." Tess scratched her head and tucked a strand of hair behind her ear. "Okay, let's map out this mess."

She drew a table, putting each family name as column headers, then the last header she labeled TGV.

"TGV?" Michowsky asked.

"Typical Garza victim," Tess replied. "We'll map discrepancies here."

"I thought you assumed these three weren't Garza's victims, right?" he asked, his confusion underlined by a hint of a frown.

"Yes, we're starting from that assumption. If Garza did kill these families, then we have nothing to worry about. He's going to fry in a few days, and no one's going to come after Laura Watson."

"Then, why are you mapping the discrepancies?" he pressed on.

"We need to uncover who this unsub really is, when he's not copycatting Garza. Which aspects of victimology, MO, and signature belong entirely to this killer? What defines him?"

"Cool," Fradella said, hopping off the conference table where he'd perched himself and grabbing a marker. "Can I try?"

Tess invited him with a hand gesture.

He added a few lines to the table and started labeling them at the far left.

"So, we have MO, weapon, signature, victimology—you said. What else?"

"That's it for now, let's populate the fields," she invited him.

He started scribbling notes in each cell.

"I think the first question we need to answer is this: Are we looking at a single unsub for all three cases? Or are we looking at more than one?"

Both men looked at her.

"Two or three copycats over such a short period of time?" Gary pushed back. "It would be highly unlikely, I believe."

"I agree," Tess replied, chewing lightly on the back end of her dry erase marker. "Let's think horses, not zebras."

"Huh?" Todd reacted.

"When you hear hoofbeats, think horses, not zebras," she quoted. "It's a guiding principle for medical students, encouraging them to not waste time chasing the improbable. It's the medical version of Occam's razor."

"So, we'll go with the assumption it's just one unsub?" Todd asked.

"For now," she replied quietly, while her frown deepened. "No, this isn't right, see?" she pointed at the signature line. "I don't think we know his signature yet. Rape and torture are not his signature, Todd, they're part of his MO. For Garza, what he did after the killings was his signature."

"Then how do you define a killer's signature?"

She liked Todd. He had an inquisitive mind and absorbed every bit of knowledge with enthusiasm. He was smart and willing to grow professionally, although sometimes a bit of an ego stood in the path of that.

"A signature is what the killer does in addition to the actual crime, the part he doesn't need to do to execute the crime. In our unsub's case, the shooting and stabbing, even the rape were his MO, but we don't know the signature yet. It's critical to figure it out, because it sheds light into his psychological makeup, into the reasons behind who he is and why he does what he does."

"We can't find that out from what we have here?" Michowsky asked.

"Maybe we can, but we haven't yet. It could be something small, a tiny thing. Maybe he takes souvenirs, something so small and insignificant no one noticed it was missing from the crime scenes. It could be as simple as taking pictures of his victims. Maybe it's something he does, that we haven't figured out yet."

She paced the floor for a while, going back and forth in front of the case board, not taking her eyes off it.

"Gary, you worked the Watson crime scene, right? Tell me what you remember."

Michowsky cleared his throat before speaking.

"Um, we found Allen Watson just where the housekeeper told us he'd be."

"Um... Hannah Svoboda?" Tess asked, after checking her notes.

"Yes, she's the one who called 911."

"Ah, yes, got it. Let's forget what's in the case file. Tell me what you felt, what your gut told you. What you smelled, heard, or sensed."

"Ugh... it's been a while, you know?" he said pensively. "I remember the TV, blaring, set on a cartoon channel. I recall we were so shocked at what we saw, it took us a while to turn that off. We cleared the house first, and I was the one who cleared the kitchen. That was the worst, worse even than the children's bedrooms upstairs. Blood everywhere, like you see there," he added, pointing at the case board.

She nodded quietly, waiting for him to continue.

"I remember thinking the blood patterns looked disturbed," he added, staring at the floor, and running his hand through his buzz-cut hair.

"Disturbed?" Tess asked. "As in—"

"You know how blood pools after the victim is stabbed and falls to the ground, right? It forms a puddle with smooth, curved edges, especially on an even, shiny surface like kitchen tiles. This one was different. It was like someone touched the blood, messed with it. The puddle was irregular, and the edge had angles and smudges."

"Could that be a signature, maybe?" Tess asked. "Did you see the same pattern with the Meyers?"

"In retrospect, maybe. I remember thinking that at the Meyer crime scene, but then concluding I couldn't be sure, because of the torture. You know, he tortured the Meyer woman."

"You mean Jackie Meyer, right?" she said quickly, drilling him with an unforgiving gaze. She didn't appreciate the apparent lack of respect toward the victims. The least they could do was say their names and treat them with the deference they deserved.

"Right," he replied with a quizzical expression in his eyes.

"But is it possible, based on what you remember, that the unsub messed with the blood pools of Jackie Meyer after her death?"

"Doing what?"

"We don't know that; nevertheless, is it possible?"

Michowsky stood and walked to the case board. He squinted and studied closely all the Meyer crime scene photos.

"Yeah, I guess so," he eventually said.

"Okay," she sighed, "let's look at the Townsends next. We have more photos in here," she added, opening the Townsend case file.

"Yeah, I see it here, and here," Todd said, pointing at one of the photos. "What the hell was he doing?"

"Is," she corrected him. "Is he doing. There's no reason to believe he stopped."

"Yeah, you're right," he replied.

She propped her hands on her hips and let out a frustrated breath of air.

"Todd, please pull a random Garza file from the box. Any case file should do it. Let's check the blood puddles."

He obliged and scattered the case photos on the table. It was a family of three from Kendale Lakes. The woman, a redhead, reminded her of Dr. Jacobs.

Tess studied the photos closely, biting her lower lip and frowning.

"Uh-huh," she eventually said, "so go ahead and add one more line to that discrepancies table. Name it blood puddles. Garza didn't mess with the blood puddles. You can see where he removed the bodies from the particular spots they were killed, but the puddle edges are intact. Entirely different."

Todd obliged, hesitating a little before adding the word "disturbed" under the three cases they were working, and "intact" under the TGV header.

"We're getting closer to discovering his signature," she said. "Is there any entry in the forensics notes on these blood puddles?"

Todd shifted through the case file, looking for the report. He mumbled as he read through it and made those sounds some impatient people make instead of tapping their fingers.

"Nope, there's nothing. Kind of unusual. They must have thought—"

"They must have thought Garza did it and stopped working it. Stopped thinking, stopped doing their jobs," Tess snapped. "Makes our job really interesting now, fifteen damn years later."

Michowsky shot her a hurt, antagonized look.

"You're so quick to judge, Winnett. People are doing a great—"

"Oh, just spare me, will ya?" she snapped. "Just don't say good job, 'cause you know it wasn't."

She slammed the case file shut and resumed her pacing. She stared into the gaping wounds of the three stabbed women, then she remembered something she'd read in the Meyer case file: "Unusual skin distension pattern in stab wound. No trace elements found." She wondered if there could be any correlation between that unusual distention and the altered blood pools. A thin theory, as thin as such theories could ever get. To her, Jackie Meyer's stab wounds looked just like Rachel Watson's or Emily Townsend's, but Doc Rizza might have a different opinion.

"Before we start pulling all the unsolved rape and murder cases in the past twenty years, we need to speak with the ME. Maybe the doc remembers something that's not in there."

17

Family Lunch

Laura studied Adrian discreetly, as he drove her SUV on the quiet Miami Shores streets, all boasting neatly manicured lawns in front of large, modern American homes, mostly hidden from view by lush greenery. Cypress trees, palmettos, flowering bushes, all trimmed and professionally maintained, completed the picturesque image of a neighborhood for the comfortably wealthy who didn't want to push the envelope and add another zero to the price of their homes, for the privilege of living in glitzy Miami Beach.

Adrian looked tense and uncomfortable in his perfectly pressed shirt and slacks, far from his normal routine, which included T-shirts, typically with humorous messages, and worn-out jeans. He'd fussed about his attire for a long, nerve-racking hour, feeling the pressure of having to impress his girlfriend's family over a long, pretentious lunch.

It wasn't the first time that Adrian had met her adoptive family, but the only other time had been a quick conversation in passing that took place in the Lincoln Road Mall, where they'd run into one another. Laura and Adrian, dressed down and having a good time eating junk food at the Chinese tray-pusher in the food court, and the Welshes, dressed to perfection, strolling through the mall like Miami royalty. It didn't go that well. Carol's kindness and pleasant demeanor felt forced, and Bradley's frown dismissed Adrian, making him feel small and unwanted. Adrian, much like any other young man in his place, never forgot the bruise to his ego.

The car turned the corner onto Grand Concourse, and Laura shifted in her seat, a little anxious herself. The familiar silhouette of the house she grew up in didn't seem so familiar anymore; almost seemed like a stranger's home. She'd moved out a couple of years before, when she'd gone to school, but that wasn't the reason. For the past few days, she'd spent lots of time dwelling in the past, the more distant past, where a white, two-story house in Palm Beach had been her home.

Bradley and Carol had sold that property on her behalf, afraid the bad memories would stay with the house and haunt her years later. They were right, but lately she'd found herself driving by that house and staring at it, trying to remember, trying to feel something more than the sense of doom that hadn't vacated her heart since that damn TV show.

She returned to her reality when Adrian cut the engine. They'd arrived, and he was parked on the street.

"Go on," she encouraged him, "park in the driveway. It's all good."

"Oh, hell no," he reacted, and hopped out of the car. She smiled when he approached her side and opened the door for her, like a true gentleman.

They walked the distance to the main door without saying a word, both immersed in their thoughts. She pushed the door handle and walked right in, and Adrian followed, after a second of hesitation.

"They're here," Amanda hollered from the middle of the stairs, then continued her descent, flying over the wide steps in a rush to get to them. She was four years older than Laura, and had been her loving, cheerful adoptive sister ever since she could remember. She had long, wavy, chestnut hair, and the face of a poster girl for cheerleader nationals. Bursting with energy and lust for life, Amanda had made Laura's life better at every milestone. First boyfriend, she was there to give good advice. First heartbreak, she snuck out and bought a quart of Häagen-Dazs for them to share, turning the bitterness in Laura's tears to laughter, sprinkled with cynicism for everything male.

Amanda hugged Laura tightly, then pulled herself away and turned to Adrian. She grabbed both his hands and held them to the sides, as if examining a model. He was petrified.

"Well, look at you. I heard a lot about you, but you're not bad at all," she concluded, in her typical direct, undiplomatic way. "Yep, you done well, sis," she laughed and finally let Adrian go. Immediately, he shoved his hands inside his pockets and took a step back.

Bradley appeared from the kitchen, wiping his hands on a paper towel.

"Hey," he said, then approached and kissed Laura on the cheek. "Adrian," he extended his hand, and the young man took one hand out of his pocket and firmly shook Bradley's hand.

"Sir."

"New lamp?" Laura asked, pointing at the modern chandelier hanging above their heads. It was different from everything she'd seen at the factory. It was metallic, all stainless steel, with each arm a custom shape, an upward pointing triangular form with irregular edges and surfaces of smooth, curvy, brushed metal. Each such irregular, flattened pyramid section hid a small light bulb behind its base, throwing multiple triangular shadows on the walls. Quite an interesting design.

"Just a prototype, something I had fun creating," he said, smiling toward the ceiling.

"Are we making it?"

"Oh, no," he laughed. "The engineers said it would be too expensive to make; it wouldn't be worth it. Too much of a hassle to supply parts for it, being that each arm is a different mold, a different component."

"Can't we standardize?"

"It's not that great, you know. Let's go, lunch is waiting," he added, and led the way to the dining room.

He seemed tired and concerned with something. Laura found herself wondering, worrying. His black hair, short-trimmed, showed an increasingly receding line, and two small but deep ridges marked the bridge of his nose, one on each side.

"Hello, my dear," Carol greeted her, then abandoned a flower arrangement to give her a hug. "You're a little pale. Is everything all right?"

"Yeah, yeah, don't worry," she replied, as Carol shook Adrian's hand.

"You know that's the precise moment a mother worries, right?"

They all laughed, a quick burst covered by chairs being drawn back and glasses being filled.

"Let me help," Laura offered, trotting behind Carol to get the food.

They'd prepared a treat, deviled eggs and bruschetta to open, and a mouthwatering roast beef with mashed potatoes.

Laura sat next to Adrian, their knees touching under the table. Amanda sat across from them and had already started her attack on the deviled eggs. Laura studied Bradley again. He ate slowly, staring down at his plate, his frown still visible.

"Bon appétit," Carol said, and raised her wine glass.

They clinked and sipped the exquisite white wine, then resumed eating in silence.

"If you'd like, I can come work with you full-time, as early as September," Laura opened the conversation, aware of how quiet everyone was. "I can step on it and finish early."

Bradley looked up from his plate and smiled, a gloomy smile that didn't touch his eyes.

"How about your MBA?"

"That can wait," she replied. "I'm thinking you might be able to use the help."

His smile widened, dissipating some of the gloom.

"I'll be fine; I can handle it on my own for a while longer. I'm not that old, you know," he replied humorously.

"I know you can," she insisted. "You look a little tired, that's all. I just want to help. Plus, Amanda's already working, so why can't I?"

"Ah, don't even go there," Amanda replied. "My daddy, yeah, him, got me an internship at a damn newspaper. Can you believe it? What a horrendous waste of my time!"

"Oh?" Laura reacted, "and what's wrong with that?"

"It's only *Miami Daily*, the biggest news house in Florida," Brad replied, then took another mouthful of delicious bruschetta.

"It's a newspaper, people," Amanda replied, as aggravated as she could be. "When's the last time any of you read a newspaper? Huh? They're the dinosaurs of the news industry, and I'm wasting my time there."

"You've got a journalism degree, don't you?" Carol intervened in her calm, appeasing voice.

"Yes, I do, but what's wrong with television? Why not intern for CBS? The only thing I'm learning at that newspaper is how to prepare a media corporation for Chapter 11."

Adrian dropped his fork and the clattering noise brought silence around the table and furtive glances. He turned red and mumbled an apology, while Amanda shot him her megawatt smile.

Carol served the roast, then she took the first bite, keeping her eyes on Laura. She swallowed the bite and said, "Never mind the newspaper drama here, we'll never hear the end of it, right?"

Amanda shot her a hurt glance. Seeing the two of them together was funny. Amanda was a younger, more rebellious version of her mother. Carol's beauty still lingered, enhancing her classy appearance.

"I'm more concerned with you," Carol continued, looking at Laura. "Are you losing weight?"

"Uh-uh," Laura replied, with her mouth full.

"What's going on with those sessions you're doing? You have us worried, all of us."

Laura swallowed and put her fork down, almost rolling her eyes.

"I have to do this. You, of all people, should understand."

Brad stared at the plate again, pursing his lips, visibly unhappy with the way the conversation was going.

"Why put yourself through this? It can only hurt you, baby," Carol insisted. Her warm voice reminded Laura of when she was younger, growing up in the serenity of their household, and having the same warm voice guiding her through life's early challenges. Her eyes misted.

"I need your help, young man," Carol continued, turning to Adrian.

"Oh, no need to ask, ma'am, I'm onboard already. But you know Laura," he replied hastily, then shrugged.

"Guys, back off, please," Laura pleaded, feeling tears choking her. "I have to do this; it's important for me. My decision is made."

She looked around the table for a sympathetic face, but found none. Brad's grim expression wasn't something she'd seen in the past, with very few exceptions. He'd always been there for her, encouraging her to do whatever she wanted, helping her forget she wasn't their real daughter. Even Amanda stared at her plate.

"Is it the media attention?" Adrian asked, clasping Laura's hand. "Is that what you're looking for?"

She sprung from the table, unable to keep her eyes from welling up. A wave of sorrow swelled her chest. In that instant, she felt completely alone in the world, while the few people she loved ganged up on her. She covered her mouth with her hand, and put all the words she couldn't speak in one tearful look she threw Adrian before she stormed out of the room.

18

Autopsy Findings

Tess led the way to the morgue, ignoring the whispered comments Gary and Todd exchanged while walking just a few feet behind her. She was eager to find out more about the three anomalous cases, and she knew that if anyone in the entire Palm Beach County area had done their job right, that would have been Doc Rizza, the medical examiner.

The automated doors swooshed open and she stepped in, greeted by a wave of chilly, humid air, heavy with the smell of disinfectant. She threw one quick glance and saw the two exam tables were vacant. She breathed out, relieved. Seeing a dead body on the cold slab always made her shiver, reminding her just how little had come between her own fate and that of any rape and murder victim who Rizza worked on. Yes, ten years ago, it could have been her on that table, but somehow she survived. And yet, seeing the morgue didn't make her feel proud that she'd survived; rather she felt an immense sorrow for all the girls who didn't.

Doc Rizza rose from his chair and came to greet them, wearing a wide grin on his chubby face. He was the only one who didn't frown on her presence there. They went back, the two of them, and they both excelled at what they did. An unspoken alliance had formed throughout the years, and Rizza's camaraderie was something Tess appreciated, by contrast with jurisdictional frictions and defensive behaviors that were the norm with the rest of the Palm Beach County Sheriff's Office.

"Well, here you are, again," Rizza said, then hugged her lightly. "You seem fine after your last adventure, but I know cracked ribs can be sore for a long time, so no bear hug for you today, missy."

She laughed, while Gary and Todd stood a little stiff, waiting. Doc Rizza was part of their team, and to see him greet her so warmly must have made them feel betrayed.

"I heard you were coming," Rizza said, "something to do with Garza?"

"Quite the opposite," she replied, pulling a chair in front of the empty evidence. "We have three cases we need you to look at, and tell us what you remember."

She laid out the three case files on the table and watched Doc Rizza put on his glasses and open the first one.

"Watson, yes, I remember this one." He flipped through the pages, mumbling "uh-huh" every few seconds. "Who else have you got? The Meyers, yes, and the Townsend family."

She waited patiently for him to refresh his memory. Then he disappeared inside the adjacent storage room, unlocked one of the large filing cabinets, and searched through it for a few seconds, then extracted his own boxed records for the three cases.

"All right, we're set. What do you want to know?"

"I believe these three families were killed by someone else, not by Garza."

"What? How come?" His mouth remained slightly open, while he ran his hand through the unruly bunch of thinning hair he still had growing near the top of his head.

"Doc, can you confirm Emily Townsend was raped? This is a major departure from the Garza MO."

"Um, yes, it's written right here," he said, pointing at one paragraph entry in his report.

"Yeah, I've seen that, just making sure." She looked briefly at the ceiling, thinking hard. Was Garza yanking her chain? How did he know Mrs. Townsend had been raped?

She turned toward Gary. "Was there a formal interrogation of Kenneth Garza on the Townsend case?"

"Must have been," Gary replied. "But it wasn't my case, so I can't be sure."

"Well, he either was questioned about the rape or heard it on the news."

"I don't recall that information being made public," Gary said.

Her eyes lingered on Todd's face, absentmindedly, while she thought of options. What Gary did or didn't recall was not solid enough for her.

"All right, all right, I'll do it," Todd said.

"What?"

"Check the media releases back then, to see if this piece of information was ever made public. Dig through archives."

"Fradella, you're the man," she replied.

"That's what everyone says," he quipped, before the doors closed behind him.

"Especially the ladies," Gary added, but there was no smile to go with that. "Countless ladies, you know."

"You're jealous?" Tess asked. "Really? He's half your age, Gary. It's his time now."

He muttered something unintelligible, and she let it drop.

"Doc, what can you tell us about these three cases? Let's start from assuming Garza didn't kill any of these people, and let's assume a single other killer did."

He rubbed his chin thoughtfully, while his eyes ran from one autopsy report to the next.

"The first thing worth mentioning is that the delay between the time of death of the men and the time of death of the women is increasing."

She frowned a little and bent over the evidence table to see what he was talking about.

"Mr. and Mrs. Watson were killed at about the same time. Their respective liver temperatures were almost the same, only a 0.2-degree difference between them. That puts their time of death within minutes of each other. With the Meyer family, we see a delay, and I've explained that by underlining the fact that Jackie Meyer had been tortured for three, maybe four hours before being killed, *after* her husband died. Finally, in the Townsend case, Ralph Townsend and Cindy Townsend, the daughter, both died at about 9:30PM, while Emily Townsend died at about 3:30AM the following day. Six hours later."

"Did it take that long for her to die? I see that the cause of death was exsanguination due to sharp-force trauma."

"No," Doc Rizza replied, and shook his head vigorously. "The fatal stab nicked her right common iliac artery. She bled out in minutes."

"But he tortured and raped her for six hours before that?" Tess asked.

"Precisely. He started by stabbing her there, superficially. The pain must have subdued her instantly, but the stab itself wasn't lethal. It was just a form of restraint he used."

She felt a wave of nausea hit her and grabbed the end of the evidence table to steady herself.

"Walk me through what happened with all three women," she asked quietly.

"Rachel Watson was the cleanest kill of all three," he replied, while his eyes searched Tess's inquisitively.

She looked away. He was perceptive, Doc Rizza, like any good ME should be.

"She was stabbed three times, two of the wounds more hesitant, superficial, while the third was the fatal one, deep, almost completely severing the abdominal aorta. She must have been dead within a minute or two."

"Hesitant? As in he's never done this before?" Gary asked.

"It's a possibility, yes," Rizza replied. "Although, if I were a betting man, which I'm not, I'd bet he'd killed before, only not stabbed someone before. The shootings of Allen Watson and the children show absolutely no hesitation."

"Stabbing is personal," Tess added. "Can we assume Rachel Watson was the intended target?"

"Strictly from a medico-legal perspective, and with the conjuncture of the other two female victims, yes. However, I can't assume. That's not my job. My job is to state the facts, and let you guys infer all you want."

"How about Jackie Meyer?"

"She was tortured. She had deep, skin-piercing bite marks on her breasts and thighs. She displays what we call overkill: multiple deep, life-threatening stab wounds made repeatedly. The lethal incision was this one here, in the lower abdomen."

Tess closed her eyes for a split second, then looked at some additional photos that weren't in the case file she had. She swallowed hard, forcing her nauseated stomach back into its place.

"One more thing," Doc Rizza said, "she was redressed."

"I was just about to ask, how was she bitten and stabbed so many times, when she was found with her clothes on?"

"That's a good question. I found some blood here, right under this button," he pointed at the top button of Jackie Meyer's shirt. "She was found lying on her back, and this button is inches above her wounds. Technically, blood shouldn't have been found there, right between the button and the fabric, unless she was redressed after the bites and the torture, by someone wearing blood-stained gloves."

"Do you think the redressing explains the smudges we see in the blood pools?"

"Most likely," Doc Rizza replied. "There could be other factors at play, but I can't say for sure what."

"Let's walk through this," Tess said. "He comes into the house, shoots the husband, then what?"

"Then stabs the wife once, here," he said, pointing at a small, gaping wound in Jackie Meyer's abdomen, on the left side. "It's not fatal; it missed all the critical organs and blood vessels, just cut into her spleen. Very painful. With an attack like that, she was immediately subdued, unable to do anything to defend herself. Then, for three to four hours, he bit and cut into her flesh, causing numerous superficial wounds, up until the final stabbing came."

They were silent for a few seconds, while Tess and Gary reviewed all the photos again, with the newly added perspective.

"Doc, I wanted to ask you, what did you mean by 'Unusual skin distension pattern in stab wound. No trace elements found'? See. Right here," she pointed at the entry in the report.

"Ah, yes. It's about this wound, the fatal stab. Are you familiar with Langer's lines?"

"No," Tess replied, then looked at Gary. He shook his head.

"They are lines of natural tension in the skin, due to the orientation of the collagen fibers in the dermis. They run parallel to the underlying muscle fibers, and they are the reason why the scar from your appendectomy is oblique. You see, if you cut along Langer's lines, there's no tension to pull the incision open. But if your cut is perpendicular to these tension lines, the wound naturally gapes. Like you see in most of these wounds on the sides of her abdomen, but not here, at the center, where Langer's lines run vertically."

"I see, got it," Tess replied.

"That comment you found in my report has to do with this wound, the fatal stab, which appears to be gaping more widely than we can attribute to Langer's lines. The head and tailing of the wound appear slightly forced open."

She frowned and felt a chill down her spine.

"Meaning what?"

"Meaning it's possible something was inserted into the wound. That something, whatever it was, left no trace elements for me to find."

"Oh, God…" Gary said. "Please tell me it wasn't—"

"We don't know what it was, and we can't speculate." Doc Rizza cut him off grimly. "No trace elements."

Tess wanted to speak, but no sound came out. She cleared her throat, then tried again.

"How about Emily Townsend?"

"Same story, only no bite marks. He raped her instead, multiple times, after she'd been stabbed, but before delivering the fatal blow. It must have been a blood bath, but no DNA, no trace elements were found."

Tess closed her eyes, trying to clear away the imagery that formed in her mind. Then she felt a wave of anger build up.

"How the hell was it possible for these three murders to be attributed so lightly to The Family Man? I see more and more discrepancies, and I've only been looking at it for a few hours."

"Back then, they didn't seem so different, you know," Doc Rizza replied calmly. "When we saw the Watson stabbing, we assumed he was evolving. The same with the other two cases. Who was to know, back then, that The Family Man would keep on killing for years to come, unchanged in his MO, or his signature? They say hindsight is twenty-twenty for a reason."

"How about that horrific Garza signature, which didn't appear in any of these cases? Didn't that bother anyone?"

Gary scrunched his lips, ready to blow up.

"It did, and I remember that conversation clearly," Doc Rizza said. "But we didn't understand the psychopathic brain back then the way we do today, after years and years of research on fMRI machines."

"How about the rest of the Garza cases? Did you notice anything even remotely similar with these?"

"No. There were no stabbings in any of the Garza cases, other than these three, which now, in our current framework, makes more sense to exclude. Most of all, Garza's signature was always the same, rigorously the same."

"Tell me. I know only what I read in the case files, but I'd like to hear your perspective."

Doc Rizza took a deep breath of air before continuing, then slowly exhaled. "With these three cases excluded, I can say all his cases were identical. Probably Garza will make serial killer history, because he didn't evolve, not in the slightest. He killed everyone quickly and painlessly, all family members. Then he posed them around the dinner table, and spent an inordinate amount of time with them. He *lived* with the dead family. He slept in their beds, ate with them at that table, watched TV, took showers. Can you believe that?"

Tess and Gary stared at Doc Rizza, both speechless, waiting for him to continue.

"Death is messy; it comes with total loss of sphincter control. Can you imagine eating at a table with dead, decomposing people? Ugh… Anyway, after thirty-six to forty-eight hours, he'd leave, just in time to prevent getting caught by housekeepers or nannies." He paused for a second. "He left lots of DNA and plenty of trace evidence at the crime scenes. It's normal, when you consider he lived in those homes for so long. The DNA we had collected allowed us to get him convicted, although in these three cases there was no DNA evidence. We just assumed he couldn't stay, so he didn't have the time to leave any behind. I think that was a big mistake, the way we discarded the lack of DNA evidence. Oh, and the dental records didn't match."

"What do you mean?" Gary asked.

"We took impressions of Jackie Meyer's bite marks. I have everything here," he showed them. He extracted an evidence bag from a case box, and unwrapped several cream-colored molds. "This is the bite impression of the Meyer family killer. They don't match Garza, but we explained it away easily. It's not that exact of a science, bite-mark analysis."

Tess's frown deepened. "What's that?"

"This one?" Doc pointed at another mold. "It's a stab impression, one of the fatal Meyer wounds. I hoped it would help us narrow the list of possible murder weapons."

"It doesn't look anything like a knife," Tess replied, examining it with curiosity.

"That's because it was an abdominal wound. As soon as the knife was pulled out, the organs rearranged in the cavity, and most of the wound pattern was compromised. It didn't bring any value, but I'd taken the mold anyway, so I kept it in the archives. Molds only bring value in wounds that penetrate muscle or bone."

"I still can't understand how these three cases were lumped together with Garza's. They are worlds apart."

"Not really," the doc replied again, his calm not budging. "Against thirty-one other identical cases, these discrepancies seemed like minor anomalies. Maybe he was interrupted and didn't have time to perform his ritual. Maybe he stabbed Mrs. Watson because he ran out of bullets. Or maybe he was disrupted. Again, maybe he was naturally evolving, like most serial killers do."

He stopped talking for a while, then rubbed his forehead with a heavy sigh. "I guess maybe we were too afraid to think we could have two monsters killing families in our town. It's possible we couldn't even conceive of that notion." He swallowed hard, then gulped some water from his uncapped bottle. "Yes, in retrospect, I think you're right, Agent Winnett. We should have seen it, a long time ago."

19

Reflections: The Art of Choosing

Just picture yourself hungry, craving, lusting for a mouthful of gratifying taste. You're standing in front of a crystal bowl filled to the brim with luscious, appetizing apples. Immediately, a Red Delicious catches your eye. You almost pick it from the pile, enticed by the heart-shaped contour in bright, vivid red, the color of pure, fresh blood. You anticipate the loud crunch your teeth will make when biting off a cool, crisp chunk.

A Gala apple smiles at you, nestled right by the Red Delicious. It's the sweetest of them all, shiny and glorious in its red and yellow skin, perfect in its uniqueness. Underneath, a Braeburn beams in green, golden yellow, and tame red, there if you crave the awakening of its rebellious, tart taste. If you like your apples to fight you, that's your choice. That, and Cripps Pink, barely visible under the others, but just as tart and crunchy. Or maybe you'd prefer the fully blossomed flavor of a sweet Fuji, to satisfy your more refined senses. Go on, don't let your hand hesitate, pick one, and enjoy! Take in that scent, with every glorious bite. Feel your lust subside, replaced by deep satisfaction.

Whatever your choice, I want to ask you, what made you choose one apple over all the others? Can you explain? Of course, science has spent valuable resources assembling countless lengthy words packed together in even lengthier phrases, to explain the act of choosing. When, in fact, it's simple.

We, as educated human beings, love the privilege of choice. It comes with wealth, abundance, and freedom, and we value it immensely. With a single apple in the bowl, there is no choice. Yes, there is science behind every choice.

But I consider it, first and foremost, an art.

It has to do with the anticipation of the reward each apple will bring. It has to do with the satisfaction we're craving, the constant quest for gratification that enslaves us. That's how I choose my apples, and probably, you choose them the same way. I always choose the one who has the most promise for a delectable experience. I choose the one most likely to satisfy my thirsting senses.

That's how I chose Jackie Meyer. To me, she was a Honeycrisp. Light, auburn-blonde hair, green eyes, and flawless skin. She walked by me one day, oblivious to who I was, and continued going about her day not realizing I was a few steps behind her since that moment. When I wasn't studying her, I was planning every detail of my feast, making sure that no one would believe The Family Man wasn't to blame. Copycatting him worked wonders with the Watsons, and there was absolutely no reason why it wouldn't work again.

Soon enough, I had planned everything and knew her life in detail. I set the date and struggled those few days before with the adrenaline rush that wouldn't cease. I couldn't sleep anymore, and my hands had this almost permanent tremor I since learned to associate with excited anticipation. I lived on coffee and adrenaline.

I took to the gym more and more. I had joined a gym after the Watsons, realizing I had to build my strength so I could enjoy those special moments without physical limitations imposed by my own body. I needed to be fit and strong, stronger than ever. I worked out diligently, six days a week, and it showed. It helped with the anxiety too. Yes, I was anxious, I have to admit. Not scared, there's a difference. A predator isn't scared, and neither was I.

I had a difficult choice to make. I wanted to possess Jackie completely, but the thought of Donna and that near-disaster in college still held me back. I felt a tremendous urge to feel that power over her, completely, with the core of my being. But I wasn't ready… not yet. I wasn't ready to do it right, without taking unacceptable risks.

I was preparing for it though, as fast as I could, without raising suspicions. I needed to learn all that I could about the forensics of rape, about DNA evidence, about the course of typical investigations. It was a lot, and I wasn't ready yet. I couldn't wait though, not anymore. I craved my Honeycrisp with every breath I took, and it couldn't wait any longer. I couldn't wait.

In my dreams, I smelled her warm skin, and every morning I woke up erect and yearning to lose myself in her softness, to taste every inch of her silky perfection. I was in pain.

The day of the feast didn't disappoint by much. Her green eyes turned almost black when she screamed, pleading for my mercy. Her thin, pale body writhed under my hands, weaker and weaker, until it conceded defeat. When my teeth pierced the pearl-white skin of her breast, my mouth filled with her incredible flavor. I took my time with her, following the steps I had so carefully planned for days in a row. The rush of exerting such power over a woman's body cannot be expressed in words. I've tried before and failed. I cannot convey the exultation, the poetry of such a heady high. I wanted it to last forever.

Nothing does, though.

The following day, I had to return to my normal life, with the memory of my recent experience to keep me company during the most tedious parts of my days, and a small souvenir, something no one will ever miss. Yes, I do have a normal life, you know, that's the tip of the iceberg that I am. For the longest time, I'd worked hard at becoming normal, at extinguishing that all-consuming fire that burns dreams of lust and power into the fabric of my soul. I spared no effort. I'd finished college and become successful at my work. I married a beautiful woman, and started a family. I even went to church every now and then; not because I'm a believer, but because that's what's expected of me, and that's how I maintain the power I hold over everyone in my life. I became really good at what's expected of me, at being the powerful, successful man with a nice family and a good life.

That means, my dear friend, should you ever become the apple of my eye, you won't see me coming.

20

The Chameleon

Back upstairs, in the conference room, no one spoke a word. Tess ruminated about the information shared by Doc Rizza, and the more she thought about things, the more everything made sense. She could see which part of the killings were the unsub's own, and which part had been done out of the necessity to emulate The Family Man. The two sets of crime scene attributes separated clearly now, like oil and water.

Fradella barged in, still panting. He'd probably climbed the two flights of stairs in a hurry.

"We didn't release it," he said. "There's no trace that the Townsend rape was ever shared with the media."

Michowsky let out a short, loud breath of air.

"Then you know what comes next?"

"The interviews?" Fradella asked.

"Yeah, all of them. We need to be sure no one mentioned it to him during an interview."

"But that's hours and hours… It's been years since they caught him, and every now and then someone goes over there and talks to the creep."

"Or I'll just go back over there myself and ask him again," Tess offered. "Might be a better use of our time."

"And he's suddenly going to open up and share, huh?" Michowsky pushed back. "How delusional can you get, Winnett?"

"He'll talk to me; I'm sure of it."

"Why the hell would he do that?"

"Because I'm the first cop to take him seriously about these three cases. No one else bothered."

"That you did," Michowsky replied morosely.

She didn't pay attention to him, and stayed focused on the crime scene photos pasted on the board. The timeline gaps before the Watsons and after the Townsends bothered her the most.

"I know what he is, this unsub," she said. "He's a chameleon. The same way he emulated The Family Man, he might have emulated others."

"But isn't this against everything we know about serial killers?" Todd pushed back. "Everything I read on the subject says each serial has his own MO, own signature, something that aligns with his specific pathology."

Tess nodded. "That's mostly correct, yes."

"Mostly? How can it be mostly correct?"

"I don't think we understand his entire pathology yet," Tess replied. "Until we can figure out what happened here," she added, pointing at the gap on the board before the Watsons, "we can't fully understand his motivations. We don't have enough information."

"He's obviously a sexual predator," Gary said.

"He is, although I struggle to understand this twisted evolution. Serial killers evolve from rape to killing, not the other way around. Any theories?"

They fidgeted a little, but stayed silent.

"All right, let's spell it out," Tess offered. "He jumped from no torture, to four hours, to six hours. Definitely evolving in terms of torture. If we consider the torture as a preamble for rape, then we know what he was building toward. If we know that, we've identified his core pathology, which is anger excitation. The rest was… camouflage. It's the women he wants. That's why the victimology wasn't making any sense."

"But you just said we can't understand his pathology, because we lack information," Fradella said.

"I said we can understand his *core* pathology, but not more. We still don't know why he evolved the way he did. Where is he coming from, this unsub? We still don't know."

Todd grabbed the marker from the edge of the board, and drew another victimology matrix.

"When we looked at victimology for the families," Todd said, "there weren't any common denominators, other than general age bracket, thirty to forty years old, and low risk, suburban families. These families never interacted, never beat the same paths. But neither did the women, because we looked at their backgrounds when we did the families."

"Yes, you did, but have you really looked at the women? Just the women, taken out of the context of their families? What do you see?" She tapped quickly on three photos, portraits of the three victims taken when they were alive.

"Oh, God…" Gary muttered.

"You see it, right?" she asked, looking at Todd.

"Yeah, I see it. Same height, same build, blonde hair, blue or green eyes. They could be sisters."

"They could. Let's discard the rest of their families. That was decoy. What do we see? How do we work these cases now? And why the hell didn't he torture or rape Rachel Watson?"

Silence engulfed the conference room again.

"Come on, guys. Maybe he was emulating someone else before. Who was active in the area back then? Before the Watsons? You know the rule. If we find his first crime, we find him."

Fradella looked to Michowsky for an answer.

"I don't recall anyone of Garza's magnitude, not since I joined the force. But the thing is, Garza killed for years before the Watson murder. Where was he, this perp?"

She sighed, frustrated. That was going nowhere. Then her eyes locked on a south Florida map hanging on the wall. She reached and took it down, then removed the print from the frame. Satisfied, she pasted it on the case board, and marked the addresses for the three murdered families with black dots.

"That's not why that's there, you know," Michowsky said.

"Do I look like I give a damn about décor, when we have a killer at large?" Tess snapped.

Michowsky raised his hands in a pacifying gesture. He seemed miserable. It couldn't have been too easy for him, but she didn't have time for his sensitivities.

"All right, so this was his hunting ground."

"His or Garza's?" Fradella asked.

"Good point. Let's map Garza's with blue. Here, you do it, I'll read the addresses."

A few minutes later, a cluster of blue dots covered the southern part of Palm Beach County, Boca Raton, Fort Lauderdale, all the way down to Miami-Dade. Two of the black dots were in Palm Beach, while the third was on the northern edge of Dade County.

"Argh... Not much luck there," Tess admitted. "I was hoping we could triangulate his hunting grounds for a DIVS search. Okay... let's start with the following parameters," she added, pushing her laptop toward Todd. "Palm Beach, Broward, and Dade counties. Go back twenty years. Unsolved cases: murders, rapes, missing persons. Add severe assaults too."

"You're forgetting these three cases show as solved."

"I'm not forgetting, only I don't have a fix for that. Tried cases disputed by the offenders are not logged in there as such. Even if they were, probably 90 percent of all cases would show as disputed. Very few people admit guilt in murder cases, even after they're convicted."

"Okay, got it," Fradella said. "Filter out victims by gender?"

She bit her fingernail, thinking. "Um... not yet. Let's see what we have, then we'll decide."

Fradella pushed enter, and the wall-mounted screen displayed the results.

"Whoa..." Michowsky reacted. "We'll never get through this. Where do we start?"

DIVS had returned hundreds of unsolved cases in their area and time span. Filtered, after removing all gang and drug-related crime, and murders that didn't involve an assaulted female victim, they broke down as fourteen unsolved murders, forty-two rapes, sixteen missing persons, and two assaults where the victims barely lived. In total, seventy-four unsolved cases that matched their search parameters.

There was no way of telling which ones of the seventy-four unsolved crimes

The Chameleon had perpetrated.

21

A Request

Tess got out of bed at 4:00AM to get an early start on traffic on her way to Raiford. She was grateful for the buzz of the alarm, after tossing and turning every minute of the few hours she'd spent in bed. She struggled, thinking of another time when she'd felt so lost, so confused during an investigation. What made it far worse was the knowledge that The Chameleon, the faceless, traceless unsub, was soon going to make his move and silence the only witness he'd left behind: The Watson Girl.

She wasn't going to lose Laura Watson, and she wasn't going to ruin her perfect case-solving score. That was the commitment she made to herself, at first the night before, when she'd decided to do whatever it took to find The Chameleon, and then that morning, when she drove pedal to the metal the whole distance to Florida State Prison.

They'd already brought Garza to the interview room. She didn't waste any time and went right in, pulled up a chair, and sat in front of him, across the dented and scratched metallic table.

He raised his eyebrows when he recognized her, but didn't say a word. Just smiled a little.

"Good morning," she said.

"Hello," he replied, that flicker of a smile now clearly formed on his face. "What an honor, Special Agent... Winnett, was it?"

"Yes," she confirmed calmly, although she knew he was faking the uncertainty he displayed.

He didn't ask anything else, resigned to study her in silence, with that faint smile still lingering. She reciprocated, unwilling to prove too eager, too desperate. She leaned back against her chair, getting ready for a long wait.

"I know you found something interesting in the cases I gave you," he eventually said, speaking slowly and calmly. "Otherwise, you wouldn't be here, now, would you, Therese? May I call you Therese?"

"No," she replied dryly. "But you can call me Tess, if you wish. Although I prefer Special Agent Winnett or Agent Winnett even."

"I see… Thank you." He smiled, then fell silent again for a while. "Ask away, Special Agent."

"How did you know?" she blurted, unable to wait any longer.

"That I didn't kill those families? Of course, I knew."

"No, that he raped the women," Tess replied, sneaking in a tiny bait.

"Woman," he corrected her impassibly.

She whistled. "Okay, seriously, how did you know?"

He smiled with superiority and shifted in his chair to straighten his back. His chains rattled. He didn't respond for a long few seconds.

"You're not that good at your job, Agent Winnett. I have to teach you how to do your job, for free? What are you offering?"

So, it had come to that, just as the rest of the world had predicted it would. He was leading her on, in the hope to gain some privileges. She felt like slamming the door behind her on her way out, just to see him defeated, punished for toying with her. She wanted him returned to the oblivion of his death-row isolation, where he had little to think about other than his nearing death. But that little ego boost she'd just envisioned for herself wouldn't help with the case. The negotiation had to continue.

"A stay of execution is out of the question, Mr. Garza. I'm afraid I can't offer what you're looking for."

"I don't want a stay. I think I told you that before, if I remember correctly."

It was her turn to be surprised.

"Then what? What can I do for you?"

He leaned back, as far as the restraints allowed, and smiled to himself, as if savoring what he was about to ask.

"Nothing that expensive or complicated, Agent Winnett. No, I'm a simple man." He licked his lips, and a spark of internal enjoyment flickered in his eyes. "I want to have dinner with you, that's all. While we review the case photos together, just you and me."

She frowned, taken aback by his request. "I'm afraid I cannot remove you from the facility, even if it's temporary."

"No need, for that, Special Agent. In here would be just fine. Bring us, say, 13-ounce ribeye steaks with fries and a nice wine. Serve the meal on a white tablecloth, without these," he rattled his chains. "Let me enjoy one dinner with real silverware, not those awful, um, sporks, they call them."

He kept his eyes riveted on hers, and she didn't flinch. What's a dinner compared to the payout of her case? What's a dinner compared to Laura Watson's life? But still, having dinner with a mass murderer, a killer of children. Enduring his presence, while having to eat and pretend everything was normal. She made an effort to repress the wave of aversion that coursed through her veins.

"We'll eat, enjoy, and discuss the case. Just you and me, Agent Winnett, just you and me. On the other side of that mirror, there can be hundreds of agents with their guns on me, but in here, just you, me, dinner, and case photos. What do you say?"

She hesitated for a while before replying. Finally, when she spoke, her voice was low and raspy, almost a growl.

"You're insane."

"Ah, but we all knew that, didn't we?" Garza laughed.

His laughter still reverberated after she'd closed the door behind her, almost running toward the exit.

22

Session

Laura sat on the edge of the wide, leather armchair, as if trying to take the least amount of space possible. She felt painful tension in her shoulders, a burning sensation in her nape, and waves of chills traveled up and down her spine. Without a word, she followed Dr. Jacobs's movements, as she was getting ready for their first regression session together.

She was terrified.

She zipped up her sweatshirt and tightened the hood strings, as if a bitter winter wind was gusting through the lush office, instead of the warm comfort of the nice, cozy fire. She shoved her hands deep into the shirt's pockets, and repressed another shiver.

She'd dressed down for the occasion, per the doctor's instructions, and had brought a number of potential memory triggers. Some of her dirty clothing in a Ziploc bag. A serving of stir fry, made following her mother's recipe, shared by Hannah after she insisted for almost an hour. A silk scarf, like Hannah said her mother wore, with a whiff of her favorite perfume, also locked inside a Ziploc bag. Now all she had left to do was hope all those sensory triggers would work, and help her take the dive into the abyss of her buried memories.

"I've made you a cup of tea, my dear," Dr. Jacobs said, handing her a big ceramic mug filled to the brim with clear, gold-colored liquid. "Chamomile. It will warm you up, relax you a little."

Laura couldn't unclench her jaws to respond. She nodded instead and wrapped her frozen hands around the steaming cup.

"How do you feel?" Dr. Jacobs asked, frowning a little as she made eye contact.

"Terrified," she admitted. "I'm... you have no idea," she eventually blurted. "I haven't been sleeping well, and I have this constant fear of... of I don't even know what."

Dr. Jacobs touched her arm gently.

"Regression is showing encouraging results as a treatment method for patients with all sorts of trauma or bad experiences they can't remember, but that affect their present lives. One of the results I'm expecting from our sessions is an improvement in your overall well-being."

"I've done it before, when I was young. I know what it's like. But I struggled," she continued, sniffling, without even being aware her eyes had moistened, "I really had a hard time with all this. Talking to Hannah about these things and preparing the food, the silk scarf, that… that was hard." She took one hand off the tea cup and covered her mouth, to repress a sob. She registered the warmth of her palm and clung to the soothing sensation it gave her.

"I can imagine how hard it must have been, and I think you're doing great. The time you took to prepare these props will help unlock that chamber in your subconscious mind. The smells, the sensations, all these factors will contribute to your success in recovering your lost memories."

She breathed deeply, steeling herself.

"I watched all your family videos, you know," Dr. Jacobs continued. "Everything you gave me, all the birthday movies. I will be able to guide you through the process. You won't be alone in there, I promise."

She inhaled sharply. "Okay… let's get it done."

"All right," Dr. Jacobs replied, then sat across from Laura on an ottoman. "Today we'll attempt to access a memory, any memory, that predates the attack. Anything you can recall is good."

Laura took a few sips of tea, then put the cup down on a side table. She looked at Dr. Jacobs intently, envying her composure, her professional attire. She was dressed sharply in a dark brown pantsuit that matched her silky auburn hair. A white shirt contrasted pleasantly with the suit, emphasizing her light complexion. Yet, to Laura, she seemed too cold, maybe a little distant, maybe a little too focused on her project. She wished Jacobs would at least remove her jacket and kick off her heels, but she didn't dare ask her that.

"I'm ready," she said between clenched teeth, not feeling ready at all.

"Lean back and feel your muscles relax," Dr. Jacobs said. "Close your eyes, and focus on the sound of my voice. I'm right here with you, and you are safe. You will be safe the entire time. Nothing bad can happen to you."

"Uh-huh," Laura mumbled, almost too quietly for Jacobs to hear her.

"Feel the armchair support your back, so you can relax. Feel the weight of your arms, as they rest on the cool leather. Feel your feet touch the ground, the firm ground that supports you. Take a deep breath, slowly, and let your mind relax. You are safe now."

Laura breathed and felt she was being engulfed into the massive armchair. She fought the sensation, but Dr. Jacobs continued to speak in the same calm, soothing voice.

"Follow the sound of my voice. You're safe, here, with me. Breathe."

Laura felt heavy, and her mind felt heavy and slow, empty of all fears, thoughts, and sensations.

"Go back with me, back to when you were young, playing with your brother and sister."

Laura fidgeted, and her eyelids scrunched and twitched, but stayed lowered.

"You're safe. Tell me what you see," Dr. Jacobs encouraged her in a soft whisper.

She didn't see anything, just darkness. She looked everywhere, but there was nothing to see. She started to panic, and fidgeted some more.

"Shh… you're safe. The little girl is safe. Little Laura is safe. I won't let anything happen to her."

She relaxed a little and allowed the darkness to engulf her more. She didn't see anything, but she started hearing things. Voices… distant. She listened intently, and the voices started to become clearer, more intelligible. Her father asking when dinner was going to be ready. Her brother hollering as he ran down the upstairs hallway; that day he wanted to be a train.

Only somewhat aware of what she was doing, she started repeating what she heard in her tenebrous memories. Her voice sounded nasal and high-pitched; it wasn't her voice anymore. It was as if someone else had taken control of her body and was using it to communicate. Someone else, but not really… it was still her, but fifteen years ago.

"I knew it," little Laura said, "I knew you'd get me a float." She mumbled something that didn't make any sense, then continues, her voice even more nasal than before. "Yes, si'. Daffy Duck… the most sensational discove'y… colossal… Sleepy Lagoon."

Laura let the sounds she heard in the deepest recesses of her mind stream loosely through her mouth, unable to fight the vortex that was swallowing her. She let herself descend freely, faster and faster, into a universe of darkness and sounds.

23

The Maze

Tess entered the conference room bringing with her a cloud of mouthwatering smells and carrying a large pizza box. Instantly, both Michowsky and Fradella grinned widely. It was midafternoon, and by the looks of things, the two hadn't stopped for lunch.

"Oh, bring it on," Fradella said, then grabbed the box from her hands and set it on the table. He made quick work of grabbing paper towels and plates. "*Calzones*? How come? That's south of here. I thought you were going to Raiford today."

"I've been there already, but I made a quick detour," she replied, then grabbed a slice and took a large bite.

"Whereabouts?" Michowsky asked with his mouth full.

"Laura Watson's school."

Michowsky let the slice drop back on his plate.

"Did you talk with her?" he asked quietly.

"No, not yet. Just made sure she's okay."

"How exactly did you do that?" Michowsky's tone didn't foretell anything good.

"Look, a few times a day I check up on her. She lives close to my place, so I swing by at night, in the morning. If it were up to me, she'd be in protective custody by now."

"Yeah, if it were up to you, the whole world would know we might have let a killer walk free for fifteen years," Michowsky replied dryly. His face turned grim. He pushed his plate away, and wiped his mouth with a paper towel.

"You know it will eventually come to that, right?" Tess asked, as kindly as she could. "At some point, it will come to that. But I made you a promise that I intend to keep, Gary."

"Yeah…" he muttered angrily. "So, what, now you're a stalker?"

Fradella choked and coughed a few times, then rushed to get some water.

"Whatever keeps Laura alive, Gary. By the way, why *is* she still alive?"

"Huh?"

"I didn't expect her to live past forty-eight hours after that TV show aired. I wonder why she's not dead yet. I'm happy that she isn't, but it just doesn't make sense to me, that's all." She took another bite of pizza and swallowed it almost without chewing.

"He could be dead or in jail for something else. Or he might have missed the show. With so many TV channels, that's not really hard to do."

"Yeah," Tess replied, her frown deepening. "Somehow I doubt she's safe though. I think he'll be coming for her, Gary. I can feel it in my—"

"Don't tell me, your famous gut?" Gary laughed. "This gut of yours, has it ever been wrong?"

She thought for a second. "Nope, not yet. I wish it were in Laura's case. We need her in protective custody, Gary. See if you can't get your captain to approve it. Pearson won't budge."

Michowsky didn't reply, just stared at the floor for a long, silent second. She knew she was asking him for a lot.

"Let's get more evidence, first," he eventually replied. "Let's build a case. How did Raiford go?"

It was her turn to avert her eyes.

"I got nothing," she admitted reluctantly. "Nothing but an invitation. If I'll have dinner with him, he'll tell me what I'm missing. No handcuffs, real silverware, the works."

"What?" Michowsky stood and started pacing angrily in front of her. "Hell, no. You can't possibly consider it, can you?"

"I might have to, Gary. If we come up empty-handed, what else is there?"

"He's got nothing to lose, and he's a psychopath with only a few days left to live. And you want to put a knife in his hand? Are you suicidal? Or crazier than he is?"

She pursed her lips and refused to answer. She took a couple of deep breaths, to help calm herself and refrain from being too abrasive with Gary. After all, if he'd done his job fifteen years ago, the whole thing would be moot, and Laura's life wouldn't be in danger. Before telling her what she could and couldn't do, maybe he should reflect on that. She managed to keep her anger to herself, and moved past it. Pearson would have been proud.

"What do you guys have, after an entire morning spent digging?" she asked, pointing at the conference table covered with scattered files and crime scene photos.

Fradella swallowed quickly and cleared his throat. He seemed excited.

"We thought of checking these cases against this unsub's established victimology. If we agree that he likes young, blonde women with blue or green eyes, and then if we filter out victims who don't match that particular description, we narrow things somewhat."

"That's excellent work, Todd," she said, smiling for the first time in hours. She'd been so tense, her facial muscles felt stiff when she did. "Tell me the counts."

"We'd be looking at only eight murders out of the initial fourteen, and twenty-three rapes out of the total of forty-two. Um, apparently, blondes with light-colored eyes are the preferred rape victims, even here in Miami, where the population is mainly Hispanic. Oh, and one of the assaults where the victim barely survived, the other one was a male victim, so we eliminated it from the pile."

"Eight murders and twenty-three rape cases?" Tess reacted. "Could he have been so prolific?"

"It wouldn't be the first time," Michowsky replied. "Remember Robert Pickton, the Canadian pig farm killer? He killed forty-nine women, and no one knew he existed until they caught him."

"You know your serials, Gary, I'm impressed. I'm not saying it's impossible. I guess I'm just saying it's a lot. Any DNA evidence in any of those rape cases?"

"Some," Fradella replied. "These days, when there's plenty of DNA evidence, the perp gets busted real fast. There was some DNA evidence, but didn't ping anything in the system. We have nothing to compare it against."

She paced the floor slowly, biting her left index fingernail and scrutinizing the crime scene photos affixed to the case board.

"Todd, have you found any serial killer in action before or after Garza that The Chameleon could have emulated?"

"No, there wasn't anyone. I pulled the media archives again to make sure."

She paced some more, thinking hard. Sometimes, in her line of work, she had to take a leap of faith and go with her gut. She had nothing else better to go with anyway.

"All right, so this unsub apparently 'evolved' in the opposite direction, from murder to rape. That's highly unusual, so unusual that it tells me that once he dared being who his true nature called him to be, a rapist *and* a killer, he didn't go back. He might have been a thrill-motivated killer at first, or something might have happened to keep him from raping Rachel Watson and Jackie Meyer, but then he added the sexual component to his subsequent killings, and that changed things for him. I'm willing to bet anything you want, he didn't go back from there. Once he discovered the thrill of killing, he couldn't revert to just being a rapist."

"So, all right, I get that, but what are you saying?" Michowsky asked.

Fradella stood and started gathering some of the scattered case files in a neat pile, then put them in the box they came in.

She nodded, and let a crooked smile appear on her lips. The young detective was smarter than he appeared. He showed real promise.

"Yeah, we scrub all the rapes where the victims lived. Keep in mind The Chameleon is a killer, not just a rapist."

Michowsky's face lit up. "Now we're down to eight murder cases that fit the profile," he said. "That we can manage."

"And manage we will," she said, then grabbed the laptop and started typing fast. "I'm setting up an alert for The Chameleon's type of victim. We'll know as soon as anyone when his type vanishes or is involved in any issue."

"This guy kills quickly," Michowsky said. "By the time anything gets reported, the victim's already dead."

"Yeah, and that's more reason for us to step on it. We need him locked up in a cage." She saved the system alert after entering all their cell phone numbers, then turned to Fradella.

"Todd, are you familiar with the concept of homicidal triad?"

He frowned a little, unsure.

"Um... not really."

"It's a set of three childhood behavioral characteristics that has been observed to be linked with later violent tendencies, particularly with serial killing. They are cruelty to animals, fire setting, and excessive bedwetting. Any of the two is a good-enough predictor."

"Bedwetting? No one reports that," Fradella replied, seeming more confused.

"No, typically no one does, not to the police anyway. Once you've shortlisted a few suspects, we could pull some medical records to look for bedwetting as an additional qualifier to narrow our suspect list even further."

"We have no suspects on that list yet. What would you like me to do?" Fradella asked.

"Look for small fires," she replied. "Let's work the timeline. If he was late twenties to mid-thirties when the Watsons were killed, and that was fifteen years ago, he might have started setting fires almost twenty years before that. Do your search from thirty-five years ago to about twenty."

"There could be hundreds of unsolved arsons. Thousands even."

"We have to start playing with maps," Tess replied. "A young kid doesn't travel far to set something on fire. He does it within a short walking distance. Same goes for animal cruelty. Typically, they prey on the neighbor's cat. Map the unsolved fires, Todd. Then map the unsolved animal cruelty cases. The two sets of map points will overlap in certain cluster areas, and those areas will mark the cradles of future Miami serial killers."

Fradella looked at her stunned, with his mouth slightly open.

"Wow, this is... just amazing you can do that."

"Yeah, it is. The hope is that science will evolve to the point of identifying and treating those who show the predisposition to become serial killers and avoid countless deaths. But that's in the future. For now, let's just catch this unsub."

"It will take me forever, Tess."

"Not really," she replied. "DIVS has a map function right here, on the search results screen. Use that, then move to the new search, filter it, then it will show a link named 'add to map,' or something like that. Then we cross-reference that map with the list of interesting people we find in these eight cases we will work. That's you, Gary, by the way."

"Uh-huh," he acknowledged. "I'll get on it."

"Include everyone related to these cases, and let's run commonalities and a separate victimology matrix for them. They're bound to have something else in common, other than hair and iris color. Don't forget to filter for suspect age. No way he killed the Watsons before he was mid-twenties."

"Got it," Michowsky replied. Then he looked up at the wall, where the once-framed map of south Florida hung, all smudged with circles drawn in black and blue marker. "If your system generates maps, why did we do that?"

"To have it in front of our eyes, all the time," she replied. "That, plus the fact that DIVS doesn't know about our Chameleon. That's nowhere in the system data; only Kenneth Garza is."

He seemed satisfied with the answer, but Tess almost chuckled, thinking of how much he seemed to preoccupy himself with that décor piece. Probably his captain will give him some grief over that, at some point, or maybe it held some emotional meaning to him.

"How about you?" Gary asked. "What will you do?"

Her entire face scrunched, and, for a few seconds, she riveted her eyes on the worn-out carpet, thinking through her options. She'd hoped she would get the chance to speak with Bill McKenzie on a personal note, before having to call on him professionally. It wasn't the way she'd anticipated things to happen, but Laura's life was at stake. Her safety trumped all of Tess's personal concerns.

"I have to call Quantico. As much as I hate to admit it, we need help."

24

Reflections: Frustration

Have you ever come within inches of fulfilling an all-consuming fantasy, only to be denied? Have you ever felt the uplifting anticipation of that nearing moment when your craving would be completely satisfied, only to be left yearning, writhing in the bitter pain of defeat? Have you ever felt like Tantalus, enduring endless thirst near receding waters and coveting the prohibited fruit?

It happened to me one night, many years ago. Unlike Tantalus, my sin was simple, yet equally grave. I denied myself too long, and when I finally gave into my craving, I was rushed, careless.

She was a tall blonde with slim legs worth dreaming about and blue eyes just like Donna's. Cathy Banks was her name. One day, fate offered her to me, right there in the grocery store checkout line. She was the customer ahead of me, and she had no idea I couldn't keep my hungry eyes off her thin waist and curvaceous buttocks.

I followed her home that day and breathed an immense sigh of relief when I realized she fit the Family Man profile. There was a husband in the picture and a young boy. What a waste of time, to deal with the whole bunch... but I still enjoyed the benefits of copycatting The Family Man back then, and every day I thought how lucky I was he was still out there, at large, so I could feast once more under his brand.

I didn't do the job right; I must have cut corners. I wish I had someone else I could blame for that defeat, like I normally do, but there's no one. Just me. I acted on impulse, driven by the all-burning craving in my gut, and forgoing the sound voice of my cold reason. I'd been looking for a tasty bite for a while, and I wasn't going to compromise, to take just anyone. I wanted the perfect Red Delicious for the celebratory feast that marked the end of a year-long period of self-denial, and you must agree not all apples are created equal.

Enough with the excuses.

That night, I approached Cathy's home at the darkest hour of dusk, right before night fully takes over. I entered the backyard, unseen and unheard, and reached the side door without triggering any sensor floodlights. I grabbed the doorknob and turned it slowly. It didn't squeak. I opened the door carefully, just a couple of inches, to get my bearings. A second door, half screen half metal, met my eyes, but that wasn't going to pose any issues. It didn't even have a lock.

As I slowly squeezed the handle, I heard a rumbling noise, then some clattering of claws approaching fast. The rumbling soon turned into a menacing, blood-curdling growl, and I instinctively pushed the screen door back, just as a huge German Shepherd hit it with all its might. He clawed through the netting with long, black nails, but I was quick to react. I shut the outer door on its growling snout and ran for my life. I managed to leave the yard and slammed the gate behind me, just as the dog turned the corner. While I ran down the street, I heard a man yelling, "Go get him, boy, get him!" The dog clawed angrily at the wooden fence, ready to tear the 8-foot gate apart.

I didn't breathe normally until I locked myself inside my car and floored it out of there. An hour later, as I walked through the park slowly, trying to subdue my anger enough to be able to go home, I finally understood where I'd gone wrong.

I'd denied myself for too long.

I had to accept who I was, if I was going to live as long as I wanted to and as freely as I wanted to. I had to understand that attempting to smother my predator nature made me weak, unstable. Vulnerable.

A year of fasting between feasts was too long.

You see, unlike most people, I'm very intelligent. Before you sneer away my statement, I'll share two things. First, statistically, I rank in the 99.99th percentile from an intelligence perspective. I'm, literally, one in a million. That means I learn from experience, I adapt, and I'm always better than I was before. My lies are believable. My manipulative strategies work. My tomorrows are always surpassing my yesterdays. That's why, I promise you, I will not make the same mistake twice.

Second, I don't believe in being modest about my intelligence. I'm open and direct about it, just as it's generally accepted to be open and direct about the color of your eyes. If you say, "I have black eyes and brown hair," everyone sees it's a simple statement of fact, and doesn't dispute it, nor do people ever think you lack modesty for admitting it so blatantly. The same goes for intelligence, DNA's winning lottery tickets. The less endowed frown on this simple statement of fact, while I, the winner, take advantage in ways you'll never comprehend.

That's why I'm sharing with you that particular event, because it marked a turning point in my life. From that day onward, instead of negating the predator inside, I accepted it with open arms and worked incessantly at making myself better. Rewards were many… I never let myself feel the same frustration again, the same unquenchable thirst like I did that night. I hunted whenever I wanted, and I got better at it. Much better.

For almost twelve years after that night, I was never denied again, and I was never kept from tasting the apples I so desired.

Until now. The curse of Tantalus is upon me again.

I have another question for you. Have you ever spent a long time waiting for the perfect reward, the perfect sensory gratification, for that perfect apple to grow, ripen, and be ready for your trembling hand to grasp? Have you ever spent your nights anticipating how it would feel to possess such a sublime creature?

That is Laura Watson to me. She's my forbidden fruit.

I've watched her grow, become a woman worthy of my wildest dreams. I've patiently controlled my urges, knowing that the day of that supreme feast will come. Every now and then, I look at her discreetly, and I feel a twitch deep inside my body, setting my blood on fire, and telling me that wonderful creature is ready for my body to possess it completely.

But no… I can't. I couldn't before, and I must deny myself again. I had to offer the ultimate feast to a stranger, a contract killer who doesn't even enjoy his work, not like I do, anyway. Some gun for hire who doesn't even know her; he doesn't dream of her curves and doesn't yearn to sink his teeth in the alabaster skin of her young breasts. I can't goddamn believe it.

Damn Laura, damn Kenneth Garza, and damn that busybody, good-for-nothing shrink who denied me my ultimate prize.

I can't talk anymore… I'm too angry. Ever since that TV show, I've been so enraged I'm afraid to go home at night and touch my wife. I'm afraid one night I'll slash her to shreds and throw my entire life down the drain.

I need… I need a fix; I need something strong. I need to spend hours and hours with someone special. I need to go to the place where no one hears them scream, so I can make such a feast last.

I built that, you know, some three years ago. It was too easy. Got a piece of land in the middle of the woods, somewhere deep inside the glades, where no one ever ventures. Bought it in cash under a fake name. Got some undocumented workers to build a log cabin, then fed them to the gators when they were done.

Yes, I got that cabin. Now I need a quick fix, someone to take there for a couple of nights. I need to hunt tonight, tomorrow at the latest. I can be denied no more.

25

Rework

The pizza was long gone, after Fradella munched on the last remaining bits, and even Michowsky had finished the last cold slice left on his plate. The sun had set some time ago, and they were still going at it.

Fradella worked on the laptop, and the wall-mounted TV showed screen after screen of search results. Fires. Unsolved arson cases. Solved arson cases with single, underage offenders. Solved animal cruelty cases with underage offenders. Unsolved animal cruelty cases. Hundreds and hundreds of results clogged the screen, spanning more than twenty years. A digital haystack, with a potential needle somewhere in there for him to find.

Michowsky scribbled, pen on paper, a victimology matrix for the eight unsolved murder cases they'd shortlisted. Much of the information was old, only available in poorly digitized files or deeply buried paper files. Every question he tried to answer took forever. He sighed every few minutes, long, tormented sighs that sounded more and more like groans.

Tess still obsessed about the three cases Garza had rejected. She twisted the information in all directions, trying to make sense of how little they had. She kept adding new information to the victimology matrix, focusing on the women. After a few hours of digging, she concluded the only things the three women had in common were age range, marital status, and physical appearance. Not nearly enough. She needed more.

She ran the back of her hand across her forehead, as if to remove the tiredness, the mental fog that lurked in her brain. She needed a fresh approach.

"Maybe we've been looking at this wrong," Tess said, breaking the enduring silence in the stale conference room.

The two men lifted their eyes from their work.

"What if we each take one of these three cases, and work them like it's the first time we see them? I'm thinking we might get lucky; we might see something that we didn't see before."

"We've been through this," Michowsky said. "You got nothing, and you keep going back, but you won't find anything new."

"I got nothing," she admitted, and her shoulders hunched forward. "But I'm not giving up either."

"No, we're not giving up." Fradella agreed. "What about this?" he asked, pointing at the wall-mounted screen.

"Yeah, keep going on that. I just—"

She stopped abruptly and turned toward the case board, hands firmly on her hips.

"Why don't we do this? Gary, you worked the Watson and Meyer cases back then. Why don't you take the Townsend now? I'll take the Watson case, and Fradella will take the Meyer. This way, we'd all have a case we've never touched before."

Michowsky scoffed angrily.

"Listen, this start-and-stop thing you got going on here is driving me crazy. Just a few hours ago, we started doing what *you* wanted. Todd's doing the database searches, which is a great idea. I'm looking at no fewer than eight new cases. What, you think we're done in three hours, and we need new assignments?"

She hated to admit it, but he had a valid point.

"All right, I get it," she said. "You guys continue for now, but I'll take the Watson case and start digging. Until Bill McKenzie comes in to help, I have little else to go on."

"When's he coming?" Fradella asked.

"Tomorrow morning," she replied, unaware she frowned.

"So soon, huh?" Michowsky replied, also frowning. "What do you think he's going to do?"

She paced the floor a little. That was a good question.

"Give us some perspective, I hope."

They were all silent for a while, and Fradella had resumed the quick tapping on the laptop's keyboard.

"Okay, so the Watsons," Tess said. "What suspects did you look at?"

"It's in the file," Michowsky replied, visibly unhappy.

She shrugged and pushed the case file toward him in a silent invitation.

"There was no sign of forced entry," he eventually said, after flipping through some of the pages and reading some of the notes. "We looked at people who knew the Watsons. We started with the business partner, Bradley Welsh."

"And?"

"Clean as a whistle. No motive whatsoever. Airtight alibi, confirmed by several people. The company was in good shape. Plus, he would have known about Laura. The two families were very close. Family parties, trips together, the works. He would have known to kill her, especially if he were after the money, right?"

"Yeah, that's true," Tess replied.

"Not to mention the kid would have recognized him."

"Yeah," she replied, thoughtful. Michowsky came with solid arguments that made sense. "Who else did you look at?"

"I checked everyone I could think of. Neighbors, business enemies, competitors, friends, and personal acquaintances, everyone the Watsons knew. Nothing… No one had motives, and most people we looked at had airtight alibis."

Her frown deepened. She needed a break, and she wasn't getting one.

"How about any lawsuits? Anyone disgruntled enough?"

"Um… there was a lawsuit," Michowsky said, checking the case file again. "A customer's house caught fire from a WatWel ceiling lamp. No one was injured. They settled out of court, a few weeks before the Watsons died. That family moved to California and bought a new home in San Diego. Must have been one hell of a settlement."

Tess felt a faint tug at her gut but couldn't place it. Someone's house burning is motive enough. Many things are lost in house fires, things money can't make whole again. Memories… family photos, videos of departed loved ones. A life's worth of emotional attachment to objects carrying precious meaning, sometimes more precious than the house itself.

"Did you check their alibis?"

"Whose?"

"The lawsuit customer and his family."

"Yeah. They were seen having dinner in California, all of them, about the time of the Watson killings."

"Unusual financial transactions?" Tess probed on, her gut still telling her she was on to something.

"Whose? Watson's?" Michowsky asked.

"No, the lawsuit family."

"There's nothing there, Winnett, trust me. I looked."

"No offense, Gary, but that's not how I work a case. I have to verify. Did you check their financials for unusual transactions?"

He turned pale and pressed his lips.

"No. There wasn't any reason to. They seemed okay with their new lives in San Diego. They'd traded up, if you were to ask me. Bigger house, fancier cars, better-paying jobs."

She had to admit his reasoning made sense, but the strange feeling in her gut wasn't going anywhere.

"What about Watson's financials?"

"All solid. The company was profitable, growing steadily for years. I spoke with several employees, and they were content. No red flags there."

"Any gambling? Vices? Drugs? Cheating wife or husband?"

"Nothing that I could find," he replied, raising his eyebrows.

She thought for a while, keeping her eyes riveted on the Watson crime scene photos. She didn't have much to go on. She didn't have anything.

"All right," she said, "I'll work this case as fast and as hard as I can, and see what I can find. This," she pointed at the crime scene photos, "is the handiwork of a very motivated killer. That kind of motivation must have left some trace somewhere. We just have to find it, before the killer finds Laura."

"You still think he'll come for her?" Fradella asked, lifting his eyes from the laptop's screen.

"Damn right he will, and we can't let that happen."

"Where do you want to start?" Michowsky asked.

"With Laura. I'll interview her."

"God, Winnett, what the hell?" Michowsky reacted, shooting her a burning glare. "Don't open that can of worms. It'll be a mess when it hits the media."

"My turn to say trust me, Gary. I'll be discreet, and make it about Garza's upcoming execution."

He still glared at her, but the intensity in his eyes had mellowed somewhat.

"Then I want to talk to this Hannah... um, Svoboda. The housekeeper. She's the one who found them. Maybe she can offer some more insight."

"After fifteen years? Most likely all she remembers now is corrupted, altered by the many times she'd told the story, every time a little different. You know how that works. Witness accounts aren't that reliable in the first twenty-four hours... What do you expect after fifteen years?"

"I'm expecting to work the case, guys. I can't sit on my ass while Laura's life is at stake."

She picked up her keys and turned to leave.

"Where you going?" Michowsky asked.

"To see Laura."

She didn't wait for his reply. She strode across the squad room and, seconds later, she hopped behind the wheel of her Suburban. She almost started the engine, ready to go, but she remembered a phone call she needed to make first. She dialed quickly, using the car's display. She got voicemail. She cleared her throat quietly before leaving a message.

"Dr. Navarro? Hi, it's Tess Winnett. Yeah... I think it's time for me to come back to therapy. Please call me when you have a minute. Thanks."

She hung up and breathed a sigh of relief. It was the right thing to do, and she knew it.

Her phone rang, and she picked it up without checking the caller ID.

"Yes, thanks for getting back—"

"Tess?" Bill McKenzie's voice interrupted her.

"Oh... Bill. Hi," she chuckled lightly, embarrassed a little. "I thought you were someone else."

"I figured that much," he replied. "Hey, I'm heading to the airport now. I'll get there very late tonight, but I wanted to see you before work tomorrow. Think we can have coffee tomorrow morning? Say... seven?"

She hesitated before responding. She dreaded the questions he could ask in private. But she didn't have a choice, either.

"Seven? Um..."

"Winnett, if I can be on the redeye for you, surely you can wake up a little earlier for me, right?"

She bit her lip.

"Sure. There's a small Starbucks right next to the office. I'll text you the address."

"Perfect," he replied, and she thought she heard a little smile in his voice. Maybe it was time to take Cat's advice and trust someone.

"Bill? Thanks for doing this, all right? And have a safe flight," she said, swallowing hard.

"Uh-huh. See you tomorrow."

The call disconnected, and she sat there, in the dark silence of her Suburban, thinking about things. Everything. Her case and how mangled and senseless it was. The dark secret in her past, and how its tentacles touched everything in her life. And Laura Watson.

26

Lies

Tess was familiar with Laura Watson's building. She'd made a point of driving by several times each day, just to make sure she was safe. Her logical brain struggled with the concept; how would she know from the parking lot, looking up at a building, that the tenant on the seventh floor was all right?

She started going up to Laura's floor and walking the hallway, listening intently at her door. Again, that didn't tell her much; if she heard nothing, Laura could very well be dead in there and she wouldn't know. But that was all she could do, before getting Pearson's approval to place her in protective custody, and Pearson wouldn't budge. Yes, her method didn't do much, but she knew her trained eye would spot things that looked out of place, minor changes, signs that a killer might be lurking nearby.

She'd thought of arresting Laura on some bogus charge, just to keep her safe for twenty-four hours. But there was no guarantee she'd catch the killer during that time, and if she didn't, it would make things worse. The killer might freak out and rush his attack the moment she had to release Laura. Nope, no option but to do those drive-bys, hoping she'd happen to be there the moment the killer chose to strike. Just until she'd get approval for the damn protective custody, to get the warrant signed.

This time she rang the doorbell, and Laura opened the door quickly, after checking the peephole.

"Special Agent Tess Winnett, FBI," she said coldly, presenting her badge. "May I come in?"

Pale, Laura stepped to the side, making room for her to enter, then closed the door behind her with trembling fingers. She gestured toward a chair, but Tess chose to stand.

The apartment was flooded in light, coming from all sorts of lamps, probably all manufactured by WatWel. A youthful arrangement, with good quality items and definite décor taste. In the generous light, Laura seemed frail and tiny. She wore a black hoodie zipped all the way up, despite a well-heated apartment, and her hands constantly tugged at the hood strings, tightening it around her neck like a scarf. A half-empty cup of tea took the table, in front of a seat where she most likely had sat just before Tess's arrival.

"What's this about?" Laura asked.

Tess cleared her throat a little.

"Um, as you know, Kenneth Garza's execution is scheduled to take place before the end of the month. We're conducting routine interviews with several people. I have a few questions for you, if you don't mind. Mostly routine," she repeated.

Laura nodded and tugged at the hood strings again.

"Right. Um, tell me anything you can remember about that night. Anything that comes to mind."

Laura took her seat and wrapped her hands around the tea cup. A cat appeared out of nowhere with a quiet meow and started brushing against their legs.

"I don't remember anything," she said, staring at the clear liquid in her cup. "I—well, that's why they're doing the regression session with me, to help me remember. I'm sorry…"

"No, it's all right. Anything you can offer is good enough."

"I used to play hide and seek with Grandma and my brother and my sister. I liked to hide where no one would find me. That's what I did that night. I only remember being scared and hiding, and then nothing, like blackness swallowed my entire memory."

"So, nothing about that night?"

"No… I'm sorry. You don't know how many times I've tried to remember. It's gone… all gone."

"What's the next thing you remember?"

Laura chuckled sadly.

"Everyone asks this question; shrinks, Dr. Jacobs, even the TV reporter. I remember my new family. Carol, my new mother, tucking me in at night, taking care of me. Amanda, my new sister, playing with me, brushing and braiding my hair."

"What about your grandmother? What happened with her?"

"I know she died shortly after my parents; she had a stroke. She couldn't deal with the loss of her daughter, two of her grandkids." She wiped a tear that welled at the corner of her eye, and sniffled. "I was told she took me in at first. I lived with her for a few days, but I can't remember anything from that time. This is just what I heard from other people, years later. Then she must have felt something was wrong with her, because she took me to the Welsh family herself. She died that same night."

Tess looked at the tiny figure, hunched over a cup of tea to warm up in eighty-degree temperature, and wondered what Laura wasn't saying.

"Has anyone given you any trouble recently?"

"Uh-uh," she replied, a little too quickly.

"Have you seen anyone acting suspiciously, lurking around?"

She shoved her hands in the hoodie's pockets and looked away.

"Why would anyone do that? Don't they have him locked up?"

"Um… it happens sometimes when an execution is approaching. All kinds of weirdos, protesting capital punishment, or stuff like that, come out of the woodwork."

"Uh-uh," she repeated. "I haven't seen anyone like that."

She was hiding something, and Tess had no leverage to get her to admit it. The whole conversation had been a useless dance of lies. She looked at her again and realized Laura wasn't cold… she was scared. Out of her mind scared. Of what?

Tess gazed at her intently, and Laura was quick to lower her eyes.

"Miss Watson, are you scared of something?"

Laura's big, round eyes shot up and met Tess's gaze. "No, I'm not scared. I'm fine."

Tess pulled out her business card and handed it to her.

"Please call me, as soon as you remember what's causing you this much anxiety. I can help, I promise."

She turned to leave, but she saw an antiquated answering machine and couldn't help but study it.

"I've only seen these in old movies, you know. It still works?"

Laura stood and approached the counter, where the phone system was plugged in.

"Yeah," she smiled shyly, "with a cassette." She popped open a lid and revealed a full-size cassette inside. "It's got, um, all their voices on it. My parents, my brother, and my sister. All of us."

She pressed a button to play the recording, and a bunch of cheerful voices erupted from the machine. "Hi, it's Allen, Rachel, Casey, Monique, and Lau'a, and we're the Watsons!"

When Tess looked at Laura again, her chin was trembling and her eyes flooded. She lowered her eyes again, and this time Tess respected that.

"Call me," she urged her one more time from the doorway. "Please."

27

Hannah

Hannah Svoboda's mouth gaped a little as she squinted in the dim light, her eyes moving back and forth from Tess's face to her FBI badge. Hannah was overweight and saggy, and her skin had myriad wrinkles, far too many for her age. No doubt a devastation brought by many years of hard labor, working physically demanding jobs as a housekeeper, cleaner, then later as a janitorial employee for a large corporation, on a permanent graveyard shift.

Tess smiled encouragingly, and Hannah invited her in. The apartment was small and modest, just what one would expect, considering Hannah's income and social status. It was clean and welcoming though, and she was quick to offer Tess a cup of freshly brewed coffee. She hesitated, given the late hour, but then Hannah offered tea instead, and she accepted it with gratitude, going against procedure.

"This is about the Watson murder, Ms. Svoboda," Tess said. "We're getting ready for Kenneth Garza's execution, coming up before the end of this month, and we're conducting—"

"They should have shot that animal a long time ago," Hannah said bitterly, suddenly overwhelmed by tears. "That monster... killed my babies... I loved them like I love mine, you know," she added, then wiped her tears with her sleeve. "Laura too. That poor child, having to live with that horror..."

Tess gave her a few seconds to continue, but she didn't. She sat hunched forward, resigned to sniffle and let the tears fall freely from her eyes.

"Were you close with the family?"

"I had been their housekeeper for many years, since before their first child was born. Casey, that sweet little boy. I hope that animal burns in hell for what he did," she added, then spoke harshly a long phrase in a foreign language Tess didn't understand. It sounded much like Russian.

"Sorry, what?"

"I cursed him good, the way only a Russian mother can curse. No one escapes that curse."

"Oh, I see," Tess replied. "What can you tell me about the day you found them?"

Hannah cleared her throat and wiped her eyes again with a now-soaked sleeve.

"I arrived earlier than usual. I had to go to the dentist that afternoon, and Mrs. Watson didn't mind me shifting my hours to make things work out for me. They were such good people. They allowed me to work weekends, just because I needed to. They didn't mind me being there at all."

She wiped her mouth with her hand, quickly, and cleared her throat again.

"I tried to unlock the front door, but it was already unlocked. I wasn't expecting them to be up yet. It was a Saturday, and Mr. Watson liked to sleep in on weekends. I opened the door and there he was, lying on the floor, in dried blood," she said, her voice overtaken by emotion, and fresh tears rolling down her pale cheeks. "There was blood on the wall, on the furniture, everywhere. I rushed inside, thinking of those babies."

She lowered her head and stared at the floor for a few long seconds.

"I found them, right after I found Mrs. Watson, cut open on the kitchen floor. I—I was hysterical back then, I know I messed up. The police gave me a hard time for it, and I was scared, you know. I had a work permit; I was afraid they'd send me back to Russia."

"Why? What happened?" Tess asked. There was no mention of any wrongdoing by Hannah or any arrest.

"They said I compromised the crime scene, running around everywhere and touching everything. I called 911 after finding the boys upstairs. But then I kept looking for Laura. I kept running through the house, calling her name."

"So, you knew she was alive?"

"I didn't... I just hoped, because..." Hannah's breath caught, and she covered her mouth for a second before speaking again. "Her body wasn't with the rest of the children, and I knew that girl loved to hide. She hid so well, no one ever found her when they played hide and seek. I did, eventually. I found her."

A new wave of sobs shook Hannah's body, and she covered her face with her hands and shook her head, unable to continue. Tess touched her shoulder, gently, giving her time.

Eventually, Hannah forced in a deep breath and continued.

"I'm sorry... I know it's been many years, but for me it feels like it was yesterday. The poor baby was curled up in the laundry hamper, in the upstairs bathroom. It was dark in there; all the lights were off. She seemed asleep, with her eyes closed tightly and sucking on her right thumb. Little did I know," she said, sounding angry with herself. "She was in shock, and I kept trying to wake her up. She'd sucked her thumb so badly her teeth had cut into the skin, right here," she demonstrated, drawing a circle around her right thumb joint. "She must have clenched her teeth. Can you imagine the terror that child must have felt? Being like that a whole night? It's a miracle she is the way she is today, normal."

Hannah took in a deep, shattered breath. Tess nodded encouragingly.

"You know she didn't speak," Hannah added, "not for years. She was in the news for a while, back then. They called her The Watson Girl, the miracle survivor. But the TV people didn't know what was really going on. That little girl was broken and needed peace. Then the Welshes took her in and ended all the TV attention, saying they were afraid the killer might come back to... Oh, God." She covered her mouth with her hand for a brief time. "We were afraid, you know. I was afraid for years, until they caught that monster, Garza," she said, adding a portion of the same Russian curse she'd incanted earlier, right after saying his name.

"Then what happened? What else do you remember?"

"Laura started to recover with the Welsh family. They were good to her. Took her to all the doctors; they did things for her. It took her a few years, but she started to grow into a somewhat normal child."

"Somewhat? Why is that?"

"There's a sadness about Laura, something that never leaves her, no matter how happy she seems. She'll always be marked by what happened. It's not something she can ever forget. I think she's depressed."

"Have you been in touch with her?"

"Yes," Hanna replied, smiling for the first time since Tess had arrived. "She looked me up when she was about sixteen. She wanted to know details about that day. What was I supposed to say? It's not like I could tell her the horror... no. It would have broken her heart. She only wanted to know her lost family better, to know about them, so I told her that. I told her stories about her parents, things they loved, what they liked to do together, places they went. It breaks your heart, you know."

"How about now?" Tess asked, wondering if Hanna might know what Laura was afraid of.

"She came to see me just the other day. She had more questions about that night. What did I see? Was the TV on? What perfume was her mother wearing? What was her mother cooking? All strange questions, but she said it was for her new therapy."

"And? Do you remember?"

"Mrs. Watson was making a beef stir fry with Worcestershire in the large cast iron. She'd finished almost, because I found the stir fry in a bowl, already cooked, but the stove was still on. Good thing the house didn't catch fire. Can you imagine? With all of them dead, and that little girl upstairs, in that hamper? Oh, my God," she said, then crossed herself quickly three times, in typical Russian manner.

"What about now? Have you noticed Laura being afraid of anything? Anyone?"

Hannah frowned and gazed at Tess, intently. A look of suspicion appeared on her face. Tess smiled encouragingly.

"There was always... She always seemed afraid of something. I noticed that throughout the years, and I asked her, but all she's ever told me was that she's afraid of what she doesn't remember. It's like fear lives inside her, she told me.

Lives inside her forever."

"How about now? You saw her a couple of days ago. Did she seem more afraid than before?"

"Um, a little bit, maybe," Hannah admitted, her salt-and-pepper eyebrows ruffled above her bleak, moist eyes. "I asked, and she told me she's afraid of this new therapy. She's afraid of what she'll find."

"Huh," Tess said quietly. It seemed plausible, but somehow she didn't buy it. The Laura she'd just met was terrified, scared for her life, of something real, more real than memories. But then again, she couldn't rule out the effect of deep-set anxiety and posttraumatic stress. Of all people, Tess knew better than to discard such effects. Maybe she wasn't hiding any pertinent information or a new threat; just a terrible ghost trapped in her mind.

"Let's go back to fifteen years ago, Ms. Svoboda. Do you remember the Watsons mentioning any issues with anyone? Anyone wanting to hurt them?"

Hannah lifted her head and stared at Tess.

"How come you ask? I thought you have the animal who—"

"We do, Ms. Svoboda. These are just routine questions."

"No, there was nothing wrong," she eventually replied, after biting her lip and frowning, a clear sign she didn't buy Tess's justification. "They were great people, living a quiet life."

Tess waited for the shabby elevator doors to close before letting out a noisy breath of air, loaded with all the cuss words she could muster. Everywhere she looked, she found nothing.

28

Early Morning Coffee

The next morning, Tess pulled over near the Starbucks patio at ten to seven, but Bill McKenzie was already there, seated at a small, wrought-iron table. The air was chilly and humid for Miami, and she welcomed the thought of a hot cup of coffee. Suddenly she wondered what Bill had ordered for her. There were two large coffee cups on Bill's table, one in front of him, and the other obviously waiting for her. She smiled, excited with anticipation.

"What's in there?" she asked, forgoing the normal greeting. Then she swallowed a curse. She could at least have greeted him properly and asked him about his flight. He didn't seem to care though.

"It's a large cappuccino, two shots of espresso, lots of foam, no sugar," he said, almost laughing toward the end of the phrase, probably reading the puzzled expression on her face.

How the hell did he know her favorite? She racked her brain, trying to recall if she'd ever ordered coffee in his presence.

She drew her chair out and took a seat, then smiled at Bill with a grateful, yet inquisitive look.

"Thanks much. What, is my favorite coffee formula somewhere in my file?"

"No, Special Agent Winnett, I just happen to be that good at what I do," Bill replied, leaning back into his chair after taking another sip of coffee.

"No way!" she reacted. "No one's that good. No. Please try again."

"All right, I'll demonstrate," he offered.

"Bring it," she replied, and her smile widened.

"You're a jeans, rather than skirts, kind of woman: direct and to the point. That means you hate fake stuff. If it can't be sugar, it won't be Splenda either. Keep this point in mind for future reference. You're sporty rather than pretentious. That tells me snobby stuff like mocha lattes are not your thing. You're in good shape, so you do watch your diet, but I have personally witnessed you wolf down a double cheeseburger with everything on it, except the bun. That tells me you watch the carb intake in your diet, but fats are okay. That translates into whole milk, lots of foam, no sugar. It's early, so a double shot of espresso would be fine with you, considering you whined a little about the time of our appointment. As for the size, I chose safely. Not too large, not too small."

"Wow… I'm speechless," Tess replied. "I'm glad I called you in for help." Her smile slowly died, when she realized just how transparent she must seem to a man with Bill McKenzie's profiling skills.

He frowned a touch, watching her get all serious.

"I was expecting your call sooner," he said, all laughter gone from his voice. "I was expecting you to reach out, just like we discussed."

She stared at the pavement, finding no words in her defense. She bit her lip, recounting how many times she'd retrieved his number from her phone's memory, only to give up and postpone what she should have done weeks ago.

"You know you can't continue with fieldwork, Tess. Not with your unmanaged PTSD. We discussed it." He paused for a short while, not taking his eyes off her. "I can't delay this any longer."

She looked him straight in the eye, unable and unwilling to hide her sadness from him.

"I know, I'm sorry. I tried… I just—"

"Do you want to talk about it?" he asked softly.

"No… not really," she whispered, keeping her eyes lowered. She didn't feel she could face him.

"What happened to you?" he probed, his voice gentle and kind, inviting and understanding.

She didn't dare tell him. After all, he was a supervisory special agent; not her direct superior, but nevertheless, he was higher up the food chain in the FBI, and, as such, he had duties. Among others, he had the duty to enter the unreported crime into the database. She couldn't take that risk. Her personal drama had to remain personal.

She stared at the pavement and shook her head quietly. In a passing thought, she felt grateful for her long hair that fell forward, covering the tears welling in her eyes.

"Tess…" he called, maintaining the same supportive tone of voice.

Now he was going to ask her to trust him. She couldn't. She forced a deep breath of air into her lungs, and looked at him, directly.

"But I did reach out to my therapist," she said, "to get back on schedule, to see him regularly."

He scrutinized her for a few, interminable seconds.

"I'll need his name, please." His voice had turned just a notch toward professional rather than friendly.

"He's off book," she protested. "If this gets out, I'm finished. Bill, please… This job is all I have."

"You don't trust me worth a damn, do you, SA Winnett?" He almost smiled, with a hint of bitterness.

"No, it's not that, Bill, I promise. It's just that I've worked so hard, and for so long, to keep this thing buried, that I freak out just by thinking someone else knows about it, that's all."

"I need his name only to make sure you're getting the help you need, from someone good enough to help you the right way; not a someone mediocre, who could do more harm than good."

"So, you're saying I can't even choose a good therapist?" The pitch in her voice escalated with her frustration. How could he trust her to do the job she did, when he didn't see her fit to choose a shrink, for fuck's sake?

He probably read her face like an open book, because he put up his hands in a pacifying gesture.

"I'm saying when you have to go off book, choices are less than stellar."

She gazed at him for a long time, searching his face for any sign of deception. He held her gaze with an open, friendly expression and didn't budge. Sure, they were all trained in various techniques of interrogation, manipulation, and deception, but she didn't feel any warning tug at her gut. She remembered Cat's advice to trust someone one day soon. Maybe that day had come.

"Dr. James Navarro," she eventually said.

He whistled appreciatively.

"It's been years since he took a new patient. You did good." He sipped some coffee, and Tess wondered if she could dare profile his coffee recipe, and how far she'd land from reality.

"Now stay in therapy, for as long as he tells you to," Bill continued. "You might not realize, but PTSD is affecting your entire life. Beyond jeopardizing your career, you're missing out on life. You're unable to trust anyone, and you can't form any meaningful relationships. It's a pointless sacrifice, a waste of a good life, Tess. Yours."

She stared at her cappuccino cup, letting tears threaten her eyes.

"All right, so how can I help you?" Bill asked, in his professional tone of voice. She smiled, grateful for the change of subject.

"Let's go upstairs, if you're ready. We have a really messed-up case."

29

Reflections: Self-Control

We could have already met, you and me; it's possible. You might have smiled after I walked right past you, thinking I looked good, a covetable, successful alpha male. You might have envied my wife or admired what a nice couple she and I make. You might have secretly wanted to date me, maybe just for one night, to taste the forbidden fruit of the dangerous affair with a charismatic, potentially dangerous stranger.

You might have seen me before, but not known me for who I am... not really. I'm the snake in your neatly trimmed grass.

You might have yielded to me in a mall parking lot dispute, when we both arrived at the same time, poised to take that perfect spot near the entrance. You might have seen me unwilling to concede the fight and might have turned away and parked elsewhere, disappointed but alive.

Not like that shmuck with the rusty, green Ford pickup.

He saw me lined up for the spot, signal on, waiting for a Lexus to pull out. Yet he didn't care, and we almost collided head-on after the Lexus finally left, both rushing to seize the opportunity. We both honked, gestured, cussed at each other through lowered windows.

Then he did the unthinkable. He muscled me out of that spot, taking advantage of the fact that his banged-up Ford was worth less than the front left wheel of my ride. Brand-new, convertible Beemer against *Deliverance* pickup truck from hell never wins. Not in a head-on fight anyway.

But he made a terrible mistake.

No one outpowers me. No one. Ever.

I waited for him to be done shopping, and I was there when he pulled out and left, unaware I was a couple of cars behind him the whole way to the outskirts of Weston. I was still two cars behind him while he stayed on I-75 west. Then I was right on his ass when he headed into the Glades, just like I hoped he would.

I cut him off and forced him to stop on the side of the road. He jumped out of his piece of shit jalopy with his fists clenched, screaming and cursing, foaming at the mouth. When he was close enough, I took a tire iron to his head and he dropped like a fly. I hit him again, just to make sure he'd stay down, then dragged him into the brush to finish him off.

I wasn't satisfied; I wanted to stomp him to death, but he seemed dead already. I stabbed him anyway, one deep stab with my tactical knife, as I roared my frustrated anger. I plunged that blade until I heard his ribs crack, then I plunged it again. And again.

No one outpowers me. No one. Ever.

There I was, panting like a dog in heat, rolling his body farther into the brush. I was deeply unsatisfied. The asshole didn't die feeling small and insignificant like I wanted him to feel. He didn't get a chance to realize what was happening to him. He didn't yield to my power; he died ignorant of his worthlessness, and I felt cheated. When I killed him, I felt nothing. I didn't feel vindicated.

I should have followed him home, tied him up, and made him watch while I possessed his wife completely, fucking her in any way imaginable, for hours. Yeah, there's a wife somewhere I'll never get to meet; he wore a cheapo wedding band. He should have been screaming too, not just her, while the restraints cut into his flesh, unable to help her, emasculated in the most supreme way a man can ever be, completely powerless. That would have been so much better. What an afterthought... Can you imagine him begging for my forgiveness, while I sliced his woman slowly, savoring every one of her screams? That's the opportunity I lost by rushing in to get quick, pointless revenge.

I was left with an emptiness inside, an immense frustration of having killed without any satisfaction. But I learned something valuable that day.

Killing doesn't do much for me anymore if I'm killing men. The rush I felt when I killed Watson was gone; my brain got used to so much more in the almost five years of killing since that first, transforming night. Like any other addict, I needed more and more to get high.

That redneck asshole deprived me of that badly, because he wasn't a woman, and because he died quickly, almost painlessly, when he deserved to die screaming. That's good to know. I won't be wasting my time on men, unless I absolutely must; and if I must, I'll make it worthwhile. But I'd rather stay focused on what matters: the quest for that perfect apple, and finding the recipe for the perfect feast.

I also had another problem emerging, about the same time I killed that hillbilly. I became more and more concerned that my wife suspected something was off about me. It probably originated when I started shaving my legs and my pubic hair. I don't think she bought the explanation I gave her, something to do with personal hygiene at the gym. I also started using hairspray quite generously and trimmed my hair much shorter. I didn't want the emerging age of DNA forensics to represent the end of mine.

You do realize I couldn't go and straight-up ask her what she suspected or didn't suspect. If she knew about the real me, I'm actually surprised she was willing to go along with it. She's always been so proper, so righteous in every way, the perfect wife by all societal norms. But didn't someone once say that still waters run deep? They definitely run deep for me, and maybe for her too. Is it that inconceivable to accept? Maybe for you, but not for me. I'd be actually quite happy to know my other half is fully worthy of being called my other half. But that's probably just wishful thinking.

I watched my wife carefully, and she seemed to behave normally, so I'm not really sure what, if anything, she might have suspected or might still suspect. That's great from a different perspective, because there could come a time when she might have to testify, if that contract killer botches up the Laura Watson job in any way, and it comes back to haunt me.

I don't think it will; I've been careful, and so has he. In any case, my wait is almost over. He said he's going to kill her tomorrow.

30

The Profiler

Tess finished summarizing the case and remained standing in front of the case board, holding a dry erase marker with both her hands. No one spoke a word. Bill frowned and bit his lower lip, while his eyes navigated from one crime scene photo to another. Michowsky and Fradella kept their eyes glued on Bill's face, waiting for him to share his opinions. As for Doc Rizza, he still panted after climbing up two flights of stairs and took a gulp of water from his bottle every now and then.

"You know," Bill eventually said, "I was asked to consult on Garza's cases when they prepped him for court. Somehow, I missed all this. These three cases were lost in the background noise of thirty-one other cases. Can't believe it," he added, pursing his lips and crossing his arms, visibly embarrassed.

Tess shot Michowsky a quick glance and thought he looked somewhat relieved. She nearly smiled. He must have felt vindicated about his own mistakes.

"So, my question is," she continued her earlier line of discussion, "if the unsub emulated The Family Man for almost seven years, and he's definitely evolving toward the lust-motivated profile, where did he start? Where did he continue after the Townsend family? We've shortlisted seventy-four cases, any number of which he could have touched. Then we eliminated some—"

"Let's start with finding out who he is," Bill said. "Let's sketch a profile. You're doing well so far, Agent Winnett, why don't you try?"

The cap of the dry eraser marker found its way to Tess's mouth; she bit on it a few times, making a faint clacking noise.

"He emulates Garza, but rapes the women anyway?" Bill added, encouraging her to continue. "What does that tell you?"

"Um, that it's his primary urge. Rape is his primary urge, not killing," she offered, hesitantly.

"Yes," Bill confirmed. "Go on, you're on the right track."

Fradella watched their exchange and took notes, thrilled to take part in the profiling process.

"But he doesn't just rape," Tess added. "He chooses to kill multiple individuals just to get to his intended victim. Why? And why did he hesitate before?"

"The issue with working multiple cases at the same time is that sometimes details clutter your mind. Elevate your judgment to the strategic level, and isolate the real questions."

"Okay… Why didn't he rape the first two women? Rapists have the sexual urge, the lust, so it can't be he didn't think about it. I can't think of a single case in history where a killer evolved into a rapist, so what the heck am I missing?" Frustration etched her voice.

"The answer is he did rape them," Bill replied.

"Um, nope, he didn't, I'm fairly sure of that," Doc Rizza intervened.

"Psychologically, he did," Bill clarified. "He stabbed them instead of shooting them, even if he was prone to emulate Garza. He bit Mrs. Meyer too. Biting is a sexual sadism practice," he clarified, looking at Michowsky, then at Fradella. "We see it much too often, unfortunately."

"So, you consider stabbing a form of rape?" Doc Rizza asked, furrowing his eyebrows.

"Almost," Bill replied. "Stabbing is personal. The blade, penetrating the victim's body, is a potent substitute for the actual sexual act. Look at the location of the stab wounds. He didn't go for the heart; he stabbed all of them in their lower abdomen; another powerful hint."

"You're saying you agree he emulated The Family Man, and, for all intents and purposes, he almost succeeded, but when he was faced with the opportunity, he couldn't control his urges and stabbed the woman to satisfy his urges with a surrogate act?" Tess asked, a long question blurted in one long breath.

"Yes, that's exactly what I'm saying. The first stabbing, Rachel Watson, was done with a kitchen knife, a weapon of opportunity found at the scene. He didn't come prepared for the stabbing, yet he came prepared for everything else. I can close my eyes and visualize the scene. He shoots everyone, then he stops short of shooting Rachel Watson. There, in front of him, he has a woman afraid for her life, trembling, pleading. A heady arousal for the power-assertive rapist. He grabs the knife instead, the biggest one in the knife block, and takes his time inserting the blade. He savors the penetration. How many stab wounds were there?"

"Three," Doc Rizza replied. "One was a little hesitant, but all were in the lower abdomen."

"She must have screamed and made him rush through the kill. For the Watson murders, I'd classify him as an organized killer and disorganized rapist, all in one." He looked at the puzzled faces of all in attendance. "I see how that can be confusing. Think impulse shopping. You go to the market for vegetables, but you also bring home a pint of ice cream, and you hate yourself. Same psychology applies here. He enters the home and does what he came to do, but then he sees the temptation: a woman, screaming, pleading, weak, and subdued. He goes for it, without thinking."

"Huh," Tess reacted, "interesting way to put it. But why not really rape her then? Why fake it with a knife? Is he impotent?"

Bill turned to Doc Rizza.

"Based on the evidence found during Emily Townsend's postmortem, I'd be willing to bet he's functional in that area."

"Maybe he needs chemical assistance to be that functional?" Fradella asked, slightly blushing.

"Like what, Viagra?" Tess asked.

"Uh-huh."

"It's a possibility," Tess conceded. "But people like that never leave home without the blue pill. I kind of struggle with it though; I can't get it to make sense in my mind."

"Here's another theory," Bill offered. "What if he didn't rape them because he was afraid of forensics? Of leaving evidence at the scene? What if instead of forgetting or needing the Viagra, he forgot the condoms?" He stopped talking and stared at the ceiling for a second, scratching his head. "Even with condoms, rape is messy. The rapist never knows if he hasn't dropped a pubic hair somewhere at the scene, or a couple of drops of seminal fluid. Most rapists get caught because of the wealth of trace evidence we normally find at the scene and on the victims."

"That's true," Doc Rizza replied.

"Jackie Meyer was stabbed multiple times and tortured for a few hours. With Emily Townsend, he prolonged the thrill and added a full-blown rape to the menu. My guess is he was afraid to rape the women until Emily Townsend, so he settled for substitute acts."

"Then you're saying he killed because he was sexually frustrated that he couldn't rape?"

Bill remained thoughtful for a while before responding, rubbing his chin with his fingers.

"It's a theory," he admitted reluctantly. "It's my turn to say it doesn't ring true to me, somehow. Those shootings were too precise, too cold and emotionless. A sexually frustrated killer is disorganized and bloody. Kills while screaming his anger and makes his victims pay for his abstinence. This was different; execution style. I don't think we understand his complex motive yet. Nor do we have any hint of what his trigger might have been."

"But you're saying it's possible he did start as a rapist then?"

"Yes, one who most likely did time for his deeds and learned to be afraid of leaving trace evidence. What kind of trace was found at the Townsend case?"

"Um, none, except for a single hair strand with a follicle attached," Doc Rizza replied.

"Did you run DNA on it?"

"Back then we didn't, because we had nothing to compare it against. Hair analysis showed it didn't belong to any of the Townsends. I put it for approval, but then Garza was caught soon afterward and it was never done."

"Okay, let's do it now," Tess replied, a little edgy.

"Sure," Doc Rizza replied.

Michowsky had been quiet the whole time. He fidgeted and hesitated, but eventually spoke, after clearing his throat.

"We shortlisted eight unsolved murder cases and started looking at the facts again," he said, pushing a pile of file folders toward Bill.

"How did you shortlist?"

"We looked at rape murders, similar MO, where the victim matches the physiognomy of these three women. All after Garza was caught. None of the earlier cases truly match."

"DNA anywhere? To match against the Townsend hair strand?"

"No. The crime scenes were incredibly clean. I think he developed a method and perfected it," Michowsky replied.

"The only thing, and I just thought of it now, Doc, can you please see if any of these eight victims show signs of that, um, distended wound pattern?"

"The what?" Bill asked.

"I noted on Jackie Meyer's medical examination that I saw an unusual skin distension pattern in one of the stab wounds," Doc Rizza replied. "There was no trace left in the wound; but it was just as if someone had forced the wound open. And yes, I'll check."

Bill frowned, but didn't say anything for a few long seconds.

"It could be part of a signature," Bill eventually said. "I think we're ready to sketch a preliminary profile. Let's get the rest of the team together," he said, then grabbed the Meyer file and opened it to the autopsy report. "I wonder what he did," he mumbled to himself.

Then he closed the case file and stood, took a last sip of his coffee, and threw the empty cup in the trash can.

"Large decaf drip, no milk, no sugar," Tess blurted out.

He turned, smiling. "How?"

"Here? Now?" she gestured at Michowsky, Fradella, and Doc Rizza. All three men seemed intrigued by the cryptic exchange.

"Yeah, let's hear it," Bill encouraged her.

"Size was identical with mine, so no profiling there; just logic. Then I noticed you have a bit of hypertension, your face, and sometimes your neck turns red. Yet you spoke passionately about coffee, which means you still love it, the taste, the smell. So, I went with decaf drip, because you were also a bit dismissive of people who go for mocha lattes or other gourmet, pretentious brews, and because you're always so direct and uncomplicated. A simple, drip kind of guy. As for no milk, no sugar, I can probably be safe betting there isn't a single ounce of fat on your body, and that doesn't happen without sacrifices."

She rushed through her explanation, embarrassed to bring up Bill's hypertension and body fat in front of other people. She had a talent for backing herself into corners from where there was no elegant way out.

He didn't seem to care; he smiled and nodded once, appreciatively.

"You know, there's an opening on the profiling team at Quantico," he said. "I could put in a good word."

Her smile died, and she looked away.

"Not now," she said with a hint of sadness in her voice. "I...can't. You know why."

"Whenever you're ready," he said, then walked out.

"What do you mean, you can't?" Fradella asked in a high-pitched tone, the moment Bill disappeared. "I'd die for that opportunity."

She stared at him, unable to find a good answer.

In the squad room, everyone was assembling, ready for SSA Bill McKenzie to formulate a preliminary profile. She thought hard and couldn't remember a single time when Bill, or any other profiler, had attempted to release a profile without fully understanding the serial killer's motive.

31

The Profile

The squad room was filling fast with many unfamiliar faces. Most people remained standing, waiting for the briefing to begin. Tess shot Michowsky an inquisitive glance.

"We've called Miami-Dade and Broward Counties to attend, considering the killer's footprint."

"Ah, that's great," she replied, a bit frustrated she hadn't thought about that herself. She'd been preoccupied with Laura Watson; the investigation progressed slowly, and no one had yet managed to secure approval for placing Laura in protective custody. While she was out there, her life was in danger.

Tess had an idea of how she could force the issue; it wasn't elegant, but it could yield the result she was hoping for. She thought of asking Bill McKenzie to issue the order, right there, in front of a squad room full of cops. She frowned. Saying it wasn't elegant was an understatement. She'd be forcing Bill into taking that action, right after he'd been so good to her. She'd prove to everyone she was the bitch they all accused her of being.

She let a long, pained groan escape; she hated situations like these. Such circumstances had earned her the reputation she was trying to outgrow, that she didn't care about anyone other than herself and her work. She *did* care; she cared about Laura Watson, and she couldn't get her terrified face out of her mind. If only they'd be any closer to identifying The Chameleon.

"Hello, everyone, and thank you for joining us," Bill said, his voice commanding instant silence over the clamor-filled room. "We're ready to release a partial profile in the following murder cases: Watson, Meyer, and Townsend. These names might not sound familiar; they are old cases, previously attributed to Kenneth Garza."

A wave of whispers and muffled sounds rose as the law-enforcement officers present processed the information and its implications.

"For obvious reasons, you are not to discuss what you learn outside this room," Bill continued. "No media whatsoever. A person's life might be at stake: Laura Watson, the Watson family murder survivor. Please take this matter very seriously. We have reasons to believe the unsub continued killing after the apprehension of Kenneth Garza and might still be active in the Miami–Fort Lauderdale–Palm Beach area." He cleared his throat quietly, then pointed at Fradella. "Detective Todd Fradella has maps showing his activity, and the eight, additional, unsolved, cold cases we are reopening. He'll share those with you."

Tess watched the detectives' reactions to Bill's statement. Most shook their heads in disbelief; it was hard for them to admit there was a serial killer at large in their backyards, without them suspecting anything. But that story wasn't new; with most prolific serial killers in history, the story played the same way. Cold cases, unsolved murders, missing persons never found, and then suddenly, a serial killer surfaced that made it all come together and make sense.

"This man is highly organized and has a high degree of self-control. He's white. He was at least in his mid-twenties fifteen years ago, when the Watson family was killed. That makes him anywhere between forty and fifty years old today," Bill said.

The audience had stopped fidgeting and whispering and was taking notes.

"He could pass for an average, middle-class man. He emulated Kenneth Garza's MO to the point that he was successful at deceiving law enforcement and was never suspected for these murders until now. That makes him acutely intelligent, with one of the highest degrees of self-control I've seen. He might have a record for rape, a single conviction, followed by an impeccable record thereafter, because this man learns. He might have been suspected in a rape case, but never convicted. Either case, he's integrated into society and could be a successful, well-adjusted man. He could be married, even have children."

Bill paused, allowing everyone to get caught up with their notes.

"The murders are spanning a large period, demonstrating he has a high degree of impulse control. During the seven years he was able to emulate The Family Man, he only killed three families that we know of. We're still trying to establish his first kill; once we do, we'll understand his motives better. The Watson family doesn't seem like it could have been the first, considering the amount of careful preparation he'd done. Almost perfectly executed, but nevertheless, one survived."

Some of the detectives lifted their eyes from their notepads. One of them raised his hand hesitantly. "Um, you're just describing an average, middle-class, white man. How is this going to help us?"

Bill didn't seem fazed by the question. "I realize that; please keep in mind this is a preliminary profile. Detectives Michowsky and Fradella will continue to work with Special Agent Winnett to refine this profile. As they do, they will communicate with you." He took a quick breath, then continued. "Laura Watson's regression sessions might hold some interesting answers."

He looked at the law enforcement in attendance, inviting more questions. "This man is a power-assertive, sexual sadist, with a strong lust motivation. Look through earlier unsolved rapes, disputed cases that have been attributed to other offenders but didn't really fit their profiles. Look for later cases, where the sexual factor is more prevalent, as in prolonged rape with torture, ending in death."

Bill invited more question with a hand gesture. Tess shifted her weight from one foot to the other, uncomfortable with what she was about to do. She decided to wait though, and she weighed the far-more-decent option to ask Bill privately to put in a word with SAC Pearson for Laura's protective custody.

"If this gets out, we're going to look like a bunch of jokers," a younger detective from the back said. "People will freak out."

"More reason to be careful about sharing any information until the unsub is caught. Only then we'll issue a statement; not a moment earlier."

"Maybe it's just me, but shouldn't we be concerned for Laura Watson's life?"

Tess smiled widely; she felt like hugging the older detective in the first row who'd brought it up.

Bill shot her a surprised glance, and her smile instantly disappeared.

"As far as we know, the unsub isn't aware we've reopened these cases. The only concern comes from Laura's statement on television regarding her decision to undergo regression therapy with a new, groundbreaking methodology. However," he continued, raising his hand to quiet the raising wave of murmurs, "there are hundreds of TV channels. The likelihood of the unsub having seen that TV show and feeling threatened by it is very slim, in my opinion. If we're careful, and don't leak any information to the media, Laura Watson's risk will remain relatively low."

The detective who'd asked the question didn't seem satisfied with the answer, and neither was Tess. What was wrong with everybody? Well, almost everybody. Why didn't they see? If she were the unsub, she'd have already taken care of the one person who could throw her in jail. The only good thing Laura had going for her at the time was that she wasn't dead yet. Since when was that a good thing?

"Thank you, everyone," Bill announced. "As soon as we have more, we'll let you know." He turned to Tess and continued, in a lower tone of voice. "Call anytime. Glad to help."

Then he turned to leave, but Tess grabbed him by the sleeve.

"Can you please put in a good word with Pearson to get Laura into custody?" She realized she was still clutching his sleeve and abruptly let it go. "Sorry," she muttered.

He studied her tense face for a second, then smiled. "Sure, I'll make a call." He turned and left without another word, while she continued to worry.

Fradella and Michowsky approached, and the three of them walked back into the conference room.

"That went well," Michowsky said. "We know so much more now," he jeered.

"We do know a few things more," Tess replied. "No need for sarcasm there."

"What if Gary and I start looking at everyone with that profile, either one rape charge, or former rape suspect, and start building a list?" Fradella offered.

"That will come back with tens of thousands of names," Michowsky said, looking defeated.

"You know that's the way it always starts," Tess replied, more hopeful than convinced. "A long list, then we filter. We cross it against age, race, and maybe, if we're lucky, he might have been bedwetting too late in his life and it's on record somewhere."

"I thought medical records were confidential," Michowsky muttered.

"They... are," she conceded, then clammed up, unwilling to go there.

She felt tired and defeated, after a whole day spent with very little progress. She felt she was losing ground, rather than gaining. She felt she was missing critical information, and not looking in the only direction she should have, from the very beginning.

"Sounds good to me," Fradella replied. "Gary and I will get to it, and—"

"How about you help me find out who can deliver a sophisticated, catered dinner to a remote place like Raiford?"

Michowsky sprung to his feet and took two steps, stopping within a foot of her, and propped his hands on his hips.

"You can't be serious," he almost yelled in her face. "He'll kill you!"

A couple of people raised their heads and looked at them through the glass wall.

"Nah... he won't. He just wants to play family dinner. That's his thing," Tess replied. Her mind was already made up.

"With dead people!" Gary shouted. "Not to mention showing him the crime scene photos? Don't those people deserve more respect than having a death-row inmate jerk off at the sight of their bodies?"

"Gary... Garza isn't the jerk-off kind of serial killer. There's no sexual component in his killings. There never was." She paused, then touched his arm in a pacifying gesture. "I've got no other option. Maybe he'll give us something."

"Like what?"

"Like I don't know what, but something that could shed some light."

"You can't be serious," Michowsky repeated, shaking his head in disbelief.

"Feel free to come and sit in the observation room," she conceded.

"You bet I will, gun in hand," he replied, almost making her smile. He liked to play the protective male partner, despite all their differences.

"Did you clear this through your channels?" Michowsky asked.

She frowned and lowered her eyes.

"Not yet."

32

Reflections: Analysis

I know you're dying to ask me what I did next. Come on, admit it, you want to know. If you could get your hands on me, you'd probably lock me in a cage and ask me thousands of questions, in your lame attempt to decipher how I think.

You'd ask all the wrong questions though. People like you can't ask people like me the right questions; your mind simply can't conceive them. Therefore, I'll save you the angst and effort and try to provide answers to the fundamental questions you're missing.

There are two types of beings in this world: the strong and the weak. Predators and prey. Goes the same for people. Some, like you, will live servient lives, burdened by a pointlessly celebrated conscience, lacking what it takes to grab life by the throat and squeeze it for all it's got, in the epic power struggle that turns sheep into wolves. Others, like me, always go for what they want, and never worry about any preconceived notions that might hinder their progress.

A preconceived notion, such as the line someone arbitrarily drew somewhere, not sure where exactly, separating what you can and cannot prey on. It's perfectly all right, by your societal standards, to sink your teeth into or carve out a piece of an apple. Yet the same conventions prevent you from sinking your teeth or slicing into another human being. Correct? With me so far? How about a dog or a cat? Not allowed, either. Hmm… they're mammals, just like humans are, protected by these preconceived notions your mind's engraved with since early childhood.

But wait… how about cows? Pigs? Sheep? Who deemed it acceptable for you to sink your teeth into a juicy ribeye? Who decided what's right or wrong? Or, even better said, who do you take your orders from? I bet you never thought of it that way.

The further down the food chain we venture, the more acceptable it is for animal life to be sacrificed for your epicurean enjoyment. There isn't a single fish species that's safe out there in the deep, unless, of course, they're toxic or bad-tasting. As for plant life, just like my metaphorical apple, it doesn't stand a chance. It gets either cultivated or mass murdered, based on a single criterion: its nutritional value.

Then, what makes some species sacred and other species game, by your twisted standards? Where's that line drawn? Mammals, in general, aren't safe. The more exotic, the more the wealthy (read, the powerful) are willing (read, able) to pay to nibble on. Of course, if the exotic mammals in discussion aren't toxic or bad-tasting. Or otherwise considered gross.

There's us, humans, sitting comfortably at the top of the food chain, and we're considered off-limits. A few other species have hitchhiked to the top with us, by becoming our companions: small cats, dogs, goldfish, hamsters, and everything else we like to fuss over on a daily basis. There's an unwritten rule that says those creatures, up there at the top of the food chain either by merit or by associated status, are off limits too.

I'm starting to see where that line is drawn; don't you?

If there's a wide-enough gap between you, reigning at the top of said food chain, and where your intended dinner resides, you can go ahead and enjoy your feast; that's agreeable by your complicated societal and even religious standards.

Who's the hypocrite now?

Now you see why, for me, picking an apple from life's generous shelf and feasting on it is perfectly acceptable, even if the apple I desire happens to be something—or someone—you'd call an innocent human being. I'm high enough on the food chain; higher than you. Much higher. Unburdened by conscience, I rose to the limit of my own buoyancy; in my case, my imagination and my zest for life. The gap between me and other human beings, including you, is large enough to allow me to feast unburdened by any concerns. Bon appétit to me.

Let me clarify another aspect you might fail to comprehend. I'm in no way cannibalistic. All references to eating, consuming, savoring, or feasting were metaphoric to spare you from the graphic details of what I really like to do. Nothing more than allegories, meant to illustrate concepts that your blindfolded mind cannot comprehend otherwise. No, I'm not a cannibal; never was, never will be.

I'm a collector. I collect a special brand of power. It might be hard for you to comprehend, but please try. I'm like a rechargeable battery, only nothing ever consumes my energy; I accumulate, and I hold on to what I store. There's no limit to my capacity; I can store an infinite amount of such power, and I'm always searching for more. Whenever I take a life, my power grows, and I feel it rejuvenating my body and mind with electrifying zaps of energy. When I possess the body of the young woman writhing and screaming under me, with my nostrils flaring and my hands slightly shaking with anticipation excitement, I revitalize my entire being. That's why I take my time... I'm savoring. It's just like dining with a fine meal, only mental, not physical.

I'm *addicted* to power, you see. That's tricky, even for me, because I require higher and higher jolts every time, just to make that needle move. So, I keep searching.

For what, you might ask?

Like most addicts, I keep searching for that ultimate fix, that enkindling hit of adrenaline, dopamine, and other wonderful neurotransmitters my body so desperately needs. Yes, I'm an addict; but I won't die in a ditch, teeth optional, clad in rancid rags, and avoided by all levels of a blind, yet judgmental society. I'm not a victim; I'm a predator. Unlike most addicts, I control my addiction; it doesn't control me.

That's why when I entered Emily Townsend's residence, I was equipped with a collection of forensic countermeasures: cable ties, large trash bags, latex gloves, and condoms. I was finally prepared to do what I've always wanted to do, ever since Donna.

That's why when a few weeks later, I heard they caught The Family Man, I felt relieved, liberated even. No more wasting time with useless distractions, such as men and children; from then onward I was free to pursue my real passion.

Last, that's why I could forego the apple of my dreams, Laura, to be picked and… There's no word for it. He won't savor her. He won't enjoy her perfect little body like I would have. He'll just eliminate a loose end, that's all. Ahh… the injustice… the shameful waste.

But he's going to do it today. My burning turmoil will soon be over. Goodbye, Laura, my forever forbidden fruit.

33

Dinner Plans

Tess caught a few moments alone in the conference room, while Michowsky and Fradella went to get refills on their beverages and probably a quick snack. Alone, she could think better, but she didn't like where those thoughts ran to.

Dinner with a serial killer! Gah! Nothing more disgusting she could think of, than sitting a couple of feet across from an unchained monster and putting food in her mouth. Food he breathed over, food touched by air that came out of his lungs.

Enough of this crap, Winnett, or you're going to barf prematurely, she admonished herself, inserting a bit of humor to untie the knot in her stomach. It didn't work too well. No matter what she kept saying to herself, there was little logic to the planned torment. She had nothing. After countless days spent digging through the three cases, then seventy-four more, then down to eight, nothing solidified as a viable investigative path. Even the profile she got from Bill McKenzie was a preliminary, partial view; even he didn't have the answers she was looking for.

Then, what were the odds a death-row monster could hold any clues? What if he was just playing tricks on her? Well, that was a possibility, but she couldn't afford to waste the tiniest hope that she'd gain a speck of valuable information out of their encounter. Somehow that monster knew Emily Townsend had been raped, and she hoped she could bait that information out of him with a steak and some fries.

She forced herself to focus on her breathing for a few seconds, to settle her stomach and silence her racing thoughts, then called Pearson.

"Winnett," he greeted her matter-of-factly.

"Sir," she replied, unaware she was frowning. "I need your approval to interview Kenneth Garza again. Tonight."

There was a brief silence.

"I sent you there myself, to do precisely that. What am I missing?"

"Um, sir, I need to go off procedure," she blurted, cringing in anticipation of his reply.

"Why the hell am I not surprised, Winnett? What do you want to do?"

"Garza is willing to trade some information for a, um, dinner. He wants me to have dinner with him, inside the interview room at Raiford."

"That can't be it, Winnett. You wouldn't have called me just for that. You're leaving something out. What is it?"

"His cuffs. He wants to be unrestrained during the meal."

"Absolutely not, Winnett. Anything else?"

"We must, sir. It's his fantasy. The moment he twitches, he'll get shot."

Pearson scoffed, disgusted. "Is that what you want, Winnett? His brain matter scattered all over your face?"

"No, sir, but it's what I'll settle for. He has information, things that were never released in the Townsend case. He knows about the rape, when that information wasn't released to the public."

A couple of seconds passed in absolute silence. Tess could visualize Pearson running his hand across his shiny, bald scalp, while the ridges on his forehead and around his mouth deepened.

"Warden's going to give me an earful, Winnett," he eventually said. "All right, go ahead with your circus. You know you've exceeded your forty-eight hours for this case, right?"

"Yes, sir, but—"

"Learn to listen to people, Winnett. I delayed your other case, the health insurance fraud investigation, but I can't delay it for much longer."

"Sir, one could argue that most of the health insurance industry is a fraud, so I think it can wait until we catch a killer, wouldn't you agree?" she spouted, then clenched her jaws and rolled her eyes, irritated with herself.

"Jeez, Winnett," he replied dryly, then hung up.

She didn't have long to admonish herself for her lack of diplomacy, because Michowsky barged in.

"Ready to go. Let's roll."

34

The Dinner

The ride to Raiford had been unexpectedly quiet. She'd managed to muscle Gary out of driving, and she white-knuckled the whole way over, taking advantage of his car's siren and letting it blare the whole time. He would have had to shout if he'd wanted to talk to her, and she didn't want any conversation; she knew exactly what he had to say.

He'd brought along a small arsenal, as if more than a handgun would be necessary. Probably that was his way to relieve his stress at the thought of the encounter. She would have preferred he stayed back at County to help Todd with the database searches and shortlisting of suspects, but, on the flipside, it was the second time he was there for her, having her back. She didn't want to admit it, but knowing he'd be in the next room, finger on the trigger, eased her fears. Did nothing for the nausea though, but made her feel safer. She smiled, a tiny, shy smile flashed in his direction.

"What?" he asked, looking tense.

"Thanks for doing this," she replied, her voice loud above the siren's noise.

He snorted and yelled in return, "If you turn around now, I promise no one will know about it. Let's just... not go through with this."

"I have to, Gary. You know that."

Not another word was spoken until they entered the observation room. The one-sided mirror showed the interview room had already been prepared for the event. The table was set, covered in a white, damask tablecloth, with real plates and silverware. Crystal wine glasses and neatly folded, matching damask napkins completed the setting. Whoever arranged the setting had done a good job.

Garza was already seated, still wearing his cuffs on a chain, but unlinked to the table. Her seat was to his left side, not across, probably to allow a direct line of sight or fire from the observation room, without her getting in the way.

She studied him for a few seconds, unaware she breathed heavily. He'd taken a shower and wore clean garb, probably a courtesy of the staff toward her more than him. His hair and beard were still moist, just like the first time they'd met, and he was equally relaxed and calm.

"All right," she said, then swallowed hard, "let's do this."

She entered the interview room and he stood politely, greeting her with a smile and a head bow.

"Agent Winnett," he said, "what an unexpected pleasure."

She put the file folder she'd brought along on the table and took her seat.

"What about these?" he asked, showing her his handcuffs.

She studied him for a couple of seconds, drilling him intently with her scrutinizing gaze. She didn't see any alarming signs in his eyes, on his face. Even her gut stayed silent.

"I gave my word," she said, "that you'll be civil and respect this dinner, just as much as I respected your wishes, against all procedure."

He nodded once, reassuring. She made a gesture toward the mirror, and someone soon entered and removed Garza's chains.

"Feet too," she offered, hoping to buy more of his cooperation. If he was going to stab her, he didn't need his feet for that anyway. She'd be inches away from his steak knife.

The terrified officer crouched down and carried out her order.

Garza put his hand on his chest, in a gesture of gratitude. He seemed to be genuine about it, but Tess knew better than to trust anything a psychopath did or said.

"I'm a dying man, you know that. I… thank you."

She acknowledged him with a faint, forced smile, then waved again.

"Shall we?" she asked, as the door opened and a scared, pale junior guard pushed a rolling table with hors d'oeuvres. Cheeses, foie gras, olives, smoked salmon, the works.

Gary must have instructed the young man thoroughly, because he never stood in front of Garza while serving and made sure he didn't obstruct Gary's line of fire.

"You must be really stuck with your investigation, Agent Winnett," Garza said, as soon as the guard left the room. He tasted an olive and studied the stainless-steel fork appreciatively. "I haven't seen one of these in a long time."

She poured water for both, then reached out for the file folder.

"Oh, please no," he said. "First we eat, then we talk about the case."

She didn't argue, leaving the folder where it was and turning toward him.

"What should we talk about then?"

"We'll find something," he said, taking a bite of smoked salmon. "This is delicious, Agent Winnett. Why don't you try a bite?"

She forced a breath of air into her lungs and stabbed a piece with her fork, then made quick work of chewing and swallowing it, chased down by two gulps of water.

"You don't enjoy it much, do you?"

She wanted to kick herself; she needed to up her game.

"I prefer cheese," she replied casually, then picked a tiny cube of Swiss cheese from the plate and chewed it thoroughly.

"Ah, I see. Have at it then, I'll stick with the fish, in that case."

She'd expected him to be rushed, to wolf down the fine foods without so much composure. She found herself studying him, trying to understand what was going on in his mind, and why that dinner was so important for him. She realized that, despite the thousands of pages of case files she'd read, she didn't know much about Kenneth Garza, the serial killer known as The Family Man.

He immediately caught her interest and replied, as if he could hear her thoughts.

"This meal reminds me of my parents," he said calmly. "I bet there isn't much in there about my childhood, is there?" He gestured toward the file folder.

"Not really."

"My father used to beat us kids at dinnertime," he said, sounding almost casual. "Whether he had a reason or not, he'd just start beating on us the moment we touched our food." He took another olive, picking it up with his fork without hesitation. "Then he starved us. He forced us to sit at the table and watch him eat, while we sat there, crying, eating nothing. He starved us, while he ate like a pig. May I?" he asked, pointing at the cheese platter.

She nodded, and he hesitated somewhat before choosing a piece of French Brie.

"I know what you're going to say," he continued, as soon as he swallowed the cheese bite, "that I blame my father for what I've become. That's typically how…"

His voice trailed off and he lowered his eyes for a second, staring at his empty plate.

"No," she replied, "I'll just ask you, what are you repeating? What story are you telling with your killings?"

He shook his head a couple of times, deep in his memories, as if unable to pull himself out of there.

"I'm just killing him over and over again. And I'm killing the poor bitch who stood there, smoking cigarettes and drinking liquor until she could bear the pain he'd given her to bear, and watched calmly how her own children went to bed hungry every night, beaten and humiliated. He was generous with the pain and humiliation he dealt out. My mother got her share, every time the pig got horny, drunk, or both."

A sad, disgusted look lingered on his face.

Tess recognized the sadness she'd seen on his face before, whenever rape was mentioned. But she couldn't figure out an explanation. Was he playing out a fantasy? He'd been a warden of the state his entire childhood; there was no mother mentioned anywhere, nor a father. She frowned, thinking. What was he trying to say? No one had ever come close to gaining any insight into Garza's motives for his blood-curdling, ritualistic murders, his terrifying signature.

"How about the children? Why do you kill them?"

"My brothers… they would have never recovered," he replied in a voice loaded with sadness. "They would have ended up just like me, lined up on death row, getting used to being called monsters by righteous people like yourself." He avoided her gaze for a quick second, then looked straight at her. "I put them out of their misery."

She hadn't realized that she'd been munching on the cheeses, entrenched in the conversation. She'd forgotten her own disgust, faced with a new mystery.

"Are you saying the people you killed abused their children?" She gestured with her fork, then picked an olive.

"No," he shouted, then slammed his hands against the table, rattling all the dinnerware and startling Tess. "No, you're not paying attention," he continued, still agitated. "I killed my own family. They're the ones I killed first, right there, at that damn dinner table. I was twelve years old."

"Oh," she reacted, and pushed herself toward the back of her chair, feeling a sudden urge to put more distance between Garza and her. "That's not anywhere in your file."

How could she have missed that? She'd taken the history in his case file as the ultimate truth and completely missed the point he was trying to make.

He shook his head, as to express his disappointment with police records.

"You're listed as an orphan with no history other than state," she said, sounding apologetic.

"He-he," he laughed sadly, "little do you cops know. Like it was the state who gave birth to me, huh?"

She watched him silently for a second, unsure where the conversation was going.

"Would you be willing to tell me—"

"Where they're buried? Sure, I'll tell you precisely where the bastards are buried, because they deserve to be dug up. Why should they rest in peace?" He ran his fingers through his thinning, shoulder-length hair, then continued, in a gentler voice. "I buried my brothers in a different place. I wanted them far from that brute, so they could find some peace, at least in death. I won't tell you where my brothers are, Agent Winnett. They have a right to be left alone."

He scraped the last piece of salmon off the platter and chewed it without raising his eyes from his plate.

At a loss for words, Tess watched him eat, and, for some reason, recounted how many families he'd killed. He was credited with thirty-four, but she'd established someone else took out three of those. That left thirty-one, and thirty-one was what she'd believed to be true up until that dinner. But now she'd learned Garza's count had gone up to thirty-two families he'd murdered. Speechless, she waved again, inviting the waiter guard to bring the rest of the food, staving off her returning nausea.

The young guard, wearing a white apron and seeming even paler than before, served the steaks and fries, and poured their wine in the tall glasses with trembling hands. Then he vanished as quickly as he could.

Garza took the wine glass to his nose, inhaling the scent with his eyes half-closed. "Thank you for this, Agent Winnett," he said, tapping his fingernail quietly against the glass. "What an unexpected pleasure, or dignity, I might call it."

She nodded in response, and he took a sip of wine, then put the glass down on the table, closer to her side. As he took his hand away from the glass, he brushed against her hand, and she jolted back. Instantly, she withdrew and cringed for a split second, averting her eyes. It didn't last long; it was a lightning-fast, instinctive reaction, before her willpower and training took over and she straightened herself, ready to fight if needed.

His eyes were riveted onto hers, as a recognizable sadness shrouded his face.

"Ah…" he said softly, in a barely audible whisper. "You've been touched. Bruised."

Her blood turned to ice cubes and she froze, averting her eyes for another split second. It took all her willpower not to scream. How could he see right through her that well? How was it possible? She wanted to run, to burst out of there screaming and never look back. But she knew she had to stay put and play it as cool as possible. After all, people were watching from just 3 feet away. And not just any kind of people; investigators, who could find it interesting to dig and find out why she, a federal agent no less, reacted so badly.

She took a deep breath and looked him in the eye, unflinching.

"You're tainted," he whispered, casually covering his mouth to make it difficult for the people in the observation room to read his lips. "How sad that makes me. If I wasn't locked up in here, I'd offer to set things straight for you."

The corner of her lip twitched, almost imperceptibly.

"But I'd be too late, I reckon," he continued, still whispering. "Good for you, my dear."

He took a couple more bites, then pushed his plate away.

"What do you need to know?" he asked in his normal voice, and pointed at the file folder.

Surprised, she cleared her throat and gathered her thoughts in a hurry.

"How did you know Emily Townsend was raped? I… We don't have any record of that information ever being released."

He leaned back against his chair and thoroughly wiped his hands on the napkin, then set it aside.

"I watched his work carefully, when they interrogated me about it," he replied, with the demeanor of someone discussing a routine business transaction. "I remember every single family I spent time with. Clearly, like it was yesterday. The moment they showed me the case photos that didn't belong to me I knew what he was."

"Who? We need to know who he is," she said, leaning forward and almost touching his hand.

"How could you? He doesn't even know who he is."

She frowned, disappointed. Was this another one of his games? Twisting words and dancing around the information?

"You said you knew who—"

"What, not who. He's a man who's transforming with every life he takes."

"Transforming into what?" she pressed.

"There aren't two of his victims who suffered the same way. He's not punishing them like I am, nor is he repeating, reliving his fantasy. He's discovering himself, who he is, who he can be."

"Who?" Tess asked, feeling more and more confused.

He hesitated a second before replying, but then looked her in the eye.

"A monster like you've never seen before."

35

Reflections: Blown Cover

For years, I was grateful for The Family Man, for his existence, shielding me from the consequences of my escapades. Then, suddenly, only a couple of months after I'd enjoyed the company of Emily Townsend, he was arrested.

I watched it on TV, and I saw his face in the flashes of tens of cameras. An average man, looking more like a hobo than someone who could get away with countless murders for so many years. He had to have something special about himself though, to pull that off. I, for one, know just how difficult that is.

His capture made me reflect on potential outcomes for my future. I saw myself in his shoes and hated it so much I took a solemn oath that day. I will never allow myself to be captured alive. Never. No one can ever cage the predator that I am.

I remember spending that evening in silent solitude; I invoked a migraine to send my wife and kids away and locked myself in the study, in semi-darkness. With him gone, out of the picture, I could be free, I could choose to do whatever I wanted to do. I could continue, unhindered, the search for the perfect high, to try all the things I wanted to try. Also, that night I made myself the promise of keeping my addiction under strict control. With The Family Man gone, I became visible. I had to be twice as careful.

Once a year, that was my promise. Maybe twice, if special circumstances arose, but not more. Never more.

Of course, there weren't any self-imposed restrictions on what I could do, those special times once or twice a year. Quite the opposite. I let my endless imagination guide me, and I experienced incredible new highs.

My new game involved several weeks of searching for the perfect apple, the one most likely to satisfy all my senses. I'd turned the neurochemical mechanism of choosing into an advanced art. Once I'd found her, I'd spend another few weeks studying everything there was to know about her. I still planned to visit the home, back then. I hadn't felt brave enough to kidnap a woman for a few more years, at least two, I think. During the time I took to study her whereabouts, her lifestyle, and her close circle of people, I spent hours daydreaming of how our encounter would play out. I'd script every step, in my mind, of course, and planned carefully to make sure I had all the needed props with me that special night.

I'm not going to bore you anymore with such tactical details. I'll just take a trip down memory lane with you and share the most memorable experiences of those days.

Janice was a Gala apple, crisp and very sweet. I saw her waiting for a bus one day, in the suffocating heat of a Miami summer. Later I'd learned she'd scored a DUI by letting herself get caught high behind the wheel. She's the one I charmed, the only one who was, at least for part of the evening's schedule, willing to participate. I'd come prepared with all sorts of drugs for her to try, and suddenly I was her best friend.

That lasted for most of the night, until I took my knife out. Then she tried to escape and fought deliciously against my possessive body. She had such stamina. I took a souvenir from my night with her; I still look at it every day and remember her long hair and thin waist. It's not an object anyone would miss, my souvenir, so don't worry.

Then there was this blonde little thing, my Golden Delicious, who was visiting from out of town somewhere. I took some serious risk with her; the only time I'd done that in a motel room, with only the television sound to cover her duct-tape-muffled screams. With her, I brought toys, lots of toys, and tried them all. I didn't like that I had to use duct tape though. I like to hear them scream and beg and shriek; it's part of what turns me on.

Then I laid low for a while, petrified at my own recklessness, but I soon emerged out of my self-imposed fasting for Karen, a fiery, auburn blonde who fought me like a ninja on crack. She was a Honeycrisp, assaulting my senses at every bite until I penetrated her deepest core. She lived inland, in a home sitting relatively isolated on some acreage, lost in the woods. I took my time with her; the conditions were perfect.

I confess I grew bolder with every one of them, but I never broke my promise, and I always kept my addiction under control. Once a year, twice sometimes, never more. I had an entire year to dream about it, and I made each encounter count. Throughout the years, I built a collection of souvenirs that still fills my heart with exhilaration every day when I see it. I still know which beauty gave me each one of these mementos, and I cherish them deeply. And every year, I add at least one new item to my growing assortment of souvenirs.

On a current and troublesome note, Laura Watson is still alive and well. Fuck it to hell. I need to contact the bastard who took my money and didn't deliver. When I get to him, I'll make that memorable too. That's a promise.

Then, there's the Laura problem I still have to take care of. It's becoming urgent.

36

Change of Plans

It was almost half past nine when Tess pulled over in front of the posh Miami Beach residence belonging to Dr. Austin Jacobs. It was much too late in the day for a house call, but she had no choice, nor was it her fault. From Raiford, she stopped at Palm Beach County Sheriff's Office, where she picked up her car, then she did her routine check on Laura's apartment, where she eavesdropped only long enough to hear the muffled conversation Laura and her boyfriend were having over dinner. Then she headed out to Miami Beach as fast as she could, but she still didn't make it before nine.

She rang the doorbell, and immediately a light came on in the living room. Good; the doctor was awake. She held her badge in front of the peephole, rehearsing in her mind the entire speech she came prepared to give.

The door opened and Dr. Jacobs appeared, wrapped in a fuzzy bathrobe.

"What can I do for you?"

"Apologies for the late hour, Dr. Jacobs. I'm Special Agent Tess Winnett with the FBI. I have a few questions regarding Laura Watson."

Dr. Jacobs invited her in, then closed the door. She led the way to a nicely decorated living room, where she took a leather armchair and invited Tess to do the same, across from a small coffee table. She obliged, weirdly aware of the squeaking sound the thick leather made when she let her weight sink into the deep cushions.

Dr. Jacobs ran her hands through her dark-red hair and tucked a few strands behind her ears. Even without makeup, she still looked imposing, much like the picture Tess had seen everywhere, from the Internet to *TIME* magazine's cover.

"All right, I'm listening," she said, frowning.

"There's no easy way to tell you this, Dr. Jacobs, especially after everything I've seen and heard about your project with Laura Watson, but we're almost 100 percent certain Kenneth Garza did *not* kill the Watson family."

Dr. Jacobs leapt from her armchair with the agility of a raging jungle feline.

"What? You can't be serious! How's that even possible?"

With every question, her tone rose higher, until she was yelling. She gestured angrily and paced the room with large strides, stomping her fuzzy slippers forcefully with every step.

"Recent developments have revealed additional information about this case," Tess gave her best shot at a vague, but at least partially true answer. Those recent developments were in fact known for years, but were chosen to be ignored out of bad judgment and sloppy police work. That was the whole truth, but Dr. Jacobs wouldn't have taken kindly to hearing it.

"My entire study is shot to pieces," Dr. Jacobs continued to yell. "What am I supposed to do now? I've secured grants, collected funds, I've talked to people. I've been on national television! It's not like I can send people a raincheck and expect to still have a career."

She stopped her rant and came to a stop in front of the small, well-assorted bar.

"Bourbon?" she asked in a more peaceful tone. "I definitely need one."

"No, thank you," Tess replied. "Still on the clock."

"Well, tell me if you change your mind," Dr. Jacobs said, then gulped an oversized shot and immediately poured herself another. She resumed pacing, but at a slower, calmer tread.

"I see this as a huge opportunity," Tess offered, "not to get confirmation for a new regression method, but to track and catch a killer no one knew existed."

Dr. Jacobs focused her piercing eyes on Tess.

"Just imagine the headlines," Tess upped the ante, gauging Dr. Jacobs's interest correctly. "You just need to adjust that method, to be openminded with your questions, and not assume you already know the answers."

Dr. Jacobs continued to keep her eyes on Tess, absorbing.

"Just… don't lead Laura on a certain path," Tess continued, uncomfortable venturing in someone else's area of expertise.

"I know how to do my job, Agent Winnett," Dr. Jacobs snapped. "Thankfully, I don't need advice from law enforcement, especially when they botch their work like that."

Tess took in a sharp breath of air, not expecting her unfiltered directness, but decided to let that remark go unanswered.

Suddenly, Dr. Jacobs plunged into her armchair and abandoned her glass on the coffee table. She rubbed her forehead, thinking, pursing her lips. Then she scribbled a quick note on a notepad she kept on the same coffee table.

"I've noticed the sessions we've had so far yielded very little result," Dr. Jacobs said, her voice now professional and level. "It seemed to me as if Laura fought me under hypnosis. I can't understand why."

"When does that typically happen?" Tess asked.

"When there's a strong emotional conflict at play, or when uncovering those buried facts is just too painful to watch and take in, even as an adult."

"Maybe this will help then," Tess offered.

"Maybe," Dr. Jacobs replied with a sad chuckle, "but don't expect me to be grateful anytime soon. Whatever the outcome, I'll have a PR nightmare on my hands. Not to mention angry investors and a compromised study."

She didn't seem that mad anymore, so Tess thought it was a good time to ask for a favor.

"I need to ask you one thing," she said, as she rose from her seat. "You can't tell Laura anything about this. Not until we're entirely sure about this whole situation."

"You want me to change the course of the study, without disclosing it to my patient? It's almost unethical," she replied.

"Almost?"

"There's no precedent we can baseline against. Thankfully though, I promised Laura we'd explore her subconscious mind searching for her buried memories, not explicitly for Kenneth Garza, and that makes the entire situation barely ethical. However, I will be withholding critical information from my patient, and that's never okay. Make it quick, Agent Winnett. Catch your killer sooner rather than later, will you?"

Tess offered her business card at the door. "I'll be in touch soon, but please call if there's any new information."

Dr. Jacobs nodded and opened the door for her.

"Oh, and one more question. Is it at all possible for you to, um, rush through these sessions?"

"What do you mean?" When she frowned, Dr. Jacobs's eyes became more piercing under her perfectly arched and waxed eyebrows.

"Could you maybe do a session each day? Instead of one per week? We need to get to that info as fast as possible."

Dr. Jacobs scoffed angrily and plopped her hands firmly on her hips. "That's unheard of in my line of work. This is not manufacturing, you know, where you add another shift to get results twice as fast. This is the human brain we're talking about. The mind needs time to heal, to process all the traumatic…" Her voice trailed off, and she tilted her head a little. "Wait, why are you asking me this?"

From the front steps, Tess hesitated for a second, then locked eyes with her.

"If that killer's still out there, there's a slight chance he could come after Laura, to shut her up."

Dr. Jacobs's jaw fell, and she stood in her doorway speechless, watching Tess get behind the wheel of her car and drive away.

Tess imagined the shocked Dr. Jacobs locking her front door and heading straight for the bourbon. She deserved it. She'd been more than cooperative, considering the circumstances.

A gnawing in Tess's stomach made her take an early exit and leave the northbound Interstate. Twenty-something minutes later, Cat put a lettuce-wrapped burger and a plate full of fries in front of her, as she sipped from her favorite drink through thin straws, leaning on her elbows at the Media Luna bar counter.

It felt good to let the rush of the day slow to almost a stop and give her time to recharge her spent batteries. It felt good to wash away the day's sinister encounter and replace it with the homey feeling of her favorite bar. She felt like home in Cat's joint, more at home than she felt in her own dreary, empty apartment. She liked to come here late at night and find him always smiling, always ready for a chat.

"Did you trust someone today, kiddo?" Cat asked, displaying a wide grin that made his teeth sparkle against his tan skin.

"Uh-huh," she acknowledged, unwilling to abandon her drink. She'd almost drained the tall glass, leaving only small ice cubes and herbs. Cat quickly obliged and brought her a new one.

"Well, who? Don't make me bite my fingernails," he insisted. He was funny without trying and probably without knowing. A warm, heart-melting kind of funny.

"I trusted a death-row inmate," she replied, as she grabbed the new glass filled to the brim.

He whistled, surprised.

"That's not what I meant, kiddo. What the hell? How about trusting someone less likely to want to harm you, huh? Why don't you try that sometime?"

"I had the chance," Tess replied, suddenly saddened, "but I couldn't. I just couldn't bring myself to do it. It makes me feel... vulnerable. Exposed."

"And the death-row inmate doesn't?" Cat stood in front of her, firm on his feet, challenging her logic.

"He's going to fry in a few days, Cat. Whatever exposure I risked was limited, so, yes, for me, the inmate felt safer than the pro—um, colleague."

"Okay, let's say I get it. You'll keep trying?"

She lifted her eyes from her disappearing food and mumbled, "Yes," with her mouth full.

"Were you in danger with that inmate?" Cat probed.

He had an uncanny talent when it came to her. He knew what was on her mind, almost like a parent would.

"Nah, not really," she replied, dreading the potential speech he could have offered, about her being more careful in her work.

The cloud of a memory made its way forward from the recesses of her weary mind and made her push the plate away, unfinished.

"Then what happened, kiddo?" Cat asked in a soft voice, taking a seat across the bar counter and bringing his head closer to hers.

She let out a long breath of air.

"This inmate... he made me in minutes," she blurted out, her voice breaking under the pressure of tears she didn't know she held inside. "I wear my history written on my forehead. What do people see when they look at me, Cat?"

He didn't reply, waiting for her to unload.

"Will they always see the sexual assault victim and nothing more?" Tess continued, letting the earlier sadness take over without fighting it anymore.

"You were never a victim," Cat replied, gently but firmly. "You refused to become one. I've always admired that about you."

She searched his eyes through a veil of tears. He touched her forearm with a warm, overworked hand.

"Thanks…" she whispered, resuming her stare at the tacky counter.

"No… I'm asking you, why become a victim now?" Cat insisted. "The past can be laid to rest. Why won't you let it go?"

37

A History of Crime

Tess arrived at Palm Beach County Sheriff's Office a few minutes before seven, carrying a coffee box and a large bag of bagels and croissants to get their day started. She climbed upstairs quickly, barely noticing the sting in her side, and stopped abruptly in the conference room door.

Fradella worked on the laptop, and he smiled with tired, bloodshot eyes when he saw her. He'd pulled an all-nighter, and it showed. He'd abandoned his tie and rolled up his sleeves, and a small pile of empty cans and food wrappers told the story of his sustenance since the previous day.

Michowsky had fallen asleep, his head resting on his forearm, slumped on the table. As for Doc Rizza, he snored lightly, leaning back in his chair with his mouth gaping.

Fradella gestured her to come in and continued typing quietly. The wall-mounted screen showed screen after screen of DIVS results, structured, filtered, but still returning names in the hundreds.

She set down the box and bag and that worked like an alarm clock for Doc Rizza.

"I smell coffee," he said, rubbing his eyes thoroughly. "Nothing like a power nap, but this will really help," he added, offering his empty mug to be filled. She obliged.

Michowsky shifted in his chair, then lifted his head, blinking, confused.

"Oh, good morning," he said, when he noticed Tess. "Um, I need some of that, please."

"You guys have been busy," Tess said, smiling appreciatively. She walked to the case board, where a new, wide table had been added since the previous day and was filled with structured information.

It showed victimology, MO, and signature for eight cases, probably the shortlisted eight they'd selected from the total unsolved murders that fit the time range. There were two additional cases at the end of the table, not identified by number but by names: Banks and Gonzales. Each table line showed a different characteristic, spanning from victim physiognomy, age, occupation, to crime scene setting, murder weapon and manner, duration of the attack, trace evidence, fingerprints, and finally, a line dedicated to the distension noticed by Doc Rizza in some wound patterns. Based on the solid line of Ys for yes, and the two Ps for possible, it seemed like they had found the killer's signature, even if they still didn't know what that wound distension meant. The table took half the case board, and above each case, a representative crime scene photo had been pasted.

"Walk me through this," she said, looking at Fradella.

Surprisingly, Michowsky replied. He'd been the last to adopt her tabular methodology of structuring information.

"We've picked apart the eight cases that we shortlisted from the pile of fourteen unsolved murders. All victims were raped, tortured, and stabbed, but there are variations. Let's see," he said, shuffling through the paper pile in front of him and taking a quick bite from a bagel.

Tess pulled up a chair in front of the case board.

"In chronological order, the first case is Janice Bennett, twenty-three, a nurse's aide. We almost didn't include her. She was a drug addict, on an active DUI suspension when she died. There were several drugs in her system, and Doc Rizza said at least part of the sex was consensual."

"What drugs?" Tess asked.

"Ecstasy, PCP, GHB, and some cocaine too. Nostrils showed signs of chronic snorting," Doc Rizza clarified.

"Then how can someone who's so high be consenting to anything, let alone sex with a killer?" Tess's voice spiked, and Fradella lifted his eyes and looked at her, furrowing his brow.

"All I'm saying is that she didn't fight the attacker that much," Doc Rizza replied. "Strictly from a vaginal tearing and bruising perspective, that is."

She clammed up, still angry, although she understood the facts. "All right, let's go on."

"I also said, 'for the most part, the sex appeared consensual,'" Doc Rizza added, "but that apparent consent ended when the assault got rough. She tried to fight him off, but with so many drugs in her system she didn't stand a chance." He checked his notes and continued. "There were several stab wounds, none hesitant or lethal, followed by one fatal stab to the lower abdomen delivered last, and showing signs of distension. She died within minutes of that blow, from exsanguination."

Tess looked at the crime scene photo and felt sorry for the young girl photographed lying in a dried pool of blood. She'd been a troubled girl, struggling, but she shouldn't have ended life like that.

"What the hell is that distension, Doc? Can you speculate?"

"I hate to do that. My job doesn't include—"

"Please," she insisted.

"I'll give you what facts I could gather. Something, an object of sorts, was inserted in those wounds. An object thicker than the knife blade, hence the distension; it forced the wounds to open wider, and pulled at the collagen fibers in the skin, at both ends of the wound. That object left absolutely no trace elements inside the abdominal cavity. That's all I have. Draw your own conclusions, although I don't think you can. I can think of many horrible scenarios, but I can't single out any one of them."

"Could he have inserted his hand?" Tess asked. "Or…" her voice trailed off.

"Oh, fuck," Fradella reacted.

"Again, there's no way of telling *what* he inserted. There was no trace element left behind. I gave you all I had," Doc Rizza replied and averted his eyes.

From his grim look and his refusal to speculate, she could follow his chain of thought and imagine several scenarios, but she decided not to voice any of them.

"One more thing," Doc Rizza said. "Because of the way things happened in her case, there's no way I can pinpoint with any accuracy how long the attack lasted. All I can tell you is that it took 90 to 120 minutes from the first laceration until she died."

She shook her head slightly, feeling a wave of rage raise bile into her throat. "Next," she signaled Michowsky.

"Rose Carrigan, twenty-two, a vacationing waitress from Colorado. He didn't have her long; two hours at the most. Also, note the unusual, high-risk location: a motel room."

"That's strange," Tess agreed. "Unreasonably high risk. How sure are we it's the same man?"

Michowsky let out a long sigh before replying. "How sure are we of anything in this mess? We've selected it from the list based on victimology, MO, and location criteria. It fits, but it's an exception too."

"Right, I get it."

"There are more of those in here," Michowsky added, tapping on the file folder pile.

"What?"

"Exceptions."

She turned and looked at the table drawn on the case board. Factors varied wildly, across the board, especially the durations of the attacks and the MOs.

"What happened to Rose?" Tess asked, keeping her eyes focused on the crime scene photo showing the body of the young woman, duct taped across the mouth and immobilized against the bedposts, also with duct tape. Some of the blood had been absorbed into the sheets, but whatever pattern was visible in the photos told the story of her painful demise.

"He brought toys and took them all with him when he left. We couldn't find any at the scene, but Doc's confident he used props on her."

She looked at Doc Rizza inquisitively. "I have here, um, 'forced vaginal and anal penetration with foreign objects,'" he quoted. "This was not my exam; I was doing my postdoctoral at the time, six years ago. But I called Dr. Gomez last night and checked every detail."

She frowned, thinking how that information impacted the profile they thought they had. "Isn't penetration with objects typically indicative of impotence of the attacker?" she asked.

"That's not the case here," replied Doc Rizza. "The objects were just the beginning."

She repressed a shudder.

Michowsky continued. "Kristen Jenkins, twenty-four, an executive assistant at a downtown real estate firm. She was found spread-eagled and stabbed multiple times in her own home, a duplex. Next-door neighbors were away on vacation. She's number three."

Tess nodded, while reviewing the data written in the table.

"Then number four, Veronica Norris, twenty, a student working on her business degree, was found suspended in her own home," Michowsky went on. "The killer brought his own tools and drove the nails into the support beam that ran between the kitchen and the living room. He, um, took his time with her; he was there for at least six hours. She was the youngest," he added and his voice trailed off.

He rubbed his forehead, then clenched his fist, and squeezed his lips. "It drives me crazy," he said forcefully, and Tess directed her gaze away from Veronica's photo to look at him. "You get one of these cases you can't close, and you just somehow make peace with it. Not enough evidence; what can you do? What can anyone do, if there aren't any leads, any suspects? You move on, because the next day another sick fuck kills someone, and you're just as busy as you were the day before, if not worse. Then this," he gestured widely with his hand toward the crowded case board. "All these women... I know it's been years, but look at it!"

Fradella had stopped typing and stared at his partner, his eyebrows raised.

"We'll catch him," Tess said, in a calm, reassuring voice. "I promise you."

"Sometimes I hate my goddamned job, that's all," he added.

Michowsky averted his eyes and cleared his throat, seemingly embarrassed at his outburst. He forced some air into his lungs, and continued. "Number five was Karen Rogers, twenty-five. She was an arts student," he stopped and cleared his throat again, "whose husband was away on a business trip. They had a home on some acreage, so the bastard had privacy. He was there for almost an entire day." His chin wrinkled, as he clenched his jaws.

"He branded her with the fireplace poker, several times," Doc Rizza added. "She fought fiercely. She cut her own skin against the cable ties she was restrained with. There were stress fractures in several of her hand and foot bones, from trying to break free. Unfortunately, there wasn't a single trace of DNA under her fingernails. It was a perfectly clean crime scene."

"Stab wounds?" Tess asked, cringing inside.

"Multiple, ending with the signature fatal stab to the lower abdomen we're so familiar with," Doc Rizza added. "The one with distended ends."

"The next one, number six—"

"Wait," Tess interrupted Michowsky, still staring at Karen's striking auburn-blonde hair. "I see a pattern here, a new one."

Fradella stopped typing and watched her intently.

"You see how the neighbors were on vacation for Kristen, how he knew to bring a hammer and heavy-duty nails for Veronica, and he knew Karen's husband was away on business? He was stalking them."

Michowsky leaned back against his chair with a long, pained groan.

"He's going into their homes before; he's a careful planner," Tess added.

"We knew that," Fradella replied. "It's in the profile."

"Not at this level, we didn't. He must have stalked them for months." She leaned against the table, focusing on the next crime scene photo. "All right, number six."

"Carla Cox, twenty-three, a service rep with a chemical company. It was repeated sexual asphyxia with her. She was found strangled in her apartment, but the lethal stab was still the sharp-force trauma to the lower abdomen," Michowsky said.

"From this point onward," Doc Rizza intervened, "he only stabbed them once, not more. Once, in the lower abdomen, all fatal blows that severed the common iliac artery, on either side. He developed surgical precision in his stabbings."

"Then Sue Bailey, also twenty-three, an intern at a major accounting firm; he carved into her body. Words, symbols, an unintelligible mess. You've seen the pictures."

"Yeah, I have."

"Number eight is Diana Webb, twenty-seven. She was a freelance computer programmer. He suspended and flogged her for hours," Michowsky said, then took a long swig of coffee, as if to wash the horror of the deaths he talked about. "Almost flayed her alive."

"No rape in these last two cases?" Tess asked, although she feared she knew the answer.

"Prolonged, repeated rape in all the cases," Doc Rizza replied grimly.

She closed her eyes for a second, but the nightmare images didn't vanish. "I see two more names added to the table," she said.

"Yeah," Fradella replied. "We're not 100 percent sure these two cases fit here, but they might."

"Okay, let's hear it."

"There was a police report filed thirteen years ago, when Garza was still out there, doing his thing. The Banks family said that their dog scared someone away, and they saw, from a distance, a man running. He had tried to enter their home through the back door. There's a vague description on file. Caucasian, late twenties, early thirties, good runner, physically fit."

"That could have been anything," Tess replied, "a burglar or a junkie."

"Everything fits, except Banks didn't die. Same age, same geographical location, isolated suburban home, dusk, attack on Friday night."

"Okay, let's assume you're right. Why are you thinking it's The Chameleon and not Garza? Our unsub plans thoroughly; he wouldn't have been scared away by a dog he didn't know existed."

"The dog was new to the home; used to live with Cathy Banks's father until two days before the attack. If you want one more reason, here's a photo of Cathy Banks," Fradella added, then clicked a button and displayed the image of a young, beautiful, thin blonde on the wall screen.

"Ah," Tess reacted. "All right, the Banks family probably belongs in the table. I'm sold. What about, um, Shirley Freeman?"

"Yes, a twenty-three-year-old store clerk who matches every criterion to the letter, except," Michowsky flipped though some notes, "she was stabbed once, in the heart. No torture, no rape. Her grandmother was also stabbed, in the neck. Weapon is a match to The Chameleon's favorite blade. The old lady pushed a button on her medical alarm bracelet before dying."

"It doesn't fit," Tess said, thoughtful. "He would have known about the grandmother. Don't tell me she was new to the home too."

Both Michowsky and Fradella nodded vigorously.

"That's Shirley," Fradella said, and displayed the image on the TV screen. She fit The Chameleon's type to perfection.

"So, he was surprised by Grandma when he was just getting started, huh? When was that?"

"Just four years ago. Emergency responders took seven minutes to get there, so he must have just run away. They didn't see anyone. He just vanished."

Tess examined the case board again, feeling her frustration climb.

"Please tell me there is some trace evidence found at these crime scenes. Something, anything. DNA, hair, fibers, anything?"

Michowsky and Doc Rizza shook their heads, seeming just as frustrated as she was.

"How the hell does one do that?" she muttered, more to herself.

"Have you seen the movie *Gattaca*?" Fradella answered. "That's what I'm thinking he did. Scraped, scrubbed, and shaved every inch of his body."

"You're probably right," Tess replied. "It's also possible he has access to forensics equipment and information. Crime scene coveralls with hood, hair covers, boot covers, the works."

"Anyone can get those online," Fradella replied. "The disposable ones are dirt cheap."

She rolled her eyes and groaned. "We need a break, guys, come on."

Michowsky frowned.

"By the way, great job with this," Tess added quickly and watched Michowsky's frown subside. "Todd, what numbers have you been crunching?"

"I entered the profile data into DIVS; one conviction for rape or rape suspect who was never indicted, age bracket between forty and fifty, Caucasian, successfully integrated, and so on. DIVS rewarded me with 788 males fitting the profile."

"Did you file against known arsonists? Bedwetters? Animal cruelty charges? How about sealed juvie records?"

"Whoa…" Fradella replied, laughing. "Yeah, just let me tell you about it. We crossed with juvie, petty arsonists who either weren't charged or records were sealed. Your analyst, Donovan, wasn't that happy to hear you asked him to help, but he did deliver."

"I asked him to help?"

Fradella looked at her sheepishly.

"Oh, yes, I remember now," Tess replied, laughing. Fradella had initiative and got the job done, at the cost of a white lie that didn't matter. She liked Fradella more and more.

"Out of the 788, only 5 are left, if we add petty arson to the mix."

"Anyone we know?"

"Nope, not even close. Based on what I've seen so far, these five men never crossed paths with the Watsons." Fradella ran his hand through his hair. "Michowsky and I will round them up anyway, speak with them."

"There was another guy who surfaced; someone who sued Watson, then his estate, a few times, all bogus claims," Michowsky added.

"Who?"

"A hotel owner who went belly up; he claimed Watson recommended the wrong model of wall sconces and that was what killed his business. Then he claimed Watson had an affair with his ex-wife and planned to ruin him. He filed that one a year after Watson died. Then another far-fetched claim against his estate, stating Watson had promised he'd feature his hotel in some magazine, but didn't. Got thrown out of court."

"Bring him in; let's hear his story," Tess replied, feeling invigorated. A business going bust could be the trigger that created a serial killer.

"He's, uh, sixty-five now, Latino, and overweight. No rape charge in his past, nothing, just petty stuff and bad business skills. He doesn't fit the profile, not a single point," Michowsky replied, letting his discouragement show.

"Bring him in, anyway. I want to know what fueled his hate for Allen Watson," Tess replied. "Apparently, no one else hated him."

She looked at the three men, noticing again how tired and drawn they looked. She hadn't caught more than three hours of sleep the past few nights. They'd worked for two days running, and for what? They still had nothing. Except…

"Garza was right," Tess said "This unsub, The Chameleon, doesn't know who he is, or what he wants. He's evolving, just like Garza said. He's exploring."

"Do you think he stopped? After Shirley Freeman and her grandmother?" Fradella asked. "We've found nothing else since then. Do you think he got caught? For something else, maybe?"

"No," Tess replied, thoughtful. "He didn't stop; not after getting this good. Not after getting used to the kill, to the smell of blood."

"BTK stopped," Fradella said, not lifting his eyes from the computer screen.

"I'm impressed with your knowledge, Todd," Tess replied. "But something tells me this unsub didn't stop. He can't stop. I feel it in my gut." She paused for a second. "I know he's out there, somewhere. He's not dead, and he's not in jail. I know it."

She half-expected them to snicker or at least stare dismissively at her remarks, but none of them did.

"Then what happened? Why can't we find any sign of his handiwork for the past three years?"

She bit her lip, thinking hard. How does someone like The Chameleon continue killing, without anyone even knowing about it? What would she do if she were him?

She shuddered, repressing the gruesome images that invaded her mind. "It's simple, really," she replied eventually. "He got *that* much better. He figured out a way to kill without worrying about unexpected grandmas or dogs anymore. I'm willing to bet that some of the missing-person cases with matching physiognomy victims are his. He's built himself a den somewhere. His own, private torture chambers."

"We'll never find it," Fradella replied immediately, voicing Tess's inner fears.

"Maybe we will," she replied. "We've got one shot, and that's Laura Watson's regression sessions."

"Really?" Fradella asked. "That's *all* we got? Then we're so screwed."

"What, you expect Laura to dream up the guy's name and social security number?" Michowsky asked bitterly.

"I've got a better question for you," Tess replied. "Admitting that I'm right, and he's still out there killing, why is Laura Watson still alive?"

38

Reflections: Lady Luck

Now that we agree you and I are not that different after all, I think I can answer your last question: how did I become who I am today? How can I enjoy my numerous, sophisticated feasts undisturbed, without leaving even the tiniest trace behind?

The final phase of my becoming started with a young lass by the name of Shirley Freeman, a store clerk who took her sweet time packing my groceries, while she smiled, batted her long lashes at me, and looked sideways with each can of tomato juice she dropped in that paper bag. She flirted with me shamelessly, with me, a man twice her age, wearing his wedding band in plain view, and shopping for tampons, among other things. I figured she'd be willing... well, at least up to some point. I sized her up, and, happy with what I saw, I decided she was going to be my next feast.

Only then I smiled back at her, and she blushed delightfully, like a Jonagold apple touched by the rays of the sun.

I did my research thoroughly during the next couple of months. I soon knew everything there was to know about her, or so I believed. I remember thinking how her house seemed way above her pay grade, an isolated home in a nice neighborhood, but, then again, people inherit things all the time. Her paycheck probably covered the taxes and the utilities for that property, but not a whole lot more. Her car, though, seemed more in line with her social status, confirming the hypothesis of an inheritance, and one of some emotional value that she didn't want to part ways with.

On the scheduled day, when all records had me traveling for business in Jacksonville, I landed in her living room ready for my feast, armed with a full kit of accessories I had learned, over the years, to pack and bring along. Large trash-can liners. Cable ties. Duct tape. Coveralls and booties, to prevent any hair or fiber to stray behind. All that and more, packed handsomely in a duffel bag I dropped quietly on the carpet the second I stepped into the house.

I looked around for her, and she was nowhere in sight. The main floor, an overly decorated open concept, proved to be a challenge. As I snuck around the dining room cupboard, a ghastly shriek froze the blood in my veins. Instantly, I turned around and saw her there, drawing breath to shriek again. I leapt forward and managed to tackle her, then covered her mouth while I crushed her with my weight. She pounded her feet against the floor and wouldn't subside until I pulled my blade and brought it within an inch of her widened eyes. Only then she quieted down.

But it was too damn late. In the living room door, clasping the doorjamb for balance and searching the room with the eyes of an eagle mother, stood a frail, old woman. When she saw me and our eyes locked, I read in there a death sentence. Mine. Without saying a word, the hag let go of the doorjamb and pressed the emergency button on her medical alert bracelet, time and again. Within seconds, the phone rang.

I had no choice.

Even now, as I look back, I realize that I had absolutely no choice than to do what I did that day. In the back of my head danced the forever-unanswered question, "How was that possible?" I had stood in that very home just days before, when Shirley was at work, and no one was there. No one, and not a trace of anyone else living with Shirley. How was it possible?

The same unanswered questions circled my brain, as my blade plunged into Shirley's chest, silencing her forever. As she stopped squirming, the old shrew screamed, not too loudly, and made a feeble attempt to get to the front door. I reached her with two large steps and grabbed her by the arm, to stop her before she could reach the doorknob, while the phone continued to ring.

The voicemail system picked up, and I heard a young man confirming that they'd already dispatched an emergency crew, that should reach the address within five minutes.

Damn! I was trapped in there, with one dead woman, and another one who was dying and saw it coming, with blue, watery eyes wide open.

But I wasn't caught yet.

I gasped as I raised my arm holding the knife and lowered it forcefully, aiming for the woman's chest. She turned unexpectedly, and my blade sliced her throat instead, severing both her carotid and jugular.

Then I knew... when Lady Luck decides to be a bitch, there's no bigger bitch on the face of this earth.

The old bat must have had skyrocketing blood pressure; otherwise, I just can't explain the arterial spray that burst all the way to the ceiling and drenched me in blood, head to toe. I grabbed my duffel bag, ran to the back door, and I slipped and fell twice on the slick hardwood until I was on firmer ground, outside, in the dusk-shrouded garden.

I heard sirens in the distance, approaching fast. I rushed to the street, chose the dark side of it, and ran without raising my eyes from the ground, clutching my precious duffel bag to my chest. I had two blocks to run to my car, and I remember thinking just how smart I'd been to park in a dark, unsecured parking lot that night, although typically I tend to be overprotective toward my new Lexus SUV. You never know who trolls those neighborhoods, right?

I didn't run into anyone on my way to the car, and the emergency crews entered the street after I had turned the corner and was well out of sight. Maybe Lady Luck was starting to smile again.

Safely behind the wheel of my car, I pushed the ignition button and drove away, stopping at every stop sign, and yielding to every pedestrian. Then, while I waited for a red light to turn green, the driver in the car next to mine gave me a stare, and I froze. I looked at my hands, my face in the mirror, the steering wheel, my clothes... all covered in blood spatter, appearing dark brownish in the dim streetlight.

I managed a smile and a quick nod to the other driver. He smiled back and looked away. Some people are such idiots... but that worked well for me. Then I disappeared into the Glades, taking the shortest route out of the city I could think of, then losing myself on some small roads.

Deep in the darkness of the forest, I finally dared to turn on the interior light in my car and look at myself.

Nope, Lady Luck remained an unforgiving, pre-menstruating bitch.

I was soaked in drying blood, and so was my car. Everything I'd touched was stained. The cream-colored, perforated leather seats, the carpeting, the door, most of the center console controls. A forensics death sentence.

Where could I go like that? Really, where?

I couldn't go home, and explain the state of affairs to my wife. She might be loyal and loving, but I think even that has its limits. I couldn't check in to a hotel, looking like that. There was nowhere I could go.

I thought of many scenarios, one more far-fetched than the other, as my overheated brain kept spinning in circles and arriving at the same conclusion.

I was finished.

39

Outcomes

Tess watched a poorly digitized recording of an old interrogation tape with Kenneth Garza, shot in an unfamiliar interview room. The light was too dim for the recording to be very clear, and she squinted and approached the wall-mounted TV to see more detail.

At the forefront, she could see the upper back and the head of an unknown investigator. He was balding at the top of his head, and his heavyset frame didn't remind her of anyone she knew. She checked the email from Donovan, who had done her a huge favor and dug up all the Garza interviews, digitized them, and arranged them in chronological order. He had labeled this one as, "Detective McKinley—Miami-Dade, Kenneth Garza, re. Watson murders." It was the same McKinley, the detective who'd passed away shortly thereafter, who had worked the Townsend case.

Tess turned up the volume and followed the exchange between the two men with curiosity, biting at her index fingernail. A younger, but just as relaxed and accepting Garza was replying to questions in a calm tone, giving quick, almost monosyllabic answers. They went through several case files like that, then McKinley presented Garza with the Watson murder file. Garza quickly reacted, by saying, "I don't know who these people are." McKinley pushed back, refusing to believe him.

They argued for a while, with Garza offering to take a polygraph, then asking McKinley what reason would he have to lie, when he'd already confessed to tens of murders. But logic got him nowhere with Detective McKinley, who obstinately insisted The Family Man had killed the Watsons too. He even taunted Garza about The Watson Girl, saying, "It must have made you feel like a fool, leaving that girl alive like that." Garza didn't flinch; he just stated calmly he didn't care one way or another, because he'd never seen those people before in his life.

Garza tried one last time, telling McKinley he wanted the record set straight for the sake of truth and honesty, but McKinley laughed in his face, and Garza called him a moron, just as calmly. Then Garza took to studying all the case photos included in the Watson file. On the low-resolution video, Tess thought she could see Garza's lips twisting in a faint, intrigued smile, as he went through the photos, one by one.

The recording ended, leaving the screen dark and the conference room quiet. That video had shown Tess exactly how the three cases were unsolved for so many years, how a serial killer was left to his own devices to continue killing for years. First Michowsky, then McKinley—they both rushed through cases, ignoring evidence and turning away from logic and common sense. Too late to dwell on that now, but she found herself wondering if there was anything else they'd missed.

The phone disrupted her fruitless introspection; it was Dr. Jacobs. She picked up immediately. "Dr. Jacobs," she greeted the caller.

"Agent Winnett," Dr. Jacobs replied. "You asked me to call with anything. I'm not sure if this is something relevant or not. I've scheduled another session with Laura Watson this morning, and it didn't yield much more than before. It followed yesterday's pattern quite closely, making me believe this could be everything we could hope to learn from this."

"I'm not sure I follow," Tess replied, frowning and scratching her forehead.

"It seems to me the few things she remembers are incoherent. For example, there are some questions I'd like answered. She was found in a bathroom in the dark. Who turned off that light? Was it always off? She doesn't go there, no matter how hard I try. However, she remembers the doorbell ring, and, in regressive state, she imitates the door chime like children normally do. Then she becomes frantic and breaks down crying, screaming, 'no, no, bad; no, no, bad, no.' She sobs uncontrollably, so I must end the sessions, always at the same point. If we could somehow go beyond that point, then maybe we—"

"What do you make of that, Dr. Jacobs?"

"Remember we're talking about a traumatized five-year-old girl. In regressive states, it's normal for patients to talk and act like they did back then, in a mirroring, or reenacting of what they did, or saw others do during the traumatic events. Laura talks with her five-year-old voice, and says things that a five-year-old would normally say under duress. Sadly, I couldn't get anywhere else with her; not yet, anyway. I'll keep trying, but—"

"Do you have recordings?" Tess asked, still staring absently into the dark TV screen. "Videos of these sessions?"

Dr. Jacobs hesitated a little.

"Yes, I do, but I would have to get her permission to share them with you."

"Please do that, and fast," Tess asked. "After that TV show, we can't be sure he won't—"

"I understand," Dr. Jacobs replied in a somber voice. "I didn't know... I had no idea. I would never risk the well-being of a patient, regardless of reason, Agent Winnett. You must believe me."

Long after the call ended, Tess still mulled over the facts in her head. No matter how she looked at all the facts, the same question bothered her, over and over again. What had The Chameleon done before the Watsons? Garza had copped to all the family killings before that one, so that meant the Watsons were relevant somehow for The Chameleon.

Could the Watsons have been The Chameleon's first kill? What kind of killer is so cold-blooded on his first kill?

She'd pored over the Watson murder details a few times, already, and had found almost nothing new. She'd spoken with the nanny, even with Laura, but there wasn't anything else she could find. Yet, her mind went there obsessively, like she'd missed something.

She let a long breath of air escape her lungs and drained her stale coffee cup with two thirsty gulps, then decided to visit with Doc Rizza again. She texted Michowsky to meet her downstairs and took to the stairs, hoping for a miracle.

40

Reflections: The Dive

I wasn't finished that night after all; I was reborn.

As my heart rate came down and my shallow, raspy breaths stabilized to a normal rhythm, a solution started appearing out of the blue. With the departure of my short-lived panic, came the arrival of sanity, of salvation.

But first, I had a few practical problems to solve. The night was dark out there in the middle of the Glades, and outside of the myriad creatures chittering in the woods, no one bore witness to my redemption plans.

I was supposed to be on a business trip to Jacksonville. I always plan my feasts carefully and make sure a convenient alibi is lined up. Most commonly used is business travel. I do the travel, make sure I'm seen everywhere, then come back a little early, right before my feast. After I'm done, I back track a couple of hundred miles on back roads and drive home on the turnpike, leaving a conveniently time-stamped paper trail. I don't need to tell you that I pay for gas in cash when backtracking, or that kind of thing.

I'm sure you can figure all that out. I sometimes use a disguise, fake ID, or even a fake plate, when I'm cutting it too close, or when my alibis involve air travel. Flying is always the worst... a lot of cameras everywhere, from parking lots to airport lounges. But it *can* be done, you know. I've done it many times.

How about hotels, you might ask? Doesn't the hotel register have me check out too early? Well, no. Not in this day and age of technology. Not when I make sure I only stay in hotels that allow Web checkout. I leave, I come back here, do my thing, then I log in remotely, via proxy, and check out of my hotel, at the right time to make sense for my alibi. I sometimes like to call the reception desk a few hours prior, right before starting my feast, and ask them some silly weather question, because I have this fierce migraine... Yes, they'll always remember me, in case they'd be asked. Then I disappear via Web checkout, unseen, and vanish without a trace in the mass of inbound and outbound travelers who drive hoteliers crazy everywhere. Or so they'll think. They'll swear they saw me leave, soon after checking out.

As a general rule, most people, if I buy them a drink or two, they'll remember I was there even if I wasn't.

I was supposed to be in Jacksonville. I still showed as checked in at a hotel there, and that was an easy fix. Just log in and check out, about six hours prior to arriving home, in Miami. Then... what?

To understand my crazy solution, you must know a bit of forensics; and I've studied a lot. There's nothing more destructive to DNA and blood evidence than water immersion. Oh, but wait, there is. That's called salt water. What do we have here, in Miami? Yep, you guessed it. An entire ocean of it.

The challenge remained to find a plausible way to leave the turnpike paper trail with all its cameras behind, then somehow plunge my car into the ocean. I wasn't thrilled with the prospect of ruining, in one single maneuver, both my impeccable driving record and my brand-new Lexus, but it sure beats the lethal injection. Okay, so my car insurance was going to take a hit. Tough luck, but it wasn't like I couldn't afford it.

I steeled my taut nerves at the thought of plunging headfirst into some bridge guardrail, then into the water, but there was no other way. After an hour of racking my brain searching for ways out, that was it, the only way out of that damn mess.

I started working on the details and the timeline. Technically, if I was in Jacksonville now, at nine in the evening, and the drive took, say, six hours, I had to check out immediately, backtrack for a couple of hours, then hop on the turnpike and start leaving the paper trail.

I still had two problems to solve. One, I needed to show clean and spotless on the many turnpike cameras. Spotless, as in no visible blood spots on my face, clothes, steering wheel, and hands. At least that. With a little imagination, a spare shirt from my suitcase, and some bog water from a puddle nearby, I got that fixed. I was clean enough to pass through highway cameras, but not more. To this day, I'm thankful I made it back into the car without an alligator or a snake taking a bite out of me. Lady Luck redeeming herself, that's what it was.

The second problem was tougher. What possible reason could I have for leaving the Interstate and ending up on the bridge, headed toward Harbor Isles, otherwise known as the Causeway bridge? But, first, why that specific bridge, you will ask? Well, for many reasons, starting with the most important: that bridge is one of the very few left with metallic guardrails instead of concrete. I'm not sure my Lexus can safely cut through concrete, but I've seen a Honda plow through metallic guardrails without much issue. I didn't want to risk it, so Harbor Isles it was.

Then, that bridge is always deserted at night; no one drives there at about three or four in the morning, my calculated time of arrival. Finally, that location held a good reason for me to leave the Interstate, a valid reason any cop would understand. Just yards from that bridge was a coffee and donut place, open twenty-four hours.

A minor detail, yet critically important, was to weigh down the duffel bag with my tire iron and let it sink in an alligator-infested lake I drove by, coming out of the Glades. Then I executed the rest of my plan perfectly.

Everything went without a glitch until I reached the Causeway bridge, where I couldn't veer off due to traffic. I needed to land in the water when no one was there, to give the car time to sit in the water long enough for the blood caked in the perforated leather seats to disintegrate. White-knuckled and hearing my heart thump against my chest with a perfectly steady, slow beat, I drove past the oncoming traffic, turned around and drove out again, then flipped another U-turn and floored it.

I didn't even hear the impact with the guardrail; the airbags deployed, cocooning me. A second of silence later, the car hit the water surface headfirst, and it smashed like it had hit concrete. Then water flooded the car rapidly through all four open windows. I stayed calm and let the water flush over me, then released my seat belt and exited through the window, leaving my beautiful Lexus behind, as it continued sinking.

I didn't climb out of the water right away; I swam around for a while, just like a confused accident victim would do. My big splash woke up a couple of boaters, but by the time they peeked out their windows, the car was long gone. I swam under the bridge, where I stayed in the water for endless minutes, rubbing at my pants, my face, my hands, cleaning all traces of blood from my body. Finally, when I thought I'd done a good enough job, I climbed on the shore and positioned myself to be found by passersby.

Believe it or not, I fell asleep, right there, on the grass, near the edge of the road. When I woke up, they were loading me into an ambulance, and they'd already fitted me with a trauma collar. Content, I closed my eyes and let them fuss over me.

I was content with how I solved my challenge. I wasn't content with how everything went down though. Not at all. Just twenty-four hours before, I was salivating in anticipation of my feast with Shirley, and now I had to deal with the memory of running for my life, of feeling hunted. The powerful predator that I was felt ashamed, unworthy, and hated it.

That could never happen again. Never.

I took an oath that day. I swore I was never again to feel the bitterness of denial, or the breath of my enemy on the back of my neck. I was angry, angrier than I'd ever been before.

That's when I decided to build my cabin, buried deep in the woods, an anonymous haven where nothing unexpected could happen, and where I could take my time with my guests. Where I could finally touch their skin with my bare, ungloved hands, and feel their silky warmth against the naked, taut sheath of my erection.

Too bad I can't take Laura there. It would have been amazing.

By the way, that contract killer swears he's got the job done. He said the trap's already set; now all we should do is wait. It will happen, soon. Apparently, that's quite common in the industry, when you want things to appear accidental.

I'm irritated and short-fused all the time; I can't stop thinking of Laura, of what I could do to her, of what I *can't* do to her. There's only one fix for the fever I'm feeling; I'm taking someone today. It's all arranged. I've had my eyes for a while on this pretty, young thing by the name of Monica. She'll make a fine guest for a couple of days, take my mind off things.

I've never had a Monica before. I wonder what her skin tastes like. I close my eyes and envision this ripe, scented Aurora apple, ready for my first bite. I wonder if she'll fight me… if her body will writhe against mine, in exhilarating spasms, or if she'll stand still, offering herself in sweet surrender, closing her eyes, afraid to breathe, afraid of my blade.

41

A Few Surprises

Doc Rizza had aligned three evidence tables, one next to the other, and had set out the archived case evidence for the three cold cases they were working on. The tables were labeled neatly with sticky notes, and he was going through all the evidence bags, one by one, probably for the tenth time already.

He straightened his back with a groan when she came in, and smiled. He had a kind smile, that didn't manage to clear all the tiredness in his eyes.

"I get visitors," he chuckled, "must be important."

"Very," she replied. "The guys are coming too."

"What's on your mind?"

"The Watson case, Doc. I want to take another look at it. Anything new in there that could help?" she asked, pointing toward the evidence table labeled "Watson."

"Maybe," he replied, just as Michowsky and Fradella entered the morgue. He nodded in their direction. "There was a hair strand with follicle attached. It was packed separately, so I didn't find it until two days ago. It was marked 'Evidence excluded,' and was never tested for DNA. Now it is; I put it through, posthaste."

"And?" Tess asked impatiently.

Doc Rizza shook his head. "No match in the database, unfortunately. It's male DNA, and it wasn't a familial match to any of the Watsons, not even to Charlie, the little boy who stayed over at the Watsons that night."

"Why the hell was it excluded from evidence?" she asked, then turned toward Michowsky with an inquisitorial look. "Gary?"

Michowsky's brow furrowed.

"If I remember correctly, that hair was raven black, just like Bradley Welsh's. Considering the hair length, we concluded it could have been his. Due to the close nature of their relationship, Welsh's hair had all the reason in the world to be at that scene. The two families were—"

"Yeah, yeah, they were close. I've heard it a million times. Not enough reason to exclude evidence, though."

"We strongly believed Garza was the killer," Michowsky replied, staring at the cement floor. "I… we didn't think—"

"Yeah. All right," she said, a little colder than she would have liked, "we've got DNA now, and it's not helping us much, is it?"

"No, it doesn't," Michowsky replied, sounding almost defiant, and raising his eyes to meet hers.

She almost reacted, dying to tell him that the fact there wasn't a DNA match in the database didn't make his decision to exclude evidence okay. It just made it forgivable. She did just that, chose to forgive, and said nothing. Soon enough, he looked away again. He probably knew, just as well as she did, that he'd been wrong about too many things in the Watson case.

"Do you want to get a DNA sample from Welsh?" Tess asked.

"I could try," Michowsky replied. "I don't think we have enough for a warrant, but I can go to Judge Santiago. He tends to approve DNA warrants."

"Okay, let's do that," Tess replied.

"You know there's a strong chance he'll laugh in my face. Bradley Welsh is not our unsub; he had a perfect alibi with more than a hundred witnesses. He raised The Watson Girl, for crying out loud. It can't be him, I'm telling you. It doesn't make any sense."

"I know," she replied, deep in her thoughts. "Let's just try, for the sake of diligence. We have nothing else, anyway. This case has gone ice cold."

As she spoke the words, a tug at her gut disagreed. She felt she was missing something, a critical piece of information, something that was right there in front of her, but she couldn't see it. She ground her teeth and clasped her hands together.

They all stood silently for a long minute, then Doc Rizza patted Tess on her shoulder.

"Why don't you call it a day, guys? Get some sleep. Start again tomorrow, with fresh eyes."

That wasn't such a bad idea; it was almost midnight, and they were among the last ones in the building. She gave Doc Rizza a quick hug, then took the stairs to the main entrance, where the receptionist hailed her.

"This just came for you, Agent Winnett," the young man said, "by courier."

She opened the envelope to find a small flash drive and a handwritten note from Dr. Jacobs. It read, "I've included relevant family videos that Laura still had, with her permission, of course. They'll help you establish a frame of reference for the regression sessions, which are also included. Call me with any questions, and good luck!"

She hesitated a second, thinking of running upstairs to watch the videos in the conference room, curious to see what more information she could garner. With a sigh, she decided to go home instead. At least she could watch those videos with her feet up and a cold drink in her hand.

She did her routine patrol rounds by Laura's apartment, but her car wasn't there, and the windows were completely dark. She wondered if they usually left the cat home alone without any light on.

A few minutes later, she had her laptop fired up in front of her, and she'd kicked off her shoes and removed her everyday sweaty clothes in favor of an oversized T-shirt and wool socks. She plugged in the flash drive and started watching the videos.

There was little to be gained from watching them. The Watsons had been a happy family, and the videos captured milestone moments in their lives: birthdays, Christmases, an Easter egg hunt with all three children, when the youngest girl was just a baby, crawling on the floor. She immersed herself in discovering what the Watsons were like, learning about their family life. She noticed the kindness in Rachel Watson's eyes, and how carefully and patiently she took care of her babies. Allen Watson seldom appeared, most likely being the one who held the camera.

Tess chuckled lightly when she noticed how little Laura had difficulties pronouncing the letter "r." That somehow sounded familiar, and she remembered hearing Laura's answering machine, with the message recorded many years ago, when all five Watsons were still alive and happy.

She continued watching the videos, almost forgetting what she was looking for, immersed in the joyous life the Watsons had shared. At every party, people were entertained by Laura's missing r's, and constantly asked her to say her name. She kept saying her name was Lau'a, and they kept smiling, giggling, encouraging her, as if it was the first time they'd heard her say it like that. They weren't mean to her; not in the slightest. They were enjoying her, like one enjoys the tricks of a sweet, little puppy.

Many of the video clips were from family birthdays and showed both families together, the Watsons and the Welshes. They were close, indeed. She scrutinized the Welshes for any red flags, any behavior or grimace that didn't belong, and saw nothing. For all intents and purposes, the Welshes and the Watsons were part of the same family.

Tess swallowed a yawn and decided to watch one more video. It was a birthday video, and little Laura celebrated her fourth year. She wore a funny birthday hat, with little bells on top, and waddled about, taking paper plates with cake on them to her many guests, children and adults. She watched Laura as she turned to the table, took another plate with a slice of cake on it from her mother's hands, and started taking it to someone who was off camera. Tess smiled, watching Laura's funny walk, but then her phone rang, cutting into the peacefulness of the home videos like a knife.

She paused the recording and picked up. "Winnett," she said.

"Tess, get to North Shore Medical Center, pronto," Michowsky said, without any preamble. "Laura rolled over in her car, on her way home."

42

Consequences

Tess arrived on the hospital floor as a doctor approached Mrs. Welsh and a young man, most likely Laura's boyfriend. She recalled a framed picture she'd seen somewhere in Laura's apartment, and that young man was in it. The three of them stood in a closed circle right in front of Laura's room, and Tess slowed her stormy approach and pulled out her badge, but waited for the doctor to finish his update.

"She should be fine in a couple of days, with plenty of rest. She's lightly sedated now, but you can see her if you'd like. The baby is fine too," he added with a smile.

Both Mrs. Welsh and the boyfriend frowned at the news and exchanged accusing gazes. Tess found their confused silence a good moment to intervene.

"Tess Winnett, FBI," she announced herself.

"What baby?" Carol Welsh asked, completely ignoring Tess, and staring at Laura's boyfriend with the look of a grizzly bear.

"Have no idea," the boyfriend replied coldly, raising his hands in the air. "Why don't you ask her. She didn't bother to tell *me* about it either."

Tess watched the exchange in disbelief. They'd just learned Laura was pregnant, and not a trace of joy was on either of their faces. She turned to the doctor.

"May I see her? I need to speak with Laura immediately."

"Sure," the doctor replied, and gestured toward Laura's room.

"You're not seeing anyone," Mrs. Welsh snapped.

She was tall and distinguished, the kind of distinction a life of plenty lends most women. She was accustomed to people doing as she wanted; Tess heard that in the cutting tone of her voice.

"Excuse me?" Tess reacted, turning toward her. She started to show her badge again, but Carol Welsh swatted the air like she was repelling an insect.

"I know who you are," she said coldly, "but that doesn't change a thing. You're not bothering my daughter."

"Since Laura is an adult, I have the right to interview her in private, by law, if her doctor agrees, and he just did," Tess replied with a smile that didn't reach her eyes. "Any effort to stop or further delay me will be an obstruction of justice, followed by your prompt arrest."

She turned and headed toward Laura's room, leaving behind a perplexed Mrs. Welsh. Once inside Laura's room, she closed the door behind her and let a quiet sigh escape. Carol Welsh was nothing more than a concerned mother, still shocked after hearing her daughter had been in a car crash, feeling and acting protective. She should have gone easier on her.

She looked at the bed and almost didn't recognize Laura. She looked pale and incredibly thin. The appearance of fear in her eyes had subsided somewhat, but wasn't completely gone. Whatever monsters Laura was hiding had come to life. Probably she felt safer here, on a hospital floor, surrounded by good people.

"Hello, Laura," Tess said gently, "I'm Special Agent Tess Winnett with the FBI."

"Yes, I remember you," she said, then licked her dry, pale lips. "I didn't know the FBI bothered with car crashes," she continued, a flicker of fear glinting in her eyes.

"Why don't you tell me what happened?" Tess asked.

"I was coming home on the Interstate, when the steering wheel suddenly got stuck. It moved hard, at first, and it took me a lot of effort to turn it, for a second or so, but then it froze completely and I couldn't stop... I didn't have time. I hit the guardrail and flipped over a few times, they told me."

"I see," Tess replied, waiting patiently for Laura to continue.

"I was lucky," she said, smiling faintly. "Just another mile farther, and I would have dropped from much higher, at the interchange. It was just an accident," she concluded, giving Tess a sheepish look. "Am I in big trouble?"

"Laura, you're an engineer," Tess said.

"Almost," she replied with a shy smile, then cringed in pain. She touched her head with a trembling, thin hand.

"Then it's time to think for yourself," Tess continued. "I want to put you in protective custody."

"Why?" Laura asked, her voice sounding desperate, almost like a cry.

Tess forced a breath of air into her lungs.

"Because it's possible that The Family Man didn't kill your parents and siblings. It's possible someone else did."

Laura stared at Tess with blue eyes that rapidly welled up. She let out a long, shuddering breath that quickly turned to sobs.

"You lied to me," she said between sobs. "You were in my home, looked me in my face, and lied to me."

She turned on her side, facing the wall and blocking Tess out. Tess stood there speechless, unable to think of a single thing she could say to make those frail shoulders stop their almost convulsive shaking.

Outside in the hallway, Tess pulled out her phone and called Michowsky. "Gary, I want Laura's car taken apart piece by piece. It was tampered with. I want to know when, how, and by whom. Oh, and post a uniform at Laura's hospital room, will you?"

Then she headed toward the exit, but felt someone grab her sleeve.

"Protective custody?" Carol Welsh yelled in her face, holding on to her sleeve with a lot of strength. "I can't let you do that!"

Tess stopped in place and stiffened.

"How would you like to be charged with assault of a federal officer?"

Mrs. Welsh released her sleeve like it suddenly burned her hand.

"I still can't let you do that," she said, somewhat subdued, pleading. "Please... We'll watch over her. We've done it before; we'll do anything you want, but don't put our daughter through that again." Tess saw nothing but worry and despair in the tearful eyes of Mrs. Welsh.

"It's what's best for her, all things considered," Tess replied. "You obviously couldn't protect her from this," she added, gesturing vaguely toward Laura's room.

"But how can you be sure? Why are you telling her that... that horrible man isn't her family's killer?"

"Sorry, I can't discuss the details of an ongoing investigation," Tess replied dryly.

"Now you suddenly can't discuss it, Agent Winnett? Well, I won't let you put my daughter in jail, that's for sure. I'll have my lawyer give your boss a call."

"Suit yourself," Tess replied, then turned and left, breathing heavily and failing to subdue her anger. Preoccupied, she failed to notice the nurse who stood right next to them in the hallway, with her back against the wall, listening to their entire conversation.

On the way to her car, treading quickly on the endless hallways, Tess couldn't keep her mind from going over her exchange of words with Mrs. Welsh. She seemed a genuinely concerned parent, yet she refused protective custody for her adoptive daughter? In what scenario did that make sense?

Eventually, she just shrugged the whole thing off, thinking it must have been the need for control, typical for people of power, that motivated Mrs. Welsh to refuse protective custody for Laura so vehemently. That, plus the notoriously bad rap that protective custody had.

43

Two Phone Calls

It wasn't seven yet when Tess grabbed her phone and dialed Pearson's number. He couldn't complain about the early hour; after all, he'd said next time she should call.

He picked up after three long rings, but he didn't sound asleep.

"What's up, Winnett?"

"Sir, I'm filing a warrant for Laura Watson's protective custody."

"Winnett, didn't we agree—"

"We did, sir," she cut him off, "but her car was tampered with. I don't think we can wait any longer."

"Do you have a suspect list narrowed down or any new evidence?"

"Um, not yet, sir, but we have a few leads we're following through."

He let a long breath escape his lungs, and Tess could visualize him shaking his head, tired of fighting her, dreading the PR nightmare that would surely ensue.

"All right, Winnett, go ahead with it, and try to keep it as quiet as possible."

"Um, sir, there could be a call coming your way this morning. Carol Welsh is not happy with the protective custody scenario. She mentioned a lawyer."

"Winnett, didn't we talk about complaints? You promised me you're going to do your job without having me pick up the pieces every time. Part of your job is negotiating, persuading, talking with the families."

"Sir, I'm sorry," she blurted without thinking, "but I can't kiss ass and do my job at the same time."

"Watch it, Winnett," Pearson snapped. He was clearly pissed. "Why don't you come by the office first thing? You probably need help with this case."

He hung up the second he finished what he had to say, leaving her no option but to comply. That was typical of Pearson, especially when she managed to make him mad. She cringed in anticipation of their meeting and decided to stop by Starbucks beforehand. She needed all the help she could get.

The drive to the Miami FBI headquarters wasn't a long one, and she normally enjoyed the morning air and the time she had to herself to organize her thoughts and plan her day. That morning though, all kinds of contradicting thoughts raced through her head, as she tried to figure out how, if ever, she was going to catch The Chameleon.

The phone disrupted her thoughts, and she picked up via her car's phone system.

"Hey, Winnett, hope we didn't wake you," Fradella's cheerful voice greeted her.

"I'm in my car… what's up?"

"We've got a surprise for you this morning, Doc and I do. We hit jackpot with that hair. It matches the Townsend hair DNA."

"What? You're not making much sense, Todd. Slow down, start over."

"Remember the black hair strand Doc sent for DNA analysis, the one from the Watson crime scene? The hair that was originally excluded?"

"Yeah, it came back male, unknown, unrelated."

"This morning, the result from the Townsend hair analysis came back from the DNA lab. It's the same guy."

"Wait, you're saying the same man left hairs behind at both the Watson and the Townsend crime scenes?" She wanted to jump up and down.

"Exactly," Fradella confirmed.

"If that hair belongs to Bradley Welsh, no way he can justify it being at the Townsends," she added.

"Bradley Welsh still doesn't make sense," Michowsky intervened on the call. "If we get a warrant, I guarantee you it'll come back as no match. Then we have nothing; just a confirmed correlation between the Watson and Townsend cases we already had."

She didn't reply; just mulled over her own thoughts.

"Gary, how sure are you of Bradley Welsh's alibi? Tell me again."

"Sheesh, Tess, what the hell," he grunted. "I know how to check a goddamned alibi."

"Just humor me, please," she insisted.

"Um, he took all his corporate staff and their spouses to a dinner. More than 130 people in total. His wife too. They reserved an entire restaurant, that sort of thing. Open bar, open menu. They had beaten the sales goals for the year, or something like that; it was an employee appreciation dinner. He went there with his wife about 4:30PM and didn't leave until almost midnight."

"You spoke with people? He was actually there, the whole time?"

"Yes, I spoke with people, what the hell," he reacted.

"How about video? The restaurant's security tapes?"

"It was fifteen years ago. It was back in the day when not everything was on video all the time. There was no video."

"How far was the restaurant from the Watson's residence?"

"I'd say about ten minutes or so."

"What if he snuck out? Disappeared for a half hour or so, got the job done, then came back?"

"You're reaching, Winnett," Gary replied. "Here we go again; I'll explain it one more time. He would have known Laura existed. He would have killed her. The kid would've recognized him. He wouldn't have raised her as his own daughter. There's nothing here; admit it. We still got nothing."

"Yeah, you might be right," she said. "I'll give you that, if you'll admit he could've snuck out of that party for half an hour without anyone noticing. People tend to forget to check attendance every few minutes during large parties with an open bar. He was their host, of course they said he was there, but that doesn't mean he was there the entire time."

"I still think you're still reaching, but yeah, it could have happened the way you're saying. Only in theory," he underlined, still acting defensive. "I don't believe it did, though. No way."

"Then I still want that warrant processed, the one for Welsh's DNA."

"Gladly, so we can end this goddamn senseless conversation, all right?"

"Gary," she asked, after a few seconds of thinking, "why didn't the Watsons attend the appreciation dinner?"

Silence took over the call, and the system amplified the background noises in the Sheriff's Office conference room.

"No idea," Gary finally replied.

"Um, is Doc there?"

"Good morning, Tess," Doc said, joining the conference call.

"Ah, good morning, Doc. Hey, can you please make sure there wasn't any excluded evidence, or any other hair strand in any of the other cases we're looking at? The Meyers, but also all the nine cases lined up on the case board?"

"I've done that already, and we have nothing. No DNA evidence in any of those cases."

"Thanks, guys. Great work, by the way," she added, then hung up.

She pulled into the FBI parking lot as her phone chimed with an alert. Immediately, her phone rang, and Fradella greeted her again.

"Have you seen it?"

"No, not yet, what's up?"

"The missing persons alert. A young girl, fits The Chameleon's type. Monica Delgado. She vanished last night from Fort Lauderdale. She never made it back from grocery shopping."

"Who's working it?"

"Broward County."

"Tell them we're taking over. Why do we hear about it so late?"

"You know the drill, twenty-four hours waiting period for any missing persons. They actually put it in the system early, because of our alert."

"Send the details to me."

Tess cut the engine and accessed her email. The alert had a photo attached. She opened it, and she felt her blood freeze in her veins. Monica Delgado could have been Laura Watson's twin sister.

44

Media

Tess arrived on the FBI floor before eight, coffee in hand, getting ready for a long, unpleasant conversation with her boss. She'd hoped for a few minutes of reprieve, to log onto DIVS and see all the details regarding Monica Delgado's disappearance, but SAC Pearson was already in his office.

She rushed over and knocked twice on the opened door. He invited her in without a word. He didn't look happy; his face was all scrunched up and two vertical, deep ridges flanked his tense mouth.

"Winnett," he said, "take a seat."

She obeyed without a word.

"Guess who called me already. Bradley Welsh, with one of the most expensive attorneys that money can buy in Miami on the call with him."

"Oh," she reacted, and locked eyes with him. "So early?"

"Yeah. Dispatch put them through to my cell; they claimed it was an emergency."

Tess refrained from asking Pearson how that call went. By the looks of it, not well, and he was going to share the details anyway.

"I'll spare you the endless list of legal threats. In conclusion, if the girl refuses protective custody, there's nothing we can do. They'll fight the warrant and they'll win, and that's even if we manage to get a judge to sign it in the first place."

"But she'll die!" Tess exclaimed, springing from her chair. "He tried already and narrowly failed. It was a matter of luck and of Laura's reactions. She was quick enough to sense that her steering was shot, and she'd already started braking when she hit the guardrail. He'll come after her again, and this time, he won't fail."

Pearson waved the argument away, then loosened his tie with an angry, rushed gesture, as if he couldn't breathe. "There's nothing you can do, Winnett. She's not testifying; she's not a gang member. I don't think anyone will sign that warrant anyway. Everything we have is speculation. And if you do convince a judge to sign it, we're on notice by the Welsh family attorney to notify them immediately. They'll fight it. I don't know why, but they will. They made that abundantly clear."

"That's exactly it, sir," she said, leaning over his desk. "Why are they fighting it in the first place?"

"That question, if it has an answer to begin with, is yours to answer, Winnett. Do you have a suspect list narrowed down? Do you have any evidence? Anything?"

"We found matching DNA at the scenes of both the Watson and Townsend cases. No match in CODIS though, and nothing to match it against. I want to go after Bradley Welsh for a sample."

"There's nothing, absolutely nothing to justify that! He's rock solid, with a confirmed alibi, a clean record, and nearly fifteen years of being that girl's parent! Have you lost your mind? The judge will throw that warrant in your face, Winnett."

"A girl went missing last night; she looks just like Laura Watson, and I believe—"

"Could be coincidental; could be nothing."

"Then I *have* nothing, and if that's the case, I'll arrest Laura as soon as the hospital releases her. It will buy us more time."

"On what charges?" Pearson asked angrily. It was his turn to stand abruptly, and now the two of them were in each other's faces, with just a narrow desk between them.

"Obstruction," she replied. "I can hold her for twenty-four hours, and that could mean she gets to live for one more day."

"Listen to me, Winnett, because I'm about to give you an order. You'll do no such thing; do you understand me? You'll—"

Pearson's desk phone rang, and he picked up, irritably, on speaker. It was the front desk.

"What?"

"Sorry, sir, but we have a crowd of reporters downstairs asking for you and Agent Winnett, by name."

"All right, I'll be there shortly," he replied, somewhat subdued. "What the hell did you do this time, Winnett?"

She repressed a shuddered sigh, feeling adrenaline rush through her body. Her already tense relationship with her boss didn't need any more tension.

"Nothing, I—"

"Come with me," he said, then led the way to the elevators. "Keep it short, and watch what you're saying."

He didn't say a word during the elevator ride down; he didn't even look at her. When the doors opened, they saw the press gathered in the visitors' lobby.

The elevator chime had alerted the crowd and they rushed forward, stopping at the locked glass doors. Pearson signaled them from the distance with a raised hand, urging them to wait patiently, as the two hastened toward the front lobby. The moment Pearson stepped into that lobby, the clamor of cameras and questions erupted.

One voice rose above everyone else's.

"Agent Pearson, we heard that The Family Man didn't kill the Watson family. Is that true? Is it true he's going after The Watson Girl?"

Pearson held both his hands up and outward, in a gesture aiming to quiet the clamor enough to make himself heard. "We have no evidence to substantiate such a claim. You are...?"

"I am sure Agent Winnett believes differently," the reporter continued, unfazed. She was a quick, bold woman with a crooked, all-knowing smile that drove Tess crazy.

"And how, might I ask, have you acquired this information?" Pearson asked, not before casting a quick, disappointed glance in Tess's direction. She stood right by his side, holding her head up, and her face cast in stone.

"A little birdie told me, sir. You know, the bird species protected by the First Amendment?" The reporter's crooked smile widened.

"Where was this bird singing? At least that much you could share?"

"In one of many hospital hallways," the reporter offered. "Now it's your turn, sir. Is it true?"

Pearson pursed his lips before continuing. "It's a theory we've explored, nothing more. Not even a viable one, for that matter."

"Agent Winnett?" the reporter asked, shoving a fuzzy microphone in her face. "It's our duty to consider any possible theory, especially when the man thought responsible for the murders is about to be executed."

"Will he get a stay?" another reporter asked, a short, balding man with a stentorian voice.

"No, we're not asking for one," Tess replied dryly. "He confessed to killing thirty-two families. His execution will take place as scheduled."

The clamor picked up a notch.

"Why thirty-two?" the stentorian voice asked. "I had him down for thirty-four, and if he didn't kill the Watsons, then that would be thirty-three? Your numbers don't add up, Agent Winnett."

"Shit, Winnett," Pearson muttered.

45

Trapped

The first light of dawn had burned through some of the darkness, making its way inside the cabin through a small window and countless cracks in the walls, where the logs didn't align properly. She was grateful for every bit of daylight she could get, after a terrifying night spent chained to the wall, seeing nothing, hearing the constant chirping of insects and croaking of frogs.

Through a haze, she recalled being hit on the back of her head, out of the blue, when she'd stopped to check on a flat tire. She didn't see anyone coming; she'd just felt the blow, then nothing. Nothing, until she woke up as the man who took her tore her clothes off and chained her to the wall.

She remembered begging him and crying endless tears, but he didn't budge. He just went through with stripping her naked, but then left her there, alone. Before he disappeared, he caressed her face, tugged gently at her hair, then told her, "Wait for me, my darling girl. You'll be... electrifying, you'll see." Then he licked his thumb, where he'd wiped her tears, tasting her pain.

It was already dark outside when he left, and he turned the light off, leaving her to scream in complete darkness and tugging desperately at her chains, while her mind imagined hordes of snakes and spiders crawling on the humid floor and all over her body. She screamed and screamed until she was breathless, then stopped, with her throat raw and her mind darkened by a panic so brutal it numbed her. She let herself slip into nothingness and spent most of the night half-faint, sobbing every time she came to, only to faint again later, exhausted. Then she realized; there was no one outside to hear her. Otherwise, the man would have taped her mouth shut.

The first light of day brought some relief to her fears. As soon as she could see clearly enough, she noticed there weren't any snakes or spiders near her. A wolf spider's luminescent eyes stared at her from a few feet away, sheltered under the bed. She followed the spider with her eyes, only to notice the floor was stained, right next to the bedposts.

She crawled as close to the bed as the chains let her and studied the stains.

"Oh, no; oh, no," she started to cry. "Oh, God, no; please don't let that be blood."

She sobbed, hugging her knees and leaning against the damp wall, forcing her eyes shut to block out the disturbing image of the dried bloodstain on the floor. Her imagination ran wild with scenarios of how that blood got there. When she opened her eyes again, the log cabin was flooded with the morning light, revealing even more details of her prison.

She was in hell, a real, tangible hell run by a sick, gruesome man.

Two of the walls were lined with all sorts of objects, hanging in a horrific display of torture implements, some reminding her of the medieval Dark Ages. Floggers, whips, belts, canes, handcuffs, all sorts of dildos, and spreader bars, arranged neatly and ready for use. A wooden cross hung from the ceiling, fitted with cuffs, and attached to a chain that could easily raise or lower it as needed. On the other wall, a collection of blades was on display, from the finest, smallest of scalpels, to full-sized military and hunting knives.

Her wide-opened eyes took all that horror in, her heart battering against her chest, as she understood she was trapped in there, with no way out. Then she screamed again, even if she knew no one would ever hear her.

46

Reflections: A Glossy Feather

Could someone please tell me, how can I be rid of The Watson Girl? What the hell is wrong with her? She escaped me, fifteen years ago, and now she managed to live, after a professional hit went down? What the hell? Is she a cat, or something? Has nine fucking lives?

Yes, I'm livid, ever since last night, when I heard about her *accident* when I was traveling for business, setting up my alibi for my feast with lovely Monica. I should have heard about her death instead.

What makes it worse is I'm constantly haunted by fantasies, by this intense urge to possess Laura's body completely. I close my eyes and I see *her*, not Monica, naked and chained against my log cabin's wall, waiting for me to return, imagining what I would do to her. I'm aching to hear her take a last gasp of air as I plunge my—

I need to stop that, right this second. It could never happen; she's too dangerous a kill.

She's ruined everything for me, Laura. I lived fifteen years wondering if her memory would ever return. I agonized year after year, watching her grow into my wildest, most consuming fantasy, and ripening into the forbidden fruit I could never enjoy.

Finally, after fifteen years of torment, she was supposed to be dead, while I celebrated the news with the next best thing I could find, to help me get over the frustration I feel about not being able to touch her. Now I'm so angry, I'm afraid I could make mistakes. I just ran a red light, minutes ago, and stupid shit like that can get me busted.

I hate feeling like this, tense, on edge, hunted. Predators like me are never afraid. I don't fret about it, I only get more careful about what I want to do, that's all. Fear doesn't rule me; it never has.

From another point of view, I can't believe what a lame hitman I hired. In my defense, it's not like I could get on Yellow Pages and browse the ads and check references. Murder for hire is a tricky business. Every time I asked around, I risked my life. Then, finally, I got to the source, some dark web directory of, um, let's call them unofficial services, and I found someone willing to talk to me.

He had a long list of instructions for how to proceed. I had to buy a new, cheap computer, pay for it with cash, and connect to the Internet from public Wi-Fi, in a busy place with lots of traffic. I had to pay him in bitcoin, and getting that much bitcoin was another challenge. Finally, he quoted me fifty grand, but then tripled the price when he saw who the mark was. Said if he'd get caught, he'd go down for the entire family's murder, not just Laura's, and there was no negotiating with him. All right, one hundred and fifty grand, in untraceable cash, half before, half after. A pile of dough, to rob me of the pleasure of killing Laura, slowly, to my heart's desire.

Then he fails? Seriously?

I got in touch with him early this morning, and he didn't even apologize. He said he'll keep going until the job gets done, but he needs to let some time pass until he can try again, that is if I still want things to look accidental.

I had no choice; I agreed and let him off the hook, momentarily. Later, once the job is finally done, I'll take care of him. I'll find him, don't worry. Anonymous logins and bitcoin can't keep someone hidden from me, when I'm actually looking. Then I won't kill him; not right away. I think I mentioned before that killing men doesn't do it for me, not even as revenge for having me endure all this… anticipation. I don't get anxiety; but I do get impatient, and I do have deadlines he completely missed. He's history; he just doesn't know it yet.

For that, for all the angst I'm suffering right now, he'll have to watch. If he's ever loved anything or anyone in his lame existence, he'll have to sit there, bound and gagged, and watch me destroy it, slowly, painfully, making it last, making it memorable. At the very end, I'll take mercy on his soul and put his lights out with one bullet to the head. He's not even worth the touch of my blade. Fucking bastard.

That aside, there was a piece of mixed news this morning. I watched the TV in my Tampa hotel room and saw a breaking-news segment. The bad part was that the FBI suspects Garza didn't kill the Watsons, and they might suspect more. The really good part is that apparently the only FBI agent who does suspect that is a woman, Tess Winnett. She's local, here, in Miami.

She looks good. Maybe a little old for my taste; she's around thirty. But she's a fine-looking creature; blonde, thin, and her blue eyes can be loaded with such passion.

Her boss seemed to be eager to close this so-called fact-checking thing Winnett is doing; but she's pushing back. She cut him off in front of the cameras. I swear to you, if you'd do that to me, they'd never find your body.

That made me think… Cops die all the time, and whenever one bites it, a long list of people they put behind bars would be suspected, before they consider other scenarios. Before anyone even correlates her death with the Watson case. They wouldn't dream it was me.

What if this Agent Winnett—no, let's call her Tess. She and I will get intimately acquainted soon. Again, what if Tess died? I don't think anyone would be so eager to pick up her work where she left off, right? The rest of the feds would be busy investigating her death and forget all about Garza, especially after he fries next week.

Of course, that won't take care of Laura, but I can't touch her, to my utmost regret. I keep saying that… It's my obsession. While Laura's waiting for what's coming to her, those shrink sessions might still yield some surprises, but is that a valid risk? I think that if she had anything locked in that brain of hers, she would have remembered by now. I heard that she's been doing sessions daily and still nothing. I think I'm good there, at least for a while.

I also believe that if I focus on Tess Winnett, the shrink will send Laura packing the moment she hears the investigation got unhealthy for one of the participants. I could always help that Dr. Jacobs see the truth with an anonymous phone call or something.

FBI Special Agent Tess Winnett. Now that's a lush feather for my cap. As I'm starting to think about it, to plan it, I feel aroused, incited. A worthy adversary, one who would fight me like none other.

I shift in my seat and crank up the car's AC a couple of notches. I won't get to enjoy Monica until later tonight, but just thinking of Tess gives me a massive, almost painful hard-on.

47

Roadblocks

Tess felt a headache starting to grip her skull with an iron clench. She rubbed her forehead vigorously, hoping to scare away the pain, then took a bite from a stale donut, the last one left in a box Fradella had picked up on his way in, early that morning.

It had been a hectic, infuriating day, filled with dead ends and roadblocks. By the time Fradella was arriving at the office carrying donuts and coffee, she'd already started her day with an unscheduled meeting with SAC Pearson at the FBI headquarters, followed by a less-than-fortunate press conference. After that had mercifully ended, the subsequent conversation she'd had with a fuming Pearson had taken another two hours. He wanted to know every single detail of the case and had countless questions about every conclusion she'd drawn and every assumption she'd made.

She'd been angry and disheartened the whole time during their talk, mostly with herself and her inability to get ahead in her investigation. Not to mention the slip of the tongue with Garza's case count in front of the press, which led to a crossfire with the reporters she didn't expect she'd survive.

Then SAC Pearson surprised her, by quoting statistics on cold cases she already knew. Four percent, nationwide, was the clearance rate for all cold cases, regardless of which law enforcement unit investigated them. Of course, local numbers varied somewhat, but overall, nationally, that was it: 4 percent. Most of the cold case success stories she'd read about were due to the scientific advancements in forensic science and little else.

She had DNA on her side now, although DNA had also been there to help investigators fifteen years earlier. Another major reason for unsolved cases was tunnel vision, and she'd encountered that in all three family murders. The previous investigators refused to consider all possible suspects, just because Garza had been conveniently available. As for the other nine cold cases on the board, they stood in testimony of the less-than-stellar national clearance case for murder cases in general: about 65 percent. Most people have no idea that one third of killers get away with it, in modern-day America.

Well, not when she's on the case. While SAC Pearson quoted the statistics, she only thought of the missing girl, Monica Delgado, and her chances of still being alive. She wanted to pore over every single missing-persons case with a fine-tooth comb, and see what she could find. But Pearson only gave her twenty-four more hours and what was supposed to be an encouraging speech, preparing her for failure.

As soon as he dismissed her, she went straight to Palm Beach County, where Michowsky and Fradella were interviewing the "arson five," as they called them. They were the five men who matched the profile—who had one rape charge in their past, followed by successful reintegration into society, had the right age, and had set a minor fire in their youth.

It was almost mid-afternoon when she told Michowsky to release the lot. One had served time for statutory rape, an obvious mistake. One look in his eyes, and Tess knew there wasn't a single violent bone in his body. The rest either had alibis or just didn't make sense, having never crossed paths with the Watson family or any other murdered family since them. As of very recently, the matching hairs found at both Watson and Townsend crime scenes served as an additional elimination factor, and it completely cleared their suspect list. None of those men had raven black hair. It was another dead end.

They regrouped into the conference room, discouraged and grim.

"What now?" Michowsky asked. "I don't see another hat trick in our future."

Tess fired up her laptop and immediately heard the new email chime.

"They found Monica's car," she said, feeling energized, then summarized the message. "It was abandoned on a side road, with a flat tire. They're looking at it now, but so far there are no fingerprints or anything on it. Last night it was pouring rain, so they don't expect to find anything on the car or around it. Inside so far, no bloodstains, nothing we can use."

The other message got them to hop on their feet and rush downstairs to the forensics lab, where the mangled remains of Laura Watson's car was being inspected.

"Hey, Javier," Tess greeted the young forensics technician, as soon as they entered the lab. "Talk to me."

"Hey, Agent Tess," he said, giving her a wide smile adorned by beautiful, white teeth.

"It's either Agent Winnett, or Tess," she replied, smiling back. "Make up your mind, already."

"Just wait until I show you what I found. You'll let me call you anything I want."

Michowsky and Fradella put their heads closer, looking where Javier was pointing, deep inside the guts of the car's engine compartment. She approached on the other side.

"Steering was definitely tampered with," Javier said, speaking with excitement. "The real surprise was how. You see this piece of metal, encroached there?"

She squinted a little, but Javier promptly put his flashlight on the object in question.

"We were lucky, you see. This is part of a microcharge device."

"A bomb?"

"A very tiny, little bomb, yes," he confirmed. "Remotely detonated by some form of transmitter, most likely radio. It blew up the steering fluid pressure hose, and the whole steering system drained within seconds."

"And she didn't feel the explosion?" Michowsky asked.

"This would have been quieter than a champagne pop. I'm talking about a state of the art, *Mission Impossible,* kind of device."

"That's awesome, Javier," she said, then hugged him. "Finally, a lead we can trace. Call me anything you want."

"How about any *time?*" he asked, then winked.

"Ah, let's not go there," she laughed, but felt her cheeks warm.

"One more thing," Javier added. "Whoever did this was very close and detonated when he thought he'd make the most damage. This device is close range; very close. Just a few yards, maybe twenty, but not more. He underestimated the speed at which the power steering fluid would drain; I think he wanted her to hit the guardrail somewhere over the Dolphin and Palmetto interchange. If he'd detonated thirty seconds later, your vic would be history, falling from a considerable height, and most likely bursting into flames upon crashing onto the freeway down below."

A few minutes later, they were back upstairs into the conference room.

"This was a professional hit," Tess said, her face reflecting the confusion she felt. "I didn't see that coming."

"Could The Chameleon be ex-military, or commandoes, or something?" Fradella asked, not even trying to hide his excitement.

"The two profiles are in serious contradiction. Our unsub is a power-lusting psychopath. You don't find those in the military, where they have to take orders all day long. They'd never survive."

"Then, what's your theory?" Fradella asked.

"If The Chameleon is not military, and this was the work of a professional, he could have emulated or hired one. A hitman. I'd go with hired."

"What kind of serial killer delegates his killing?" Michowsky asked. "I've never heard of it."

Silence engulfed the room for a second.

"A very smart one," Tess finally replied. "Now we know a little more about him. He's not only incredibly smart, but he's loaded, can move cash freely, and he's probably got an alibi for that night. I know just whose finances I want to look at."

"Come on, don't start, not again," Michowsky said.

"Speaking of Mr. Welsh, how's that warrant coming along?"

"The judge said he needed a few hours to think about it. He really grilled us over it, though. How about the warrant you filed for Laura's protective custody?"

She scrunched her lips and frowned.

"The judge threw me out of chambers; I got nothing. If Pearson had made the call, maybe the outcome would have been different, but he didn't, and that's that. Is your man still at the hospital?"

"Yeah, and he's off the clock," Michowsky replied. "He's doing it pro bono. Our captain pulled the plug; until this moment, we had no probable cause. Now we do, so guess where I'm going."

"I'll try that warrant again; maybe now we'll get it signed," Tess offered, sounding unconvinced.

A young uniformed officer knocked on the door, then put his head in.

"This is for you, Detective," he said, then handed Michowsky a letter.

He opened the envelope and extracted the papers inside.

"Just like I expected. The Welsh DNA warrant has been denied. It made no sense to begin with; I'm not surprised. Listen to this," he muttered, then read from the judge's letter. "'There's not nearly enough evidence to support the invasion of privacy of a church-going, outstanding pillar of our community and substantial contributor to numerous charities.' Can you believe it?"

Tess hopped to her feet, muttering a long, detailed curse. She couldn't sit idle and feel better, just because the cold case statistics were on her side if she failed. Not with Monica Delgado still missing.

"Yeah, I'm not surprised either, but I won't give up, you know." She grabbed her keys and headed for the door.

"Whoa, take it easy, partner," Michowsky said, "where you going?"

Her frown deepened, as she weighed her options. Bradley Welsh had just filed a formal complaint with the Bureau that very morning, so she stood no chance of asking him nicely for a DNA sample. But she was going there anyway, and somehow she was going to get that sample.

"You two follow the contract killer lead. Not many places supply microcharge detonators. As for me, I will tempt fate. I'm going to pay the Welsh family a visit."

"Tess, it can't be him. Why are you risking your career over this… nonsense?" Michowsky insisted.

"I know it's most likely not him. But wouldn't you like to be sure? Absolutely, positively sure? Sorry, Gary, but I can't settle for anything less."

48

A Visit

Tess waited in front of the Welsh family residence for a good minute after ringing the doorbell. She had her badge out, but doubted she was going to need it, being that at least Mrs. Welsh knew her personally. She'd decided to speak with Mrs. Welsh, and not ask for the man whose DNA she was after. Not at first, anyway.

The property was surrounded by its own private oasis, a landscaped paradise with palm trees, palmettos, and flowering shrubs, providing privacy and shade, and hosting a plethora of birds. Their evening chirping was the only sound she could hear; all the greenery surrounding the property muffled the distant city noises, creating an atmosphere of complete serenity. She'd expected nothing less from the founder and CEO of WatWel Lighting, but she couldn't help admiring the imposing home and its peaceful surroundings.

Carol Welsh opened the door and stood in the doorway, rigid and tense in her business pantsuit, staring Tess down with a direct, condescending look. Then she stepped to the side, making room for Tess to walk in.

"You have some nerve showing up here," she said through clenched jaws, almost spitting the words out. She closed the door behind Tess, slamming it to make her point. Then she turned to face Tess, with her hands propped firmly on her hips, and the same glare filled with contempt. "What can I do for you?"

Tess looked around, taking in as much information as she could. She was in the two-story foyer, and Mrs. Welsh was blocking her access to the massive living room.

Just like Laura's apartment, only on a much bigger scale, lamps and fixtures of all sorts and designs adorned the home, from what she could see. The foyer's walls were covered in hundreds of small, triangular shadows, projected by a one-of-a-kind chandelier. It had three staggered circular layers of triangular elements carved in brushed metal, pointing up, each hiding behind it a small, but powerful light source, probably LED. Each triangle seemed unique, with bases of about two inches and about three inches tall, but irregular shaped and almost wavy, as if made of soft fabric and blown upward by the wind. The effect was exquisite;

each light source projected shadows on the walls, multiplied countless times.

"Are you here to stare at the lamp, Agent Winnett?" Mrs. Welsh asked.

Tess snapped back to reality and met Mrs. Welsh's burning glare.

"No, although it's a striking piece. I've never seen anything like it."

"My husband dabbles with design sometimes. What can I do for you?"

"Not for me, for Laura," Tess replied. "Please convince her to go voluntarily into protective custody."

Mrs. Welsh dropped her glare to the ground and with it, her shoulders dropped too. When she looked up, all the contempt was gone; only the worried mother was left. She absentmindedly browsed the collection of family photos framed on the wall. Throughout the years, the Welshes had been good parents to both their own daughter, Amanda, and Laura. Ski trips, Christmases in Lake Tahoe, summers in the Caribbean, smiling faces, lots of fun and color, with the two adults always there, watchful while enjoying the two girls participating in their games.

"It took years, you know, to get that girl back on her feet. Can you imagine? Having to live through what she did?"

For a second, Mrs. Welsh looked like she was about to cry. Her chin trembled slightly, and her eyes misted. But she took a sharp breath of air and recomposed herself. "Did you know she didn't speak for years?" she continued, hiding her emotions better, but not entirely. "Not a single sound, no laughter, nothing. For years. We worried she might have been lost forever, unable to forget the most terrible nightmare a child could live through."

Mrs. Welsh lowered her eyelids for a second and took another deep breath. "Therapy, struggles, countless socialization efforts, a painful few years. Then one day she spoke; she called my name, like she used to do before that night. Auntie Carol, that's what she called me. That's what she still calls me. I was so happy... we celebrated, we played music and danced with the girls, both of us. Slowly, from that day onward, she recovered, got caught up with school, and grew up as a healthy, normal child. She's about to finish school and join Brad at the helm of the company. She was happy until a few days ago." Her voice had hardened somewhat, as if she was getting angrier with every word. "Then you come in, and blow everything out of the water. I just wish you'd disappear and leave her alone."

"If Kenneth Garza didn't kill her family, wouldn't you want the real killer held accountable? Wouldn't you like Laura to be safe again?"

"How dare you talk to me about her safety, when you people lied to us all these years? *You* put her life in jeopardy, you and the other troublemaker, Dr. Jacobs, that busybody, that wild goose chaser who's responsible for Laura's returning nightmares and panic attacks. And now you want my help to put my daughter in jail? Or send her to Montana somewhere, to pack groceries at Walmart for ten an hour, until you incompetents catch a killer you didn't manage to catch in fifteen years? I think this conversation is over, Agent Winnett. Please leave."

Tess raised her hands in the air, in a pacifying gesture. Somehow, the rapport she thought she was building had vanished, dissipated by very rational arguments that fueled Mrs. Welsh's parental anger. But she couldn't leave; not just yet, not without having a shot at the DNA sample she'd come to get.

"Before I do," she replied calmly, "may I please speak with Mr. Welsh?"

"He's not in right now. Contact our attorney and set up a meeting. He'll be happy to help when he comes back from travel. Your boss has his number."

"Oh, I see," she replied. "Can I please use your restroom?"

"There are gas stations, you know," Mrs. Welsh replied, her old condescending glare returning in full force.

Tess remained calm and smiled. "Please. It won't take long."

Mrs. Welsh pointed at a door just a few feet away, then promptly crossed her arms at her chest.

Tess nodded once, then entered the small half-bathroom. She closed the door gently, then turned on the sink faucet. The perfectly clean marble counter was completely empty, except for a brand-new liquid soap bottle and a neatly folded hand towel. The medicine cabinet was also empty and wiped clean.

She opened drawers quietly, one by one, only to find two spare rolls of toilet paper, nothing else. No toothbrushes, no loose hairs on the sink, nothing.

She kneeled on the soft, blue carpet and squinted in the dim light, but saw no hairs anywhere. Finally, she shoved her fingers in the shower drain and dug in there, but came back empty. She frowned, wondering who cleans their shower drain that perfectly. Then she realized that the small half-bath was probably reserved for guests, wanted or not so much, and that shower stall had probably never been used.

She flushed the toilet, then washed her hands and dried them on the small towel. As she opened the door to step back into the hallway, Bradley Welsh was coming through the door leading to the garage.

He froze when he laid eyes on her, then his eyes filled with the same burning contempt she'd seen in his wife.

"The nerve you have—" he started, but his wife cut him off.

"My words, exactly. Agent Winnett was just leaving."

Tess straightened her back and extended her hand to Mr. Welsh, but he ignored it, continuing to stare her down.

"Please, Mr. Welsh," she said, as persuasively as she could, "Laura will be released from the hospital today. Please help me help her."

Their eyes met, and Tess felt a chill down her spine. There was something in his cold, blue stare; not just contempt or hate; it was something that reminded her of her own personal ordeal, of the look her attacker had given her years before, as he was tying her down, ripping her clothes off, and getting ready to rape her. A look of lust, of blood thirst, of anticipation.

But how can that gut feeling be reconciled with the family pictures she saw on the wall? That man on the wall was the real Bradley Welsh; years and years of photographic evidence, lined up and displayed on the wall for everyone to see. The love his daughters had for him, that meant something; that was a testimony to who Bradley Welsh really was. And still... those eyes...

She repressed a shudder; she didn't have time to worry about that; instead, her eyes desperately screened his jacket for any loose hairs that could have fallen from his head. He wore his hair much shorter than before, less than half an inch in length. He probably dyed it too, because not a single white hair was visible.

There it was, right above his elbow, a barely visible strand of hair, black against the light gray of his jacket. She calculated her move and clenched her jaws. It was going to be now or probably never.

"Please call me if you—" she started saying, and offered her business card.

"I can't tell Laura what to do, Agent Winnett. I can't and I won't," Mrs. Welsh said, and opened the door for her.

As she headed toward the door, she passed Mr. Welsh and pretended to trip. To stabilize herself, she grabbed his sleeve, in apparent reflex.

"Christ!" he growled, moving away from her and pulling his sleeve from her grasp. He didn't even try to help her get her footing back, but she didn't need him to.

"I'm so sorry," Tess said in a humble voice. "I... well, thank you," she added, and stepped outside. She heard the door slam behind her and didn't look back. Her hair still stood on end at the back of her head, and a chill traveled up and down her spine, restlessly.

She didn't open her right fist until she was in her car, and when she did, she saw a hair there, as black as a raven's feather. With a wide grin, she took out an evidence bag and sealed the tiny hair, then drove off with a smile.

"Got you now, Mr. pillar-of-the-community, church-going, gives-me-the-creeps Welsh."

49

A Sensible Plan

The main difference between you and me is, I don't hesitate. When something needs to be done, I get it done. No delay, no denial. Normally, you *do* hesitate, and waste countless hours, days, even years, weighed down by your conscience and by your overwhelming anxieties. You endlessly ask yourself, What if I get caught? What if something happens? What if… What if?

I don't worry, I plan. Hence, I don't get caught, because I plan well.

Someone once said something that stuck with me and helped me shape my life. I think it was a historian, something-Parkinson was his name. He said, "Delay is the deadliest form of denial." It applies to everything, no matter the circumstance, from your always procrastinated cancer screening to everything else your anxiety enslaves you into fearing, but never facing. You think that if you don't get that cancer screening done, you're in fact healthy? No, it just postpones the moment you, a terrified, vulnerable human being, must deal with your reality, while your initially small problem grows unseen into a death sentence. But how do you know that you won't celebrate, once negative results come your way, eliminating all that angst? Why do you always expect the worst?

I don't.

My problem is now still small, but it has the potential of growing into the killer of me, if I let it. Therefore, I won't. Thankfully, I don't have the ball and chain normally referred to as conscience to hold me back, and that means I will deal with my lovely Tess this very evening. She's becoming a nuisance, and delay is, as I was quoting, the deadliest form of denial.

I'm also getting ready for my evening with Monica, and for a few minutes, I close my eyes and envision the two of them together, Tess and Monica, all ready for me, waiting for me, screaming for me. How would that play out? How incredibly delicious would that be? What kind of rush would that give me? I bet it would be unprecedented, a new level of exhilaration, a new beginning.

But let's get real here, despite the already bothersome erection that's been keeping me company the whole day. We're talking about an experienced federal agent, someone trained to kill. Someone who's killed before, and, who knows, might even enjoy it. Mmm… just how awesome would that be, if I could possess a killer, a true hunter, slowly, enticingly?

It's a good thing I have a steeled willpower, you know. I can always take a cold shower, and kill her quickly and effectively, without taking the risk that she kills me instead. No woman is worth that. No matter how wonderful, there are others better than her out there. If I want a night of fascinating sex with a federal agent, I can always pick me another one, someone who's maybe a little younger, and who won't see me coming.

Long story short, I need to deny myself this rush in favor of pragmatism, and get the job done quickly, quietly, and without getting shot in the process.

Tess Winnett is not an apple for me to enjoy; she's a countermeasure.

I don't think I ever mentioned how grateful I am for people being so vain and so careless, leaving their windows uncovered after dusk and allowing me to see everything there is to see from a safe distance. My work would be infinitely more difficult if it weren't for this… honestly, I don't know what *this* is. A trend? A fashion? Vanity, to let everyone see what nice furniture they have and all that? I've always wondered about people who watch TV with their curtains wide open at night, so that everyone sees their new LED screen and surround system, don't they like to watch their movies half-naked, like I do? Don't they need to scratch their balls occasionally? Do they ever do it? Do they care that they're seen by people like me? Are they, in fact, exhibitionists? Do they secretly get off, knowing people like me are out there, watching? Craving? Dreaming?

It makes my life and my work so easy, I was saying. I just walk down the street, in a strolling pace, and take it all in. What neighbors are home, what time, what do they do? What time is dinner? How many kids? Is there a husband or a dog? I will know. Is she coming home every day at about the same time? I'm there, watching, and, thanks to the age of all-window transparency, I'm seeing.

The same happened with Tess, you know. I already know she lives alone, in a high-rise apartment. Yes, even if the object of my desires lives in an apartment on the umpteenth floor, I can still see, from the building across the street, using binoculars, even infrared imaging if I need to. All it takes is uncovered windows.

I know she comes home late at night, and sometimes she skips dinner altogether. I know she rarely leaves her gun out of her reach, and that's what changed my plans, from savoring her to just eliminating her. I know she likes things simple, and her apartment doesn't have a lot of furniture, which will make my mission even more difficult, if I plan on surprising her. Finally, I know I must be patient. I'll be there, waiting for her to come home tonight, but it could be hours before she arrives.

However, after she's left this world, I can immerse myself in the wonderful Monica.

50

At the Morgue

Tess waited impatiently, propped up on a three-legged stool next to Doc Rizza's lab table. Not saying a word, she watched him turn the knobs on his microscope, while he mumbled something only he could hear.

She'd pulled him away from his home at that late hour and felt guilty about it, seeing the deep, dark circles under his eyes and his tired gait, but she couldn't bear to wait until the following morning. If she was right, despite all evidence and all logic, and Bradley Welsh was a serial killer, she wanted him arrested immediately, not a moment later. Maybe there was still hope for Monica.

"I'm sorry, Tess," Doc Rizza said, then took off his glasses and pinched the bridge of his nose, where the frames had left reddish indents from prolonged wear. "There's no follicle attached to this hair. We can't pull DNA."

"You can't be serious, Doc. Please don't tell me that."

"Unfortunately, I got nothing else I can tell. I even compared the hair you took today, with the ones we had on file from the old crime scene."

"And?" she pressed on impatiently and hopped off her stool. It was easier to maintain her calm if she paced the floor in the quiet, dimly lit morgue.

"It's not definitive, either way. The new strand is thinner than the old one. Could that mean it's not the same person? Yes, but it could also mean his hair thinned with age. It happens; it's quite common actually. I ran a mineral analysis, and it's not a match with the old hairs. Again, that's not definitive either way. Environmental factors, toxins, nutrients, even drug prescriptions vary over such lengths of time."

"We got nothing, that's what you're saying, Doc?"

"To begin with, hair analysis is only admissible in court to exclude someone; never to include. We couldn't do that either. The new hair isn't so different from the old ones to exclude Bradley Welsh. But it doesn't include him either. In fifteen years, the man's hair could have changed enough to warrant the differences we see today, but I can't be sure; not even off the record." He sighed and flipped off the switch to his electronic microscope. "I guess you could say we have nothing more than we had before you went to visit the Welshes."

She swallowed a long, detailed curse. Doc didn't deserve to hear her outburst, so she clammed up. After a few seconds, she felt her calm slowly return, bringing clarity of thinking with it.

"All I wanted was to be 100 percent sure, Doc, one way or another," she said sadly, staring at the floor's cement mosaic pattern.

"Life isn't precise, you know," Doc said. "We try our best, but we don't always succeed."

"You're right, Doc," she replied with a faint smile. "You're a wise man." She paused, but Doc didn't interrupt her chain of thought. "I struggle with this one, Doc," she eventually said. "You should see the pictures on their walls. You should see how Laura looked into his eyes, holding his hand, when she was seven or eight years old. No way in hell she did that if he'd killed her parents, right?"

"You'd think so, yes."

"And yet, when *I* looked into his eyes, I froze. There was something in there that… I couldn't explain," she said, avoiding specifics that could have led to countless questions about her personal history.

Doc sighed again and shifted on his lab stool.

"Sometimes rich and powerful men are fierce like that. They're used to everyone obeying, and whenever something or someone is in their paths, they can turn aggressive. That doesn't make them killers though."

"Yeah, I guess," she admitted, but the uneasy feeling clung to her like a drenched coat.

"Who else have you got on your suspect list?"

"No one yet, but Laura's car was sabotaged, you know that."

"Uh-huh, I know the details."

"We caught a break there. The device they used is traceable. The FBI has a database of all known dealers of such devices, because they're normally used by terrorists. It's our only break. Gary and Todd are closing that one."

"Good," Doc said, and slapped his palms on his knees. "That's something. Once you find the device maker you'll get him to talk; you'll find a way."

"Yeah…" she said, almost distracted. "I checked Bradley Welsh's finances. Donovan helped me. He didn't move cash, and he was away on business travel when Monica disappeared."

"Oh, so you got a warrant after all?" Doc asked, seemingly surprised.

"You had to ask," Tess sighed with a crooked smile. "You really had to ask."

"I didn't ask anything, my dear," Doc replied with a smile. "It must have been the wind outside. It's quite nasty out there."

They both laughed.

"Now, get some rest, young lady. Welsh doesn't seem to be your guy. Maybe tomorrow you'll start fresh."

She gave the Doc a quick hug, then started toward the elevator. She stopped next to the three evidence tables, still lined up with the Watson, Meyer, and Townsend case evidence, her eyes fixed on a stab wound mold in a clear, sealed evidence bag. The more she stared at that mold, the more her gut churned, and she felt the grip of fear twisting her insides. But why? It didn't make sense.

"What's up?" Doc Rizza asked.

"Um, nothing. Just trying to figure out where I've seen this before."

"Probably in here," Doc said, and started shutting down the many pieces of equipment that furnished his lab.

Her face scrunched up, and she shook her head, as if she rejected Doc's explanation with all her being.

"Nowhere else you see these, except in a morgue or a forensics lab."

"I'll figure it out," she finally said. "Can I hold on to this?" she asked, picking up the small bag.

"Oh, no, not that one. You'd break the chain of evidence on an active case. I'll find you another one, from the autopsies I do with students, when they come in for practice."

Minutes later, she walked out of the morgue with a yellow-white piece of flexible silicone in her pocket.

51

At Home

It was late when Tess got home, but she didn't plan on going to bed; not yet. She still had a good portion of Laura's videos to watch, and she wanted to watch them all, unsure what she was going to find, but unwilling to give up the tiniest shred of hope.

She unlocked the front door and turned on the light, then locked it back up. She kicked her shoes off, and wiggled her toes against the soft carpet, feeling her soles relax after a long day, spent mostly on her feet. She took off her jacket, inspected it briefly, then scoffed with disgust feeling the faint smell of sweat and dust. She rolled it into a bunch and threw it in the laundry hamper, then pulled her shirt loose and undid a couple of buttons.

She opened the fridge and took out a can of tomato juice, then grabbed her laptop bag and put both items on the table. She fired up the laptop, then removed her holstered gun and dropped it on the table, next to the can of juice. One pop, then she gulped half the juice can thirstily. It felt good, the salty-sweet taste of fresh tomatoes, the soothing feeling of a no longer empty and growling stomach.

She let herself drop onto the couch, and promptly put her feet up on the table. With the computer on her lap, she opened the memory drive with Laura's videos. She searched a little, trying to figure out where she left off, but finally found the one she wanted to watch next.

It was a video shot on Laura's fourth birthday, because people not only asked her what her name was, but also her age. She kept giggling, and telling everyone her name was Lau'a and she was fou'. Everyone laughed warmly, ruffled her hair, or pinched her cheeks, and she only giggled more.

The two families were celebrating together. Carol Welsh and Rachel Watson were getting ready to serve the cake. Tess knew that Rachel had been a medieval history teacher, on faculty with Florida International University, had a kindness in her eyes that lit up whenever she looked at the kids. She arranged paper plates and plastic forks and didn't stop smiling. Carol Welsh carefully put four little candles on top of a big chocolate cake, with a message written in white icing, "Happy 4th Birthday, Laura!"

On the patio, the Watsons's other two kids played with oversized Legos, and, at times threw the Legos onto the lawn, competing over who threw the farthest. Rachel admonished them, then the little boy, Casey, reluctantly got to his feet and wobbled over, collecting the scattered Lego blocks and bringing them back.

To the side, the Welshes's only daughter, Amanda, who must have been about eight or nine years old at the time, sat on a patio chair a little stiff and indignant, as if offended to find herself at a party for small children. She was the only one who didn't smile; she kept her eyes stubbornly fixed on the horizon line, ignoring everyone as if she were a captive princess.

It must have been Allen Watson holding the camera, because at some point, Bradley Welsh appeared on the screen; he popped the cap off a Bud Light and, after gesturing "cheers," gulped down a good portion of the cold liquid. He then wiped his mouth with his hand, unceremoniously, then leaned back in his chair, smiling, relaxed. His half-closed eyes expressed contentment; everything was going well for Mr. Welsh that day.

Rachel summoned the kids to gather around the cake, and they all squealed as they came; of course, Amanda didn't even budge from her remote seat. Rachel patiently instructed Laura what to do, then watched over her daughter as she took a deep breath and blew out the candles. They clapped, cheered, and then sang the birthday song for her, a little out of tune and dragging.

The video cut abruptly to where Laura carried paper plates with slices of cake to everyone present. She took a paper plate out to her sister, then wobbled back to the table to get another plate. Her mother handed one to her, and she turned and started to walk unsteadily around the table.

That was the exact point where Tess had to stop watching the video the day before. She propped herself a little straighter on the couch and frowned as she concentrated on the screen.

Little Laura walked around the table, a little shy and hesitant, heading toward someone who was off camera. Then the camera followed her, and Tess watched as she headed toward Bradley Welsh. "Fo' you, Uncle B'ad," she said, and Brad tousled her hair while accepting the plate.

Tess felt a tug of uneasiness in her gut. Frowning, she paused the video and rewound a few seconds. She played the scene again. Little Laura, handing Brad the paper plate. "Fo' you, Uncle, B'ad." Brad tousling her hair, smiling, and accepting the offering. All mundane stuff.

Tess took another mouthful of tomato juice and watched the scene yet again. She couldn't figure out what was wrong, not at first. But then she realized.

"I'll be damned," she muttered under her breath. "I'll be completely damned. Illogical like hell, but what if?"

She minimized the video player window, then went to the memory card folder and sifted through the regression session videos, until she found the one she was looking for. She fast-forwarded through the sections she didn't care about, then played the scene right before Laura broke apart, time after time.

The video showed Laura lying down on Dr. Jacobs's sofa, her eyes squeezed shut, while tears ran freely down her cheeks. In her childish voice, Laura kept saying, while shaking violently, "No, no, bad; no, no bad."

What if the "bad" in Laura's regression sessions, was, in fact, "Brad"? The name she couldn't pronounce correctly as a child, just like she couldn't pronounce her own? What if, instead of remembering what she, herself had said, back then, during that terrifying night, Laura remembered what *her mother* had screamed? It could have been Rachel Watson shouting, "No, no, Brad," as her attacker plunged his knife into her abdomen.

Paper thin, illogical, not even close to the concept of evidence. Michowsky, Fradella, and most likely everyone else would say she was grasping at straws, and that she was fueling her overactive imagination with information that was irrelevant, coincidental at best.

Yet, the only question she still had in her mind was how could someone be the loving father she'd seen Bradley Welsh to be and also be the serial killer she believed he was? How can the two personas coexist within the same man?

She let her mind wander for a second or two and remembered a lecture Bill McKenzie had given some years before at Quantico. He'd said, "There's a common misconception that all psychopaths are lower intelligence, poorly integrated rejects and savages. While some of them are, the most gruesome of serial killers can appear perfectly normal on the outside. They can be loving fathers and devoted husbands. They can have successful businesses or significant professional achievement. They can lead perfectly healthy and prosperous lives on the surface, while deep within, just as the shark is circling under the gleaming, serene surface of the summer ocean, the predator lurks and waits for the opportunity to strike. These predators are extremely rare; we call them *perfect psychopaths*, people who easily switch between the two aspects of their lives, making them both seem incredibly real, showing no hint of their other reality. These rare psychopaths score at least thirty-six points out of forty on the Hare Psychopathy Checklist. As a frame of reference, the average individual scores four points, while the average death-row inmate scores about twenty-nine. The perfect psychopath doesn't have a diminished conscience; he or she doesn't have one at all. Thankfully though, most of you will live your entire professional lives without encountering a single one of these killers."

Huh... so much for that prediction, Tess thought, then grabbed her phone and dialed Michowsky's number. She got voicemail, but she left a message in an excited voice.

"Hey, Gary, there's something you need to see in the old Laura Watson videos. Call me when you get this, all right?" Then she ended the call and dropped the phone on the coffee table.

Suddenly feeling refreshed and optimistic, she hopped off the couch and scampered into the bedroom. She wanted to put on a fresh set of clothes and be ready to meet with Gary and decide what to do with the new information she'd uncovered.

But was it really new information, or was it her imagination? She wondered if maybe Dr. Jacobs might be able to offer some insight.

She opened her closet and reached inside to get a fresh shirt, when something ripped into her back, and she collapsed, gasping. As she fell, she saw the attacker's feet right next to her. She grabbed the man's ankle and held on as tightly as she could, ignoring the burning pain in her back.

The man kicked himself free without much effort and disappeared. A second later, she heard the front door latch shut. She tried to crawl back into the living room, where she'd left her phone, on the coffee table next to her gun, but a wave of darkness clouded her vision and wiped all her strength away.

52

Emergency Calls

The coolness of the bathroom floor tiles helped Tess regain consciousness, or at least that's what she thought. The first sensation she became aware of was how cold the tile seemed against her cheek. Then she felt the soaking of blood on her back, and, with a pained groan, she felt around with her hand, trying to assess the damage.

She reached the wound and almost screamed when she touched it. It was a deep gash in her lower left back, bleeding heavily. She reached above her head to grab the edge of the counter and lift herself up. Her hand, covered in blood, slipped a couple of times, but she wiped it against her shirt and managed to pull herself standing, using the counter for support. She looked in the mirror, turned halfway right, to examine her stab wound.

It was big and gushing blood at an alarming rate. If that kind of blood loss continued, she'd be dead soon. No time for an ambulance to get there. She reached into a drawer with a trembling hand, and, after rummaging through the many items in there, she extracted an emergency medical kit. She opened it and found what she was looking for, a sealed XStat syringe, filled with little sponges.

She tried to unseal the wrapping, but her fingers trembled too much and couldn't pull hard enough. She used her teeth instead and ripped through the foil, exposing the syringe. Then she took a small towel and bit on it, while positioning herself to see the wound in the mirror. After a second of hesitation, she shoved the tip of the syringe deep into her wound and pushed the plunger.

Then she screamed, a long, agonizing scream only partly muffled by the towel she bit on, as the sponges filled the wound and expanded, absorbing the blood and putting hemostatic pressure on the sliced blood vessels inside. When she was finally able, she threw some cold water on her face and drank some too, trying to remain alert and not go into shock.

She unwrapped an H-Bandage and applied the dressing to the wound, tightening it as much as she could. When she finished, she splashed cold water on her face again, feeling the queasiness of a fainting spell approaching.

There was a painkiller syringe in the emergency kit, and she took that next.

She unsealed it and injected the contents directly into her thigh, through the fabric of her blood-soaked pants.

A long minute later, the excruciating pain had subsided somewhat, and the hemorrhage had stopped. She dared to leave the support offered by the bathroom counter. She dragged herself slowly to the living room table, grunted when she leaned to reach down, and grabbed her phone. She redialed Gary's number and left another message.

"Gary, go to Laura's right now. He's going after her…" Her voice trailed off, but she forced air into her lungs and continued, almost whispering. "He got me, Gary, and I didn't even see his face."

She ended the call, then dialed dispatch and instructed them to send all available units to Laura's apartment. She asked them about their response time; they replied that it would be ten to fifteen minutes.

She took another long, raspy breath of air and made her decision. Laura lived three minutes away from her; three minutes she should be able to drive. She grabbed her keys and slowly, unsteadily walked out the door, wincing, groaning, and cursing at every step.

She didn't even bother to close the door behind her. She knew that after the voicemail she'd left Gary, the place would be swarming with cops in no time.

53

Arguments

Laura managed to postpone the looming argument with Adrian, but it wasn't avoidable. He was in a gloomy, sour mood when he'd come to pick her up from the hospital and stayed unusually silent while she checked herself out. He started the conversation in the car, but she'd pleaded with him to be patient and not argue, not before they got home.

That transpired half an hour earlier. Now they'd finally arrived at their apartment, and Boo was happy to see her. He weaved intricate patterns with his tail straight up in the air and waited for her to take her usual seat on the sofa, to jump in her lap, purring. She stroked his back gently and rubbed behind his ears, savoring the smooth silk of his fur and the warmth of his little body.

Adrian put a steaming cup of chamomile tea on the coffee table, and pulled himself a chair across from her. "Talk to me," he said, in a tone that didn't accept any argument. "Why didn't I deserve to know that you're pregnant with my child?"

She closed her eyes. She was still a little drowsy from the medication they'd given her in the hospital, and she just couldn't find her words. The reason he was going to hear was a complex one, with the potential to end their relationship.

She arranged her left arm, still immobilized in a sling, and fidgeted until she found a position where it didn't hurt.

"I'm listening," he insisted, throwing her another dark glance.

She sighed. Like always, she had to do what he wanted, when he wanted. Maybe it was time to have that conversation, after all.

"Adrian, please try to understand. You're too overbearing for me to handle. Most of the time, I don't get a say in things, and I don't think that's the right environment to raise a child."

He sprung off his chair and shoved his hands into his jeans pockets.

"What are you saying, Laura?" he asked, sounding deceivingly calm.

"I'm saying that with you, either I comply with whatever you want me to do, or we argue until I'm too tired to fight, and I comply, just to end the argument. See my choices here, Adrian? It's like that, all the time!"

"When did I ever want anything bad for you, Laura? I just care about you, that's all. I'm worried like hell."

"There's no need to be," she said, then sighed and closed her eyes again, knowing just how futile it was to try to convince Adrian of anything.

"No need? What are you talking about? There's someone out there who wants to kill you; isn't that enough reason to worry?"

She met his gaze and maintained eye contact firmly. "I've lived like this all my life, Adrian. My family was doomed; I survived because... I really don't know why I survived. You have no idea how many times I wished I was dead too. Whatever will happen, will happen."

"You're going to sit here and do nothing, wait for that guy to kill you? That's ridiculous, and you're crazy. I need you to call that fed woman and tell her you're going into protective custody."

She remembered the man she'd seen at the car dealership, the one who followed her one night, and wondered if that was him, the man who killed her family, the man who tried to kill her. She wasn't going to run away, regardless of how scared she was.

Sometimes, she was so scared she felt she couldn't breathe, couldn't move. It was paralyzing. But every time she ended up doing the same thing. She went out there and took a stroll on the streets she loved, rain or shine. It was like provoking whoever lurked in the shadows; it was as if she invited him to finish what he'd started fifteen years ago.

She hated to admit it, but finding out that Garza didn't kill her family didn't come as a complete surprise to her. She'd always doubted that, without any rational reason or evidence, and without a clear memory of the real killer. She just didn't believe it that much. That's why fear had been a constant in her life, making her wonder every now and then when it would be her time to die. She lived on borrowed time, borrowed from a killer who didn't lend.

She'd faced that fear so many times she felt strong, unyielding, and prepared. She wasn't going to start running now. *Que sera, sera,* an old song used to say. "No, Adrian, I won't call her, and I won't go in protective custody. End of story."

"Why?" He seemed literally puzzled.

"I can't live like this. I can't run away, and I can't have you telling me how to run my life anymore, pregnant or not."

"You're crazy, you know that?" he snapped, then kicked the chair over. It toppled, and Boo reacted, jumping promptly from her lap in favor of his hiding place behind the sofa. She almost hated Adrian, for taking Boo away from her, for scaring him.

"I don't think you and I should be parents," she said calmly. "I don't think you're ready to be a father. I'm not sure if I can be a mother. I think there are other people more qualified, more balanced, more willing."

"It's my kid too, Laura!" he yelled.

"Yes, and I know you'd drive both of us crazy, Adrian. You can't compromise, and you can't take risks. Both are mandatory if you want to raise a family. It's not your fault; you simply can't, that's all."

"I won't let you do this, you hear me? I won't!"

He leapt over the fallen chair and almost ran to the door. Then he left, and before he slammed the door behind him, Laura heard him curse her name.

She breathed deeply, ashamed at how relieved she felt with him gone. She didn't want to argue anymore, and maybe they *were* doomed; they didn't have a future together. She couldn't remember the last time she'd been happy. There was always something making Adrian miserable, something he could object to, something that she didn't do right, something he'd criticize her for. All that, while she had her own monsters to battle, her fears, the sadness she still felt when she thought about her parents and siblings, the terrible sense of loss. The painful void that sometimes took all the space of her heart.

The doorbell chimed and she lifted her chin, unaware of the tears running down her cheeks. That was quick. Adrian was quick to anger and slow to heal. Maybe he wasn't coming back to make up; maybe he was coming back for his stuff.

"Come in, it's open," she shouted, unwilling to get up and open the door.

Carol Welsh entered and closed the door behind her.

"Laura?" she called.

"In here," she replied.

Her face lit up when she saw Carol. She wiped her tears with a quick gesture and started getting up. Carol stopped her with a hand gesture.

"I'm so happy you're here," she said. "I'm having a hell of a day."

Carol stopped in front of Laura, after shooting the fallen chair a quick glance, followed by a raised eyebrow. She looked imposing, in a dress pantsuit and slimming jacket. She always looked imposing and perfectly groomed, elegant, no matter what she wore.

"You should lock your door, especially when people are trying to kill you, don't you agree?"

Laura stared at the floor for a second, feeling a wave of sadness wash over her. She always disappointed the people who loved her.

When she looked back up, she gasped. Carol was holding a gun aimed at her chest. Her eyes were cold, merciless. The eyes of a stranger, a killer.

"What… Why?" Laura managed to articulate, fighting the choking claw of fear that didn't let her breathe.

"Because my dear husband is too much of a coward to tie up his loose ends, that's why," Carol replied, holding the gun with a steady hand.

"No… This isn't happening… You're the only family I've ever known, you and Uncle Brad," Laura whimpered, while tears sprung from her eyes. "You're telling me… Oh, my God!"

She pressed her right hand against her chest, trying to steady herself, to be able to think clearly.

"It wasn't his fault; it was your father's. Brad just did what he had to do, that's all."

Laura looked into Carol's eyes, with an unspoken question.

"They were young when they started the company, and for a few years they didn't make much money," Carol explained, sounding annoyed. "Allen wanted Brad to cut costs from manufacturing, because he had to offer deep discounts to get deals signed up. Brad did exactly that, and things went well for a while. Then a house caught fire, from one of the lamps. They settled, no one was hurt, but your father was adamant. He wanted a full investigation into what caused the fire and a massive recall of all the fixtures that had low-grade insulation. There was no talking him out of it. He would have ruined all of us, and Brad only did exactly what he'd told him to do."

Laura's vision blurred, partly because of the constant stream of tears, and partly because the nightmare she was living was too much to handle. Her stomach started hurting badly and she pressed her hand on it, trying to settle it.

"Brad did what he had to do, just like I'm doing now."

She heard Carol's words and turned pale, fighting her nausea and losing.

"I'm going to be sick," she whispered, and started to get up.

"I'm going to be sick," Carol mocked her, and the mockery hurt almost as badly as the story she'd just heard. "You were always such a wimp. Sit down," she ordered.

Laura forced herself to breathe deeply, to curb the queasiness.

"Why... why did he let me live?" she managed to ask? "Why not kill me too?"

"He thought he did. You know him; always preoccupied, not paying attention to anything. He made a mistake."

Laura's eyes opened wide, in shock.

"You two discussed—"

"No, but I could tell by his reactions, the following day."

The room started spinning again, dragging Laura into a vortex of pain. She loved them dearly; they were her family, the two people she knew as parents, despite the faint memories she cherished about her real mother and father. She tried to comprehend that all those years she'd loved her father's killer. She'd held his hand, fell asleep in his arms, and cherished his presence.

A new wave of nausea surprised her, and she desperately gasped for air. She dry-heaved in place, there on the sofa, then managed to steady herself, to control the raging scream of unspeakable pain she felt bubbling up inside her.

"Why raise me?" Laura finally asked, when she could articulate between suffocating sobs. "Why not send me to hell, to die in some foster home? Why pretend you loved me, when you must have hated me so much?"

"You, my dear, were Brad's perfect alibi," Carol replied, and cocked her gun. "Now you've become a liability."

Laura closed her eyes, accepting her fate just like she always thought she would. Somehow, the thought of dying seemed like a relief, promising to end the immense pain she felt ripping through her soul. Soon, she'd be with her real family. Yet somewhere, in a remote corner of her mind, she sensed the new life blooming inside her and remembered she had something to live for. Someone to love, someone to hold and cherish and protect. Someone worth fighting for.

She was going to be a mother.

She opened her eyes just as she heard the gunshot, but didn't feel anything. She saw Carol collapse on the floor, and that FBI agent who'd lied to her, barely standing, with her gun drawn.

"Are you all right?" the agent asked in a weak voice.

Laura couldn't bring herself to answer. Instead, she felt a new wave of tears flush over her, the grip of unspeakable pain choke her, and she gave in, sobbing hard.

Michowsky rushed through the door, with his gun drawn.

"Tess?" he called.

"We're all clear," she replied. "Not in great shape, but clear. I think we should call Dr. Jacobs."

"I'll get you an ambulance," Gary replied. He holstered his weapon and crouched down to check Carol's vitals. "She's gone. Let's take care of you now."

"No, not yet. Got something I have to do first." She turned toward Laura, and touched her shoulder. "It's hard to believe it right now, but you'll be all right."

Laura looked at her and grabbed her sleeve.

"I have to tell you something," she articulated amid shuddering breaths and sobs. "He…"

"I know," Tess replied, and walked away, followed by Gary.

54

Encounter

It was almost completely dark when Bradley Welsh pulled into the driveway in front of his home and cut the engine. He grabbed his briefcase and got out of his car, then locked it with the remote. The Audi chirped and flashed once, but its headlights stayed on for a few more seconds. He strode toward the main entrance, while checking the time on his phone, unaware of his surroundings.

"You know, it took me a while," Tess said, and watched how Brad startled and froze in his tracks. She moved closer, appearing from behind a large shrub, holding her gun aimed at him. "Now I know where I've seen these before," she added, and threw the silicone wound mold at his feet.

He took a step back, almost jumping, as if he'd seen a snake.

"I don't know what you're talking about," he said, seemingly unperturbed.

"Your lamp, Mr. Welsh. You couldn't go a single day without contemplating a memento of what you did to all those women, could you? You wanted to come home every day, and look at the fatal wounds you gave them, replicated in hundreds of shadows on your walls. In plain sight, where everyone could see them, but no one would know."

He stood tall and stiff, without saying a word.

"You took your souvenirs from the crime scenes. You poured silicone in each of their fatal wounds and cast a mold. When you had enough of them in your collection, you built the lamp. Quite original, and the lamp design isn't bad at all. Until now, we couldn't figure out why those wounds had distension marks. We speculated, but we couldn't imagine *this*. We couldn't imagine *you*, Mr. Welsh."

"I still don't know what you're talking about," he repeated, then took a few steps toward her. She aimed her gun a little higher, and he stopped in place.

"There's something keeping me up at night," Tess said, giving him a pensive look. "How does someone so intelligent, so organized, leave a witness behind?"

His eyes almost rolled before he covered them shut with scrunched eyelids. He seemed aggravated with himself, almost angry.

"Ah, you made a mistake," Tess continued. "Were you that self-absorbed, engulfed in your dense shell of superiority, that you never even bothered to notice those kids? And then you killed the wrong one. Huh... That must have hurt like hell, with that monster ego of yours!"

Bradley's nostrils flared and his jaws clenched, but he didn't say a single word.

"That's it, isn't it?" Tess chuckled. "Wow, that's something. Then you had to live with your mistake, all this time."

He shot her a poisoned glare, and two marked ridges appeared on his forehead.

"To think you were so close to Laura, all her life, looking at her, touching her, just makes me sick. You kept her close, to make sure she didn't remember anything, and if she did, that you could easily kill her. That poor girl, to be raised by such monsters." She curled her upper lip in disgust. "I bet you didn't expect to see *me* alive, did you?"

He shook his head and shrugged, and Tess reflected how perfectly composed and calm he seemed, how natural and genuine, denying any involvement or knowledge. Under normal circumstances, she might have believed him, if it weren't for that tug in her gut.

"We've got DNA, you wiseass," she said, letting a long, pained sigh escape her scorched lips. "You're over. Finished."

Not even the reference to DNA fazed him; he continued to stand calmly, waiting.

"Okay, let's get this over with and done with," she said. "Hit the deck, face down, hands behind your head."

He didn't move, staring at her with fiercely cold eyes.

"Or what?" he eventually whispered. "I nailed you good; there's not much you can do to me anymore. You're drawing your last breath, only you don't know it yet. I might take a mold out of you yet." He smiled as he finished talking, then licked his lips. He was enjoying the situation. Seeing her in pain, seeing her agonize.

"I can still kill you," Tess replied dryly. "Instead, I'll let him arrest you."

Brad flinched when he felt Michowsky's gun against his back.

"I promised my boss," Tess continued, watching how Michowsky propped Welsh against the hood of his car and forced his hands behind his back, "no, I *swore* to him no more killing; just catching."

He continued to stare at her with chilling eyes.

"One other thing I don't understand," Tess said, her voice sounding weaker. "Why weren't the Watsons at the company party that night?"

The corner of his lip twitched a little, while his nostrils flared. "Why... People like you never question when people like me do them favors. They consider they somehow deserve it, and even feel grateful, in their immense simplicity. I offered to handle the company party on my own, so he could spend more time with his kids. The idiot accepted with gratitude." He sneered, his derision outing a glint of vileness in his eye. "Easy."

She took a few steps closer, until she could shove the barrel of her gun into the side of his neck. "Where's Monica, you sick son of a bitch?"

"I don't know what you're talking about," he replied calmly, with a hint of a wicked smile in his eyes. "But I'm sorry," he continued, looking Tess straight in the eye, with that chilling gaze that awakened nightmares in her mind. "I'm sorry I didn't take my time with you. I'm sorry I didn't allow myself to enjoy you."

Michowsky holstered his weapon and grabbed the handcuffs. Suddenly, Welsh pivoted and kicked Michowsky in the stomach, while shoving Tess out of his way. Michowsky, bent over, groaned in pain, while Tess, disoriented and weak, had to hold on to the car for balance. When she recovered, Welsh was already far, running fast, about to disappear behind the bushes.

She didn't hesitate; she pulled the trigger twice, calmly, and watched how Welsh went down and didn't move. Michowsky rushed over and checked his pulse.

That was the last thing she saw. Too weak to continue standing, she let herself slide against Welsh's car, until she hit the ground. Feeling grateful for the support, she let herself fall, and felt the coolness of the asphalt against her face.

As in a dream, she heard Michowsky yell in his phone, "I need that ambulance right now, dammit, we have an officer down. You hear me? Now!" Then he crouched next to her and cradled her head on his knees.

"Hang on, partner, they're coming," he said, and swallowed with difficulty. "Hang on. Talk to me."

"Don't worry," she whispered. "People die hard. Monica…"

"We'll find her—"

"No," she interrupted, barely audible, but he stopped talking and listened. "Car's GPS must have it. Remote… Glades…"

"I don't know how to—"

"Call… Donovan," she managed to articulate, then faded away in a world of silence and darkness.

55

Deductive Reasoning

They rolled her with the gurney so fast it made her queasy. She wanted to tell them to slow down, but they didn't hear her. She tried to speak louder, forced herself, but only a whimper made it out. She gave up and watched the white ceiling tiles alternating with fluorescent, embedded lamps, as they moved by, fast. Too fast.

Lamps... why were lamps important? What was she forgetting? She struggled to remember, but failed, and conceded that fight.

The gurney suddenly stopped, and she thought she recognized Michowsky's voice.

"How is she?"

"She's stabilized now, but weak. She's lost a lot of blood, and she's still bleeding internally. That XStat saved her life, but she should've..." His voice trailed off, and he cleared his throat and changed the topic. "We'll let you know after the surgery."

Tess reached out and grabbed the man's sleeve. Pearson's head appeared, leaning over the gurney and looking at her. He was frowning and seemed upset. She was in trouble.

"Sorry..." she whispered.

"Winnett, what the hell are you sorry for?"

"I'm sorry, sir, I tried..." she managed to say, but Pearson had to come closer to hear her.

"She did," Michowsky intervened. "She had no choice, but she did try."

"What?" Pearson asked, frowning deeper.

"Not to kill him," Michowsky replied.

Pearson scoffed and turned away.

The gurney started to roll again, but she flailed her arm. "No," she said weakly, "Monica?"

"They found her, just like you said," Michowsky replied. "She's all right."

She swallowed hard and licked her dry lips, but it didn't soothe her. She looked at Pearson intently. "Why did you send me to interview Garza?"

He furrowed his brow and leaned over the gurney, to hear her faint voice. "Never mind that," Pearson replied kindly but firmly. "We'll talk after the surgery."

"Please... You knew about the Watsons and the others?" she insisted.

"Yes, I did," Pearson admitted reluctantly, then rolled his eyes.

"Then why send me?" she insisted, feeling weaker. She drew a deep breath, willing her brain to stay alert.

A male nurse wearing a white lab coat waited with a loaded syringe, ready to push it into her IV line. He was growing impatient and made that clear without words. He must have been the one who'd given Michowsky the update earlier.

"Because you can't trust anyone worth a damn, whether cops or serial killers," Pearson replied, then signaled the medical team to proceed.

"Then it was you who recalled me," Tess said, a little louder, and the man stopped short of injecting the contents of the syringe. "If you hadn't, I would've returned from leave *after* Garza fried." She summoned her last bit of strength and lifted her head off her pillow an inch or two, searching Pearson's eyes. "It was you... Am I right?"

Pearson made another gesture toward the man, this time more demanding.

The nurse pushed the plunger, and Tess felt darkness engulf her. Before letting herself sink into an all-forgiving sleep, she heard Pearson's voice once more, clearly at first.

"Jeez, Winnett, just shut up already." He then turned toward the nurse, his voice fading away with the rest of her world, but she thought she heard him say, "She's amazing, you know. Take good care of her."

56

New Beginnings

The WatWel boardroom was engulfed in silence, and the lowered window shades kept the fierce sunrays at bay. Outside of the distant noises of the building buzzing with activity, the occasional truck horn, or the beeping sounds of operating forklifts, nothing disturbed the peace of the large room.

Laura sat at the wide conference table, flipping absently through the numerous pages of a business sale agreement, the document that, if signed by both shareholders, would make WatWel part of her history. Instead of poring over each paragraph, her unfocused mind counted the yellow tags where her lawyer had marked the document for signature or initial. Twenty-seven such places in total; four signatures and the rest initials. Only lawyers could call that logical for a twenty-two-page document.

She lifted her eyes from the pages and looked at Amanda's slim figure. She hadn't moved from the window since they'd arrived. She stood there with her back straight and her eyes fixed on a distant point, somewhere on the Miami horizon line, waiting. She hadn't said one word, nor looked at her once.

"I never thought this day would come, you know," Laura broke the silence, and her voice resonated strangely against the walls of the immense room, as if she'd spoken loudly in a mausoleum.

She waited for Amanda to say something, but she didn't, so Laura continued. "This was my legacy, the last thing I had to remind me of my parents. This, a few photos, and a recording of their voices on an obsolete answering machine is all I have left."

Silence took over again, and Laura flipped through the pages some more, still unable to read a single word. Yet she unscrewed the cap off her pen, getting ready to sign.

The sound of a baby fussing disrupted the eerie silence.

"Can I hold him?" Amanda asked, still staring at the horizon.

"Sure you can," Laura replied without any hesitation. "I think he's hungry, but I don't have a bottle with me."

"I can sympathize," Amanda replied, gently picking up the baby and holding him in her arms. "I'm hungry too."

Eventually, the fussing subsided, while Amanda rocked him gently, holding his head on her shoulder.

Laura watched the two of them together and a felt a lump in her throat. The only remaining pieces of her family were in this room, and one of the two beings she called family was about to leave her life forever, with a signed sale agreement. She probably wanted to run out of there and never look back, and Laura couldn't blame her, not a single bit.

She started initialing the document with trembling fingers. "No matter how hard I try, I don't think I can look at lamps the same way again. I can't be in this business; I don't want to talk about lamps ever again in my life."

"I thought of switching to candle lighting," Amanda said with a sad chuckle. "You know, live like the Amish, strictly from a light-fixture perspective though. I'd die without Internet."

Laura almost smiled. Amanda was never going to change. Half diva, half businesswoman, a fierce combination.

"The thought had crossed my mind," Laura admitted, and initialed a few more pages, but something made her stop. She cringed a little, but decided to say what was on her mind. "You know, the only thing I regret when signing the business away is losing you. We'll go our separate ways… there'll be nothing left to hold us together."

Amanda didn't say a word; she kept walking with Laura's son in her arms, back and forth along the large, shaded windows.

"Anyway, I'm almost done," she added, looking through a veil of tears at the final page of the document, where her last signature was about to seal the fate of WatWel Lighting.

"What are you planning to do after this?" Amanda asked, and her voice seemed a little coarse, choked. "We'll be loaded, you know. We could park our butts somewhere in the Caribbean and never look back."

"That's not for me," Laura replied, "I want to build something worthwhile, something that Allen will enjoy taking over from me. I also have a list of charities I want to get involved with. It's time to bring some good into our lives, some bright, lively colors."

"How does fashion sound?" Amanda asked shyly.

Laura covered her mouth and fought back her tears. "You'd work with me?"

"I'd work with no one else," she replied quietly, careful not to wake Allen up. "You're awesome at everything—operational, manufacturing, logistics, you're a natural. I can do media, marketing, sales, distribution, the whole nine yards. And I'd die to see us at the Paris Fashion Week, strutting our stuff. What do you say?"

Laura stood and walked over to Amanda, then looked her straight in the eye from up close, while a wide grin flourished on her lips. "I'm in, on one condition."

"Name it," Amanda replied in her business tone, then laughed quietly.

"We are never to talk about the past again, about any of it. Ever again."

"It's a deal." Amanda put Allen back into his carrier, then hugged Laura. "Sisters forever?" she whispered.

"Sisters forever," Laura replied, then wiped a rebel tear.

"Awesome, now let's eat. I'm starving!"

~~ The End ~~

Read on for an excerpt from

Glimpse of Death: Tess Winnett Book Three

She saw his eyes, and the sight of them chilled her to the bone. She saw his hands, the hands of a killer.

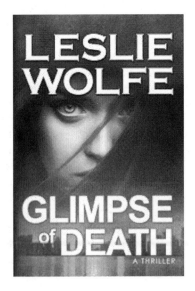

The Science behind the Character

Bradley Welsh

I've crafted Bradley Welsh's character as a psychopath, showing traces of malignant narcissism. Unlike typical psychopaths, those with traces of malignant narcissism are somewhat different from the norm, combining the pervasive pattern of grandiosity (as described by the fifth edition of the *Diagnostic and Statistical Manual of Mental Disorders—DSM-5*) with the typical characteristics of the psychopath: reckless risk taking, lack of attachment, dishonesty, and, the most distinct of all, the absence of conscience.

Narcissistic psychopaths are extremely self-absorbed, to the point where they don't notice anything around them that doesn't benefit them directly. As such, Bradley could have attended, out of obligation, countless kid parties, without even noticing or remembering how many kids the Watsons actually had. A narcissistic psychopath doesn't have real friendships; he has a strategy and subsequent obligations that he endures with a polite mask on his face.

In the first chapter, Bradley Walsh goes into the Watson home, assuming the kids he finds are all Allen Watson's children. He knows there are three of them, but in the heat of the moment, he doesn't recall how many boys and how many girls. He's also stressed; it's his first time killing. After he leaves the house and sees the decal on the car, he notices the discrepancy, and only then he starts paying attention, but it's already too late. As mentioned by his wife in later chapters, Bradley made a mistake, because he didn't pay attention.

Think of it this way: if you don't care at all about guns, and every time you meet your brother-in-law at family events he talks about guns—calibers and brands, and rifle versus shotgun—chances are you'll space out, fake a smile, and forget everything he says. In one car, and out the other, right? You won't remember what kinds of guns he has, even if your life depended on it. You'll just remember he likes guns... a lot, because that's the part that bored or bothered you.

Bradley did the same, and then some, because he's a completely self-absorbed narcissistic psychopath, not a neurotypical individual, like you and me. Bradley just knew Watson had three kids... as for the rest, he couldn't be bothered to care.

I found the research into the world of psychopaths a fascinating journey. If you'd like to know more about how someone like Bradley Welsh could be your neighbor, boss, or coworker, here are some highly recommended titles.

- ***The Psychopath Whisperer: The Science of Those Without Conscience***, by Kent A. Kiehl, PhD. Dr. Kiehl describes years of working with jailed psychopaths and studying their thought processes, in fascinating detail.
- ***Snakes in Suits: When Psychopaths Go to Work***, by Paul Babiak, PhD, and Robert D. Hare, PhD. Dr. Hare developed the ***Psychopathy Checklist—Revised (PCL-R)***, a reference test for the clinical diagnosis of a psychopath. He is a world-renowned researcher and an advisor for the FBI. The book, *Snakes is Suits*, is dedicated entirely to the study of "the functioning psychopath," specifically how certain psychopaths thrive in corporate environments, where they manage to build careers and success at the cost of everyone else.
- ***The Sociopath Next Door***, by Martha Stout, PhD. While sociopaths are clinically different from psychopaths, the two terms have been used interchangeably because of the numerous characteristic similarities. Dr. Stout presents the behaviors of the well-integrated sociopath, from the youngest age to adulthood, and the depths of damage sociopaths might cause, even if they're not homicidal.

Finally, let me remind you of one scary (fictional) fact from the Thomas Harris masterpiece, *The Silence of the Lambs:* Before being incarcerated in a maximum-security facility, Dr. Hannibal Lecter was a successful psychiatrist with a blooming practice, a well-integrated individual.

Ultimately, Bradley Welsh is nothing more but a fictional character, created for your enjoyment and to give you something to ponder about the people who live in this world.

Thank You!

A big, heartfelt thank you for choosing to read my book. If you enjoyed it, please take a moment to leave me a four- or five-star review; I would be very grateful. It doesn't need to be more than a couple of words, and it makes a huge difference.

Join my mailing list for latest news, sale events, and new releases. Log on to www.WolfeNovels.com to sign up, or email me at LW@WolfeNovels.com.

Did you enjoy Tess Winnett and her team? Would you like to see them again in another Miami crime story? Your thoughts and feedback are very valuable to me. Please contact me directly through one of the channels listed below. Email works best: LW@WolfeNovels.com.

Connect with Me

Email: LW@WolfeNovels.com
Twitter: @WolfeNovels
Facebook: https://www.facebook.com/wolfenovels
LinkedIn: https://www.linkedin.com/in/wolfenovels
Web: www.WolfeNovels.com

Books by Leslie Wolfe

BAXTER & HOLT SERIES

Las Vegas Girl
Casino Girl
Las Vegas Crime

TESS WINNETT SERIES

Dawn Girl
The Watson Girl
Glimpse of Death
Taker of Lives

SELF-STANDING NOVELS

Stories Untold

ALEX HOFFMANN SERIES

Executive
Devil's Move
The Backup Asset
The Ghost Pattern
Operation Sunset

For the complete list of Leslie Wolfe's novels, visit:
Wolfenovels.com/order

Preview: *Glimpse of Death*

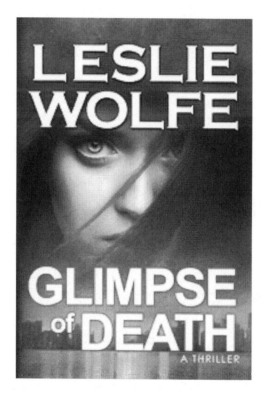

1

Taken

He watched her from across the street as she left the coffee shop. She was beautiful, this one. Her long, wavy, brown hair coiled and bounced in thick, silky strands around her shoulders, dancing with every step she took. Her smile was dazzling, even from a distance, and her eyes were half-closed, the way they get when laughter touches them and lends a glow of happiness.

He licked his lips and swallowed hard. Soon enough, those eyes would be looking at him. He felt a twitch below his waist, and a crooked smile curled the corner of his mouth.

She stopped right outside the coffee shop and turned around to look at the man who'd held the door for her. Then she reached out and took his hand, weaving her fingers through his, and her smile widened. The man leaned forward and kissed her on the lips, lingering a little, then turned away and quickly disappeared around the corner. She unzipped her purse, her eyes still following him as he vanished, and took out her car keys.

That was his cue. Time to move.

He ran his sweaty palms against his thinning, blond hair and arranged it into place, although not much could be done with the few remaining strands, pushed backward by an aggressively receding hairline. He straightened his posture and arranged the knot of his tie, then buttoned his jacket. He scrutinized the reflection in the tinted car window and saw a moderately attractive, professionally dressed man, looking the part he was about to play.

He quickly crossed the street and caught up with her just as she was about to get behind the wheel. He delayed his arrival long enough to give her time to be seated but caught the doorframe before she could close it.

"Dr. Katherine Nelson?" he asked, flashing a wallet with his fake police ID.

The young woman didn't bother to check his credentials. They never did. But even if she checked, the fake he carried was quite good; it could probably pass for the real thing with most uneducated civilians. He'd paid good money for it, worth it to the last dime. It made things so much easier. He didn't have to lurk in the shadows anymore, worrying about muffling their screams and getting kicked, bit, and scratched. He could go out in broad daylight and get the job done.

"Yes, that's me," the young woman replied, her voice trembling a little.

"I'm afraid I have some bad news for you. Your husband, he—"

"What happened? What's wrong?" she almost yelled, panic instilling a crystalline, high pitch in her voice.

He didn't even have to be creative. They never let him finish his damn sentence anyway.

"It's better if you come with me, Dr. Nelson. It's faster that way."

She grabbed her purse and slammed her car door, then trotted quickly behind him, as he crossed the street and headed toward his car. The rhythmic sound of her high heels hitting the asphalt made it unnecessary for him to look over his shoulder to make sure she was still coming.

He led her to a black, unmarked Crown Victoria he'd bought at a police auction a couple of years before, and held the door open for her. Then he took his seat behind the wheel and shoved the key in the ignition.

"Please," Katherine said, turning toward him, "tell me what happened to Craig. Is he okay?"

He reached into his pocket and pulled out a syringe, then quickly removed the cap. She watched him with bewildered eyes, turning pale, faltering. She pushed herself backward as far as she could, flailing desperately for the door handle, but unable to take her eyes from the approaching needle. Her mouth opened, but no sound came out.

"Your husband is in a world of trouble, Dr. Nelson." He grabbed her shoulder with a steeled grip and shoved the needle into the side of her neck, swiftly pushing the plunger, before she could react. "You see, his cheating wife was kidnapped today."

2

Waiting Room

The three men knew one another well, but barely exchanged glances. The occasional word was muttered under their breaths, almost whispered, although no one else could hear them talk. Other than that, they waited.

Hospital waiting rooms are all the same, no matter where they happen to be. Fluorescent lights, with undecided hues of bluish purple, and the nonstop humming of the ceiling-mounted lamps. A vending machine, also humming every now and then, holding the typical offering of junk food, rich in chemicals and empty calories. A few wide chairs in green, faded fabric, and a wall-mounted TV, with the sound set on mute.

At least they had their privacy.

Hospitals tend to be courteous to law enforcement, probably due to the repeat business the profession tends to deliver. Passing, or even enduring, relationships are formed among officers, agents, and their family members on one side, and nurses and doctors on the other. They cross paths, unfortunately, much too often. In their case, the small, private, waiting room was the least the hospital could do.

The three men had been waiting for a while—a few hours now. Not a word.

FBI Special Agent in Charge Alan Pearson had loosened his tie an inch or two, then crossed his arms at his chest. That had happened more than an hour earlier. He hadn't budged since, although somewhat irritated with the restlessness of Detective Todd Fradella, from Palm Beach County Sheriff's Office. The young detective couldn't sit still; he paced the floor like a caged animal, annoyingly running his hands through his shoulder-length hair, randomly stopping in front of the window, as if something of any interest could actually be seen through it, in the late-afternoon sunlight.

As for Detective Gary Michowsky, he didn't move much either; but his lips did. He sat in the same chair, his hands clasped together tightly in his lap, and stared into emptiness. His jaws clenched spasmodically, and he constantly bit his lips, munching on them from the inside, angrily. He tried to stay calm and quiet, but his anguish showed.

Fradella stopped his pacing in front of Pearson.

"It's taking a while," he said, breaking the tense silence.

The two men stared at him disapprovingly.

"I hope she's okay," he continued, almost apologetically. "I mean, when it takes so long—"

"Shut it, Fradella," Michowsky snapped.

Pearson unfolded his arms and sighed. "Come on, guys, take it easy," he said, staring at Michowsky.

Michowsky fidgeted in his seat, then gazed at the shiny, floor, following the random design of the cement mosaic tiles.

"It's on me," he eventually muttered. "All this. On me."

Pearson frowned, and Fradella turned to look at his partner.

"How d'you figure that?" Pearson asked.

Michowsky remained silent, biting his lips some more.

"Did *you* stab her?" Pearson pressed on. "Was that you, detective? Or was it a psychopath you two eventually put in the morgue?"

Michowsky shot Pearson an angry glare, then lowered his eyes again. There was nothing to say, and he didn't want any consolation coming from any of them.

"When this is over," Pearson continued unfazed, making a gesture with his hand, "I'll need a statement from you. I know it was a good shoot, but she's under internal rev—"

Michowsky glared at Pearson again, just as briefly, interrupting him.

"Yeah, I heard about that nonsense. I'll give you my statement anytime you want. It *was* a good shoot."

The door opened and a tall man dressed in a surgical gown walked in. The three men gathered around him, all talking at the same time, asking the same question, but with different words.

The doctor raised his hands in a pacifying gesture. "Hello, I'm Dr. DePaolo. We met earlier, I think," he said, locking eyes with Pearson and then Michowsky. "She's strong and she's a fighter; she has a good chance to make a full recovery," he said, and smiled encouragingly, while wiping his brow with his sleeve. Tiny beads of sweat had accumulated there, and the edge of his surgical cap was moist.

"It was a close call for a while," he continued, "but I believe she'll pull through. The next few hours are still critical. She waited too long." He cleared his throat, then continued in a stern tone. "XStat is designed to stop the bleeding while help is on the way, officers. You can't get stabbed, XStat the wound, patch it up with a bandage, and go back to work like nothing happened."

The three men looked at one another, then, one by one, lowered their eyes.

"She lost a lot of blood," Dr. DePaolo continued. "She's in ICU now, still sedated. I'll show you where that is, if you follow me."

He scampered quietly on the endless corridors, then led them to a room on a restricted part of the floor. The room had a glass wall and a French door, also made of glass. Inside the room, surrounded by stacks of beeping equipment and digital screens, a tiny figure lay immobile on the bed.

Tess looked thin and pale against the white bed sheets; Gary almost didn't recognize her. By her side, a nurse took readings from the machines and jotted notes onto a chart.

Pearson frowned and tapped gently on the glass. The nurse quietly opened the door.

"Why is she restrained, Nurse… Henderson?" he asked in a curt tone, reading the name off the ID tag she was wearing.

Gary hadn't noticed the restraints, but now that Pearson mentioned them, he frowned as well. Her wrists were tied to the bed rails, and she constantly shook her head, slowly, without opening her eyes, moaning.

"She's very restless, although she's heavily sedated. We can't risk her moving too much and tearing her sutures."

"I'll place a uniform at the door," Fradella said. "Just in case."

That wasn't a case Gary could think of, but he didn't find it necessary to disagree. After all, it was Tess Winnett in there, fighting for her life.

"Are you family?" the nurse asked.

"Work family," Michowsky replied, earning himself a curious look from Pearson. "Why? Need anything?"

"She's worried about her cat. She keeps mumbling something, I can't understand what, but it's something to do with a cat. Can someone check her home and make sure her cat's okay? Maybe then she'll be able to sleep better."

He stared at Tess, puzzled for a few seconds. He wished he could ask her what she needed. Cops had turned her apartment upside down, and he'd been there too; it was still an active crime scene. No one had mentioned a cat, and he didn't remember seeing food bowls or cat toys anywhere.

Then he remembered something else.

He pulled out his phone and said, "I think I know what that's about."

He dialed 411, then requested the information, "I need the number for a Media Luna Bar and Grill, or something like that. Yes, in Palm Beach. Yeah, connect me; I'll hold."

A few seconds later, Michowsky broke the silence again.

"Yeah, um, hey, Cat, you might want to know that Tess is in the hospital." He stopped talking for a split second, then continued. "University of Miami Hospital, third floor, room 3104."

The call ended without any additional words. Michowsky had expected a few questions, but none came. All for the better. He felt exhausted, the exhaustion brought by feeling some relief, after a long period of tension.

The nurse smiled and nodded a silent thank you in his direction. He sat on a vinyl chair across the hallway, and let out a long breath of air.

"She won't be up for a while," the nurse said. "Why don't you go home? I can call you when she wakes up."

"I'm not going anywhere," Michowsky replied, resuming his earlier posture, with his hands firmly clasped in his lap and his shoulders hunched forward. Pearson nodded and did the same, leaving an empty chair between them and taking the one next to that. Fradella resumed his pacing, including the occasional stops in front of a nearby window, now completely engulfed in darkness.

A few minutes later, a uniformed officer arrived, quietly greeted Fradella and Michowsky, and pulled a chair for himself right next to Tess's door. The nurse frowned when she saw him sit there, but then got absorbed in her work and her frown vanished.

Michowsky's phone chime raised disapproving eyebrows everywhere on the hallway, even from passersby. He took the call immediately, shooting apologetic glances in all directions. A minute later, he stood up, ready to leave.

"Fradella, I've got to go. They found Lisa Trask, the missing person from last week. She's been dead for at least a day. You stay here; I'll do this solo. Call me as soon as Tess wakes up."

"You got it. Where did they find the body?"

"You're not going to believe this… in her own backyard."

He nodded an acknowledgment toward Pearson and hurried out, not noticing the worried look that appeared on Pearson's face the moment he'd mentioned where the body had been found.

~~~End Preview~~~

Like *Glimpse of Death?*

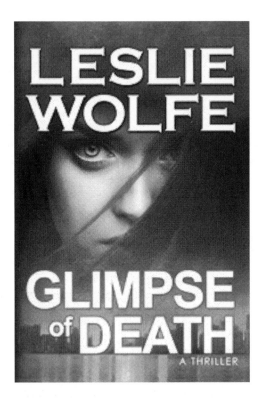

Buy it now!

About the Author

Leslie Wolfe is a bestselling author whose novels break the mold of traditional thrillers. She creates unforgettable, brilliant, strong women heroes who deliver fast-paced, satisfying suspense, backed up by extensive background research in technology and psychology.

Leslie released the first novel, *Executive*, in October 2011. It was very well received, including inquiries from Hollywood. Since then, Leslie published numerous novels and enjoyed growing success and recognition in the marketplace. Among Leslie's most notable works, *The Watson Girl* (2017) was recognized for offering a unique insight into the mind of a serial killer and a rarely seen first person account of his actions, in a dramatic and intense procedural thriller.

A complete list of Leslie's titles is available at https://wolfenovels.com/order.

Leslie enjoys engaging with readers every day and would love to hear from you. Become an insider: gain early access to previews of Leslie's new novels.

- **Email: LW@WolfeNovels.com**
- Follow Leslie on Twitter: @WolfeNovels
- Like Leslie's Facebook page: https://www.facebook.com/wolfenovels
- Connect on LinkedIn: https://www.linkedin.com/in/wolfenovels
- Visit Leslie's website for the latest news: www.WolfeNovels.com

CONTENTS

Made in the USA
Columbia, SC
25 October 2018